A ⊺

CW00531368

A JOURNEY OF FAITH

✳

A Novel

David Willington

Ashgrove Publishing
London

for

Ben and Abby

Chapter One

❋

1912

James Millward walked slowly back to the Pavilion, took off his pads in the changing room and, wearing a blazer, went to sit on a deck chair by the boundary; he ignored the condolences of his team mates. Gloomily he lit his pipe and watched his successor at the crease settle into his innings. After some minutes someone sat down in the next chair. He turned to James.

'This is a very nice day.'

'True,' said James. The Parks in May looked lovely and a larger number of spectators than usual was watching Oxford play Sussex.

'I don't know much about your game of Cricket, but you had some good hits. Twenty-four can't be bad.'

'Could have been so much better. I was beginning to read the bowling and became too confident. I played across the line to a good length ball and was LBW. Silly. Anyway, there goes my chance of a Blue.'

'I don't understand those terms… but I find it a pleasure to watch this aspect of English culture. Perhaps I should explain. Haase, Stefan, St John's.'

'James Millward, Trinity.'

They leant across and shook hands.

'I am over here from Heidelberg to write a paper on your Bible, the King James Version and the sources the translators used in their work. I am a Rhodes Scholar, one of the first, I believe. What are you reading, Millward?'

'You mean when I am not playing cricket? I am reading Greats. I got a decent First in Mods but I will have to work a bit harder during the winter to get the same in Greats. They say that an Oxford Blue is worth a First in the outside world, but…' he sighed, 'I don't think I will get either. Are you a theologian, Haase?'

'Yes. I have a sabbatical from my studies at Heidelberg. It takes bit of time to become a pastor in Germany, but in a year or so I will be a Reverend Doktor.'

James digested this information. Then he asked:

'What is the difference between Lutheranism and our Church of England?'

Haase looked at his watch with an exaggerated gesture. 'How long have we got?'

James laughed. 'Don't let's spoil this conversation with a lecture. I can read it up for myself. But I assume we worship the same God.'

'We do indeed, Millward. What are you going to do with your degree in Greats? It is a course of study much respected in Germany.'

'Well, Haase, I am not really a reading man. To tell the truth, I have really no idea. I suspect that I will end up as a government official somewhere in the Empire. My father was a Resident in India and I grew up there, surrounded by servants and living a pampered life. So I was sent off to boarding school in England, a Spartan existence by comparison.'

'My parents were quite rich, too. My father owned a factory, but he and my mother died three years ago…'

'I'm sorry.'

'They both had cancer and died within a few weeks of each other. I think it was a mercy for them both. My brother now runs the firm. I have no head for business but I have an income which enables me to follow my calling.'

'Do you mind me asking a personal question? Have you always wanted to be a priest?'

Haase smiled. 'We all have our struggles in life. I resisted the call for some years but when I was thinking about university, something, someone, guided me towards Theology and made up my mind for me.'

'Come to think of it, I have never had to struggle... really struggle. I enjoyed school, did pretty well academically and on the games field, became a praepostor and got an exhibition to come here. A gilded youth, you might say. Perhaps in the long run it would have been better for me to have a little more rain fall in my life.'

'Don't be ashamed of your gifts and privileges. It is what you do with them that is important. Forgive my preaching. Here endeth the lesson, as you say in the service.'

The players were coming off the field for tea.

'Look, Haase, I had better go.' He got up. 'Hang on, why don't you come for a cuppa as well?'

'Thank you. But I have a meeting with my supervisor. Perhaps we could meet again. Do you know the Lamb and Flag?'

'I have been known to patronise it.'

'I'll send you a note to arrange a time.'

'I'd like that.'

Over the next few weeks the two men met several times, either at the pub or on walks along the river. Soon they were on first name terms. Although Stefan's English was excellent, he had not made any close friends so far during his time at St John's, because not many other people were pursuing similar studies, and also because there was a growing suspicion of Germany in the country. At first he cultivated James as an example of young English manhood, but soon came to like him for his personal qualities; he did not show the air of effortless superiority so characteristic of his fellow countrymen. James was impressed and a little abashed by the width of Stefan's knowledge: he was proficient in the Classical languages, could read Hebrew and was working on Aramaic and Syriac.

'But what impact will all this learning have on your duties as a priest?'

'A very good question, James. I might become Herr Professor and then I could teach other people Hebrew and so forth. And they could teach other people in turn, and so on *ad infinitum*. How far that would advance the Kingdom of God is open to question. Until very recently, ordination was requisite for membership of the Theology Faculty, but I don't want to end up as a dry-as-dust academic. I think that my studies into the basis of our beliefs will help me to be a pastor of souls, not directly, obviously, but as essential background for dealing with matters that confront people in their daily lives.'

'Wouldn't you be better served with a course in Psychology?'

'I have read Freud's *The Interpretation of Dreams* and some of his articles, but I found them hard going, and German is my native language! Anyway, I am not a mind doctor. Everyone has a touch of the Divine in them as a child of God, and I conceive my job is to interpret the Divine to them, as best I can. That means sharing with people their experiences of life.'

'You mean, by being a sinner along with the rest of us?'

'I have put it badly. I mean being aware of and understanding their experiences. And trying not to be a sinner, but a good example, with God's help.'

'I don't believe you are a great sinner, Stefan.'

'You'd be surprised at what I have done. I repent of my sins daily.'

'But I must ask. Would you be really content serving a parish in some village far off the beaten track, with no intellectual stimulus? There can't be very many different types of spiritual or personal problems around. All much of a muchness. I think you would be bored after a year or so.'

'Bored in a good cause, would be the official response. I am here to serve. However, you have a point. And after you have preached to the same people every Sunday for a few years, you run out of new ideas and your congregation will have heard it all before. That is why our church likes to move pastors around to different parishes after a bit. But I have known of pastors spending thirty years in one post.'

'Where would you like to serve?'

'I come from North Germany, a village close to Bremen and I

am familiar with the people, farmers mostly. It would do me good to get my pastoral hands dirty with industrial grime.'

One day just before the end of term, when they had not met for a week or so, James happened to meet Stefan coming out of the Bodleian.

'I have been meaning to ask you. What are you doing this summer? My parents take a house in Pitlochry in the summer and I wondered if you would like to spend a few days with us – somewhere for you to blow away the dust of the Bodleian.'

Stefan looked a little surprised at the invitation.

'You would be very welcome,' James went on. 'My sister Beth will be there, and some cousins nearby.'

'But I have never shot anything. And I don't have suitable clothes.'

'We don't shoot and we don't dress for dinner. We can kit you out with weatherproofs. Just turn up and leave your books behind. For a few days.'

Stefan thought for a moment. 'You know, I was at a loose end this summer. I have no particular wish or need to go home. I have never been to North Britain. You're right. I need a complete break. Thank you. I will come.'

* * *

On the second day of his visit, there was an expedition to climb Ben Vrackie, the hill behind Pitlochry. James had not been sure how fit Stefan was and worried that he might find the climb difficult. However, he had kept up well and spent much of the ascent listening to Beth talking about her favourite topic of the moment, Women's Suffrage.

'We have a very active movement here. What about Germany?'

'I must confess it is not a matter that, er, comes to my mind very often.'

'Do you have a sister, Stefan, or a young lady you are interested in?'

'I much regret having neither,' he declared.

'But priests of your persuasion can marry, can't they?'

'Yes, of course. But at the moment I am so wrapt up in my studies, and... I have not yet found the right person.'

'Well, let me tell you about Women's Suffrage. I have been looking at things in Germany. I believe that the Socialists are keen to press for women's rights at work and also for the vote. A few years ago there was a Women's Congress in Stuttgart but it was all talk. All men have had the vote since 1871. You are a very paternalistic society; the role of women is *Kinder*, *Küche*, *Kirche*. Having no vote is shameful when women work in factories and can qualify as doctors.'

'But not as priests.'

'No. I suppose not. That would be a step too far. Now take New Zealand. Women have had the vote there since 1893. New Zealand is a dominion like Canada or Australia. It rules itself. So why can't the mother country learn from its children?'

There being no possible response to this rhetorical question, Stefan changed the subject.

'Tell me, Beth, if I may ask, what is your ambition?'

'You mean, as well as being a *hausfrau*? Travel the world, write a book, perhaps even become an MP, when we get the vote. Any one of these. Actually, my immediate ambition this summer is to climb Ben Nevis. James will come with me. He doesn't know it yet but I have booked him for the trip.'

'Has he been doing much reading this summer?'

'James has brought books with him, so he says, but with this fine weather I expect they will remain unopened.'

'He told me to leave my books behind.'

'That was good advice since you are here for just a few days. But James will be here for three weeks.'

At the top they ate their sandwiches. James lit his pipe.

'Stefan must be getting the wrong impression of Scottish weather,' said Beth.

'I'm sure it is like this always,' Stefan replied with a twinkle.

There was not a cloud in the sky and even distant mountains stood out clearly.

'Which one is Ben Nevis?' Andrew, one of the cousins asked.

'Difficult to tell,' said James. 'There are so many high mountains round about it and from this angle it does not stand out except as a flattish top slightly higher than the others. Look over there.' He pointed in a north-westerly direction. 'It will be over fifty miles away.'

'Do you have high mountains like this in Germany?' asked Peter, the other cousin, who was twelve.

'Oh yes. We have high mountains in the south, higher than here, but they don't look quite so wild. For a start, they have many more trees on them, and a lot of folk live in the mountain areas. People come to ski and climb, all year round. Where I live, in the north, the land is flat and there are a lot of farms. Very boring.'

'In India,' said Beth, 'in the hot season we used to go up to a hill station, usually Simla, at seven and a half thousand feet. That, Peter, is more than twice the height we are now. Father took a small house on the outskirts and we had magnificent views of the mountains. We came up by railway, narrow gauge, with some very tight bends. It took an age, but it was a relief to be cool and breathe mountain air. Lots of pine trees, like your Alps, Stefan.'

'I am ashamed to say that I have never seen them in person. We Northerners usually take our holidays by the sea. My father had a small yacht at Cuxhaven and we sailed every summer. So I have never been on skis, but I have sea legs.'

Peter, who had never been in the company of a foreigner before, was eager to ask him more questions.

'Stefan, what is your yacht called? How many masts does it have? Can you sleep aboard it?'

'It was called *Victoria*, after the former Kaiserin. She was the daughter of your Queen. It had a main mast and a smaller mast near the stern. And a bowsprit. Actually, Peter, it was originally a fishing boat, which meant that it was not very fast but it was very seaworthy, good in a rough sea. We used to sail to

Helgoland, to look at the seabird colonies. But we have not been there recently, because the Imperial Navy is busy fortifying it and discourages visitors, unless there is an emergency. Did you know, Peter, that you British had it until 1890, when we swapped it for Zanzibar?'

'Gosh. I didn't know that,' said Peter. 'If I visit you in Gemany, can I have a sail in *Victoria*?'

'You would be very welcome to visit, Peter, but I am afraid my brother sold it a year ago.'

Peter looked crestfallen.

'Never mind. There will be plenty of other ships to see. New battleships, for instance.'

'You mean, like HMS *Dreadnought*? It is supposed to be the best battleship in the world. I have been reading up about it. It weighs 21,000 tons, it has steam turbines and can make 21 knots. They use coal sprayed with oil to increase the burn rate. It has ten twelve inch guns which can fire nearly twelve miles.'

'I am not a naval architect, Peter,' said Stefan, 'but it sounds pretty powerful. As I said, we are building new battleships, too. I just hope that they do not meet in battle.'

'There hasn't been a real naval battle since Trafalgar,' Peter went on. 'It's about time there was another one.'

Beth was about to say something but Stefan spoke first.

'Don't get romantic ideas about war, Peter. It is a very terrible thing. And those who win wars never get what they were aiming for. Have you read the short story *The Monkey's Paw*?'

Peter shook his head.

'It's a cautionary tale. It was translated into German. The moral is "Be careful what you wish for".'

'Oh', said Peter. 'Am I not allowed to wish for something, like a birthday or Christmas present?'

'Of course you can,' said Beth, sharply. 'But you might not get it.'

'That's not fair.'

'Life's not fair,' she replied.

'What am I to do if I want something?'

'The thing, Peter,' said Stefan, 'is not to be too disappointed and to be grateful for what you have been given.'

'Like when we say Grace?'

'Exactly. And what you get may be even better than what you wanted. Have you thought of that?'

Peter looked at Stefan for a moment and then nodded reluctantly. 'I suppose so.'

James intervened. 'That's enough Moral Philosophy for one day. Let us just be thankful for a warm day, clear skies and'… he looked around him… 'and for love and friendship.'

'Amen to that,' they all chimed in.

James looked at his watch. 'If we start down now, we will be in time for tea. On your feet. Last one to the lochan is a sissie.'

After several tumbles, Peter and his brother Andrew reached the lochan first, and sat there mocking the slower progress of the older members of the party. When they arrived, James went ahead with the boys, while Beth asked Stefan to wait with her. She took out a packet of cigarettes.

'I don't like to smoke in front of the boys, though I am sure they have had exploratory puffs at school.'

She offered one to Stefan.

'I don't usually.'

'No one will know. Have one to keep me company.'

Stefan took one and they lit up.

'Women are not supposed to smoke, according to the men,' she said, 'but it is a symbol of our independence. Besides, I enjoy it. Just as James enjoys his pipe.'

'What does James think about the suffragettes?'

'I don't really know. He never says very much. If I start talking about them, he, like my father, will smile and talk vaguely about "When the time comes". They never specify what that time will be. To be fair, they have never said, as some men have, that women are not responsible enough to vote.'

'I have read in our newspapers of Emmeline Pankhurst and her campaigns.'

'The Womens' Social and Political Union, "Words not deeds", rallies in Hyde Park, breaking windows, arson, throwing stones at the Prime Minister's car. Bills for Women's Voting Rights have been in Parliament for forty years, but have got nowhere. But I'm with Millicent Fawcett on this. She says that these antics are the chief obstacle to the Suffrage Movement in the House of Commons. Another thing. Emmeline is a socialist and a friend of Keir Hardie, and that is seen by some as a sufficient reason for opposing her. She has been arrested several times and has spent time in prison. We had a debate about her in College last term. Some of the girls supported her actions but most of us, while applauding her overall aim, thought that she was an embarrassment.'

'Which college do you attend?'

'Newnham Hall in Cambridge. Millicent Fawcett founded it. I am coming up to my last year.'

'Same as James.'

'Yes, but I am a little older than him. I went up after a spell abroad. I went as a lady's companion all over Europe. We spent quite a lot of time in Art Galleries or taking energetic walks in the mountains. I can converse rather clumsily in a number of languages. Will you help me with my German? It's a bit rusty now, since I haven't spoken it, or rather tried to speak it, for three years. I am reading English Literature, a suitable course for young ladies. But I never did any Science at school and I am not interested in Law or Medicine. I am doing an option on Comparative Literature. There are learned articles which we are supposed to consult, some of them in German. I can get by well enough with a dictionary. But it takes me a bit of time to start thinking in German again. Would you mind?'

'*Es wird ein Vergnügen sein, gnädige fraulein.*'

'*Er... Vielen Dank, freundlicher Herr.*'

They ambled down the path, making no attempt to catch up with James and the boys. Stefan was fascinated to hear about her childhood in India. By comparison, he said, his own childhood had been much less adventurous.

'Apart from storms at sea in the *Victoria*?'

'My father was most careful to watch the barometer and he would never venture out if there was undue risk. He employed an old sailor, Conrad, to look after the boat and come with us on occasion. Conrad had become more cautious with age. He had a saying, which was, roughly translated: "There are old sailors and there are bold sailors, but no old bold sailors." But it was fun to career along with the spray breaking over the deck, especially if one was allowed to take the helm.'

They were still chatting when almost without noticing they came across the other three sitting outside the inn. James had a mug of beer and the boys had lemonade.

'We gave up waiting for you at the gate, so we came here and had a drink. Join us?'

* * *

When dinner was over, Beth and her mother retired to the drawing room while James, Stefan and Mr Millward sat over glasses of port. He had lit a cigar and having helped himself to a liberal measure pushed the decanter towards Stefan, who took a half glass and passed the decanter to James.

'Tell me, Herr Haase. What is happening in Agadir?'

To collect his thoughts, Stefan sipped carefully; he was unused to the rich flavour.

'Well, sir,' he began, 'I only know what has been written in the English newspapers. You will know as much as I do.'

'Yes, yes,' said Mr Millward impatiently, 'but what is behind it?'

'I think… I think it is because the Kaiser wants to expand German influence. You see, Germany came late to the colonisation of Africa and therefore he wants a greater presence there.'

'He has territory in East and South West Africa.'

'Yes, sir, but he wants more and closer to home. France has North Africa and Britain has Egypt.'

'Understood, but why send a gunboat?'

'There was an agreement between France and Germany two

years ago that France should have exclusive political control but would uphold German economic interests in the country.'

'Sounds pretty vague to me,' said James.

'This year there was a rebellion against the Sultan,' Stefan went on. 'The French forced him to accept French troops on the pretext of protecting French lives and property in Fez.'

'Well,' said James, 'I can understand that.'

'But the rebellion was in the remote interior far from Fez. The French agreed to make concessions to Germany if she recognised its position in Morocco. There would be negotiations. But the French have not negotiated so far. Germany sent the gunboat *Panther* to Agadir at the beginning of last month, and the cruiser *Bremen* soon replaced it.'

'Hm,' said Mr Millward. 'That explains what Sir Edward Grey said recently, that the French are not being wise; they should know that Britain would accept a German presence in Morocco. Then France said that would break the Entente Cordiale. And of course, if Germany had access to a port on the Atlantic, that would constitute a threat to our trade routes.'

'We can't have that.' said James, 'As Germany has sent a cruiser we should send a battleship. I read that Mr Lloyd-George said that national honour was more precious than peace and peace at any price would be a humiliation, when our vital interests are threatened, for a great nation like ours to tolerate.'

'He's a Welsh windbag,' said Mr Millward. 'He doesn't have the support of most of the Cabinet.'

He turned to Stefan. 'Have some more port. What do you think, Haase?'

'I am a man of God, and so I must be a man of peace. In Germany there are people who regard war as inevitable. I am worried also by the financial troubles in Germany, and how that will affect my brother's business. A run on the banks is starting. There could be great unemployment if factories close.'

'All the more reason for the Kaiser to get his own house in order first before throwing his weight around,' said James.

'Sorry, Stefan. I shouldn't be criticising your Emperor. I wouldn't like it if you criticised King George. But he does seem, from what I have read, to be a bit of a loose cannon.'

'He is a difficult man, yes. The trouble is, I think, that he listens to the generals and admirals rather than civilians and even his chancellor.'

Mr Millward looked at his watch.

'Time we joined the ladies.'

Chapter Two

※

The next two days were damp but the weather cleared thereafter. All the family took the opportunity to go by train to Aviemore for the day. From there, they hired a charabanc to take them through the forest to Loch Morlich, where they had a picnic. Afterwards, Mr and Mrs Millward sat in the sun and dozed. The younger members walked round the loch. James and the cousins strode on ahead. Stefan and Beth walked together. Stefan remarked on the trees he saw round about.

'Scots pine,' said Beth.

'Ah, yes. *Pinus silvestris*. We have some in North Germany, but not round Bremen. The soil is too rich for them there. I have seen them along the coast where the soil is poor. There are some splendid specimens here.'

Suddenly there was a loud clattering of wings on their left.

'Look, Stefan.' Beth pointed into the trees. 'Can you see it? A large bird.'

It ran along and rose into the air sluggishly.

'It's a cock capercaillie. Rather like a turkey. We were lucky to see one so close. They tend to hide in the undergrowth. I'll show you a picture when we get back.'

'Are they good to eat?'

'Not really. It's a pity to shoot them, because all you can do with them is to stuff them and put them in a glass case. Now if you were to offer me a grouse or pheasant...'

'Are they tasty?'

'Very. I'll ask Father to get some grouse for us. The season has just started and there are bound to be some in the butcher's.'

She took his arm.

'You don't mind, do you, Stefan? If anyone notices, I will say that I took your arm in case I tripped over a tree root.'

There were indeed tree roots across the path.

'Beth, I will have to go back to Oxford the day after tomorrow. I have known you only a few days but may I write to you in Cambridge?'

'My dear Stefan, not only write, but visit me. Regulations don't allow you into my rooms, but we can have lunch or tea together, and a walk along the Backs.'

'Thank you. I would like that very much.'

'You're not just being polite, are you?'

'*Ich meine es wirklich ernst.*'

Beth paused for a moment. 'I can't think how to say it in German, but if you don't come to Cambridge when term starts again, I will certainly descend on you in Oxford. Trains run regularly through Bletchley.'

A squawking came from nearby. A brightly coloured bird flew across the path.

'Whatever's that?'

'It's a jay,' said Beth. 'A beautiful bird, with a raucous call.'

As they walked, Stefan told her about his plans for the ministry. She replied that she wasn't sure that there was a god but she was open to persuasion.

'I can't persuade you by argument. It is not an intellectual exercise, but a matter of faith, and faith comes from trust. It doesn't descend from on high. It has to be worked at.'

'I see. At least I think I see.'

'As has been said many times, God moves in a mysterious way. Do you want to believe in a god?'

'I think so. It would make attendance at church more worthwhile. At the moment I just sit there and let it all go over my head. Actually, I do like to go to Choral Evensong, to hear the music.'

'Ah. A strict Protestant would say that beautiful music was a distraction. One should be meditating on one's sins and striving to repent.'

'I'm not sure I have committed many sins, at least not big ones. I have been unkind and thoughtless like everyone else. I haven't broken the seventh commandment, for example. That was not difficult since the opportunity has never arisen.'

'I go to Choral Evensong as well. We have nothing quite like it in Germany, though there are many fine choirs. Let me try this idea on you. Does it please you that you are attending a service that has not changed substantially since the days of Queen Elizabeth, and that she herself would have heard anthems that are still sung today?'

'Yes. I like the feeling of continuity.'

'Then something that has survived so well over three and a half centuries must be based on people's real conviction that the God they are worshipping exists. Surely if it was based on a false premise someone would have exploded the myth during that time.'

'Sounds a bit Jesuitical to me. But in general I agree with you about the historical validity argument. It's just that I have no…' She fumbled for words. 'The Chariots of Fire have not come my way.'

'I understand. I don't want to preach, but keep an open mind. Then one day, whether you like it or not and probably not at a time of your choosing, you will become certain. Try praying.'

'The last time I prayed I was about five years old. What should I pray for? I remember girls at school. They used to pray the day beforehand that they would pass examinations. I thought that they should have prayed at the start of the year. And it seems wrong somehow to pray for one's personal gain or success. I can understand praying for other people.'

'Your Prayer Book has the answer to this, if I remember it correctly: "Fulfil now, O Lord, the desires and petitions of thy servants, as may be most expedient for them." Start off by using the traditional forms, the Lord's Prayer, for example. Quite apart from running over the words you are opening yourself to God in a sort of meditation. This will gradually make a difference to your life and you will be guided into Faith. But don't be impatient.'

'You know, Stefan, you will make a very good pastor.'

'Well, let's hope the Bishop agrees.'

It had taken them just over an hour to walk round the loch.

'We had wondered where you had got to,' said Mr Millward, looking at his watch. 'The others have been here for some time.'

'Well, Father, we have seen some interesting birds and have been admiring trees. We have seen an osprey's nest.'

Stefan looked at her in some surprise.

'I didn't tell you at the time, because we were having such an interesting conversation. But here we are. Does our carriage await?'

* * *

For Stefan, the week in the Highlands came to an end all too soon. As he took the train back to Edinburgh and thence to London and Oxford, he went over in his mind all the conversations he had had with Beth. Even in his reading of the Daily Office he was distracted by thoughts of her. She was not conventionally pretty, but was spirited and carried herself well. He was already composing in his head the letter he would write to her when he got back to Oxford. It would await her arrival back at College. In the meantime he would write a letter of thanks to the Millwards. He wondered how much he should tell James about her.

Back in his rather shabby rooms at St John's he sternly reminded himself that he was in Oxford to complete his thesis and not to find a wife. Nevertheless he kept a corner of his daily devotions for her and hoped that his prayers might be expedient for her and himself.

Progress in researching his thesis was slow. He had begun by examining the use made of earlier English translators of the Old Testament, William Tyndale and Miles Coverdale, by the Authorised Version. This had led to an examination of the texts used by Tyndale and Coverdale, whether Hebrew, Greek or Latin. There were considerable differences between the versions in the three languages which could impinge on the tenets of the Christian faith. Study of the New Testament would have to wait for another period of research and would concentrate on Greek,

Syriac and Aramaic. He was working on these last two as a sideline for the moment. There were times when he wondered whether he had bitten off more than he could chew. But his supervisor had been encouraging, saying that textual criticism of the Bible, a feature of studies in Germany, should be better known in England and America. He had suggested that the thesis should be published in English as well as German; he was sure that a translator could be found to carry this out, in consultation, of course, with Stefan. Meanwhile, he should be thinking about publishing interim reports of his work in learned journals. This would be of benefit on two counts, as a useful self-discipline, and to make his project available for scholarly comment.

All in all, this was a pretty daunting prospect. But he had chosen to embark on an academic exercise and he must see it through. Thoughts of pastoral work, and even marriage, must be shelved for the time being. He could envisage himself staying in Oxford for another two years at least.

One Sunday afternoon, he took a long walk along the Isis. Back in his rooms, he wrote to Beth. After describing the progress and scope of his researches he went on:

> …Sometimes sitting down at my desk in the morning requires a great effort of willpower. I could instead take a walk through the Parks, or spend time with the newspapers, or write letters. But if I am to get anywhere with my studies I have to apply myself rigorously, postpone my walk till the afternoon and settle back again after tea until time for dinner. Then I read through my notes, say the Office and allow myself a small nightcap, as you call it. Since my visit to Scotland I have developed a taste for whisky, *uisge-beatha*. A curious language is Gaelic. The spelling had seemingly no relation to the pronunciation. Another language for me to tackle.
>
> I hope you have had a good start to your term and I would be interested to hear about what you are studying.

I will try to come over in October. As you can see from the above, I need a break from time to time, and how better to spend it than in your company. *Ich denke sehr oft an dich.*

Please write when you have time.

Stefan

Shortly after term had started he sent a message to James, asking to meet him at the Lamb and Flag. He received a swift response and the following evening they were drinking in the small front room.

'You know, James,' said Stefan, 'at last I am getting a taste for your flat warm English beer. It has taken some time.'

'This brew is pretty decent, one of the best. So, how are the dusty books?'

'No longer dusty. I have done a lot of work since Scotland. The only thing is, the more I look into it, the wider the scope of my thesis will be.' He told James what his supervisor had said. 'So it looks as though it will take some time yet. But my funds can cover it.'

'It's obviously a big undertaking. As for me, I have my Finals at the end of this coming Trinity, and I wish I had a clear idea of what will come after. It might depend on whether I get a First. Should I read for the Bar, or have a go at Civil Service or Colonial Office exams? My father might be able to pull a few strings at the India Office, but I am not sure I want to go there. Too hot and dirty, and, I suspect, a bit of a backwater, in the long term. There are the Colonies; South Africa looks interesting. I have pretty well ruled out the Bar. After four years here the last thing I will want is another bout of books. By the way, did I tell you that I have been awarded my Blue? We had some away matches in the late summer and I made a century and a couple of fifties, much to my surprise. I ended the season with the highest average.'

'Congratulations. You must explain to me what that means.'

James did so at considerable length.

'Can you take your cricket further?'

'I shall have to limit my appearances next summer. There is always the possibility of a county trial. But the fact remains that my future will depend not on my prowess with the bat but on my academic performance. I will have to knuckle down.'

Stefan wanted to ask about Beth, but adopted a roundabout approach.

'I wrote to your parents to thank them for the holiday.'

'Yes. They much appreciated your letter.'

'And are they well?'

'In good heart, thank you.'

'And your sister?'

'Just back in Cambridge, so I hear. When the family got back home, she went on one of the Suffragist marches, much to the Pater's disgust. She was nearly arrested. Did she talk to you about the Women's Movement?'

'She said something on the subject.'

'She has strong views on that, and other things too, as you may have gathered.'

'I can well imagine.'

'We used to quarrel as young children, but then we went our separate ways, and now we get on well enough. I haven't been in touch with her since I came down from Scotland. She stayed on and they all came back together. I assume she is now hard at work in Cambridge.'

'What does she want to do after university?'

'I have no idea. I think she can do anything she puts her mind to. I hope that she will choose something where she can make the most of her talents, and not fritter them away on public posturing.'

'You don't believe in Women's Suffrage?'

'I have never really given it much thought. I suppose I have nothing against it in principle – Beth would not allow me to have any other view – and so I go along with it in the interests of sibling harmony. What do the politicians in Germany think?'

'If I were to belong to a political party in Germany, it would be the *Sozialdemokratische Partei Deutschlands*.'

'What in Heaven's name are they?'

'SPD. Social Democrats. They are not Communists, though the Conservatives like to call them that. They have the greatest number of seats in the Reichstag but the government simply ignores them. I suppose they are closest to your Labour Party. There are extremists in the party, but they are on the fringes. Like you, James, they are in favour of Women's Rights, but the Trades Unions fear that women will put men out of a job, since they will be paid less. And the Trades Unions have industrial power.'

'That had never occurred to me.' He laughed. 'There is so much I have to learn beyond the world of Cricket and the Classics. What do the Communists want?'

'The usual stuff: abolition of the monarchy and titled aristocracy; the ending of worker exploitation achieved by the destruction of Capitalism; establishment of the public ownership in all sectors; the breakup of landed estates; the overthrow of state religion.'

'Goodness! Is that what they want in Germany?'

'I've had to think about it quite a lot, since we as a family own a factory. My brother has to deal with a few hot-heads. But they don't have much of a following. So long as the state provides pensions and welfare and workers are paid a reasonable wage, resentment is tempered by prudence. Most people see that there is no gain in turning everything upside down for ideological reasons.'

'I see. What do you, as a man of God, say to this?'

'We are all men of God, even you, James. I say that workers, male or female, should be paid fairly, that their health should be supported and provision made for old age. Quite how this is done is a question for politicians. I tend to retreat from taking sides in political discussions. Instead, I listen to see what people are thinking, so that I will know what I will come across in my ministry.'

'Didn't Christ say that my kingdom is not of this world?'

'He did indeed. His disciples wanted him to lead a revolt against the Romans and restore Israel. He had another kingdom in mind. That is why I am suspicious when politicians invoke Christianity. The only people who are honest about it are the Communists, who don't believe in God anyway.'

'There's so much I can learn from you, Stefan. I have sat through endless school chapel services, and I avoid College Chapel here as much as I can. My parents never made me go to church in the holidays. But some things stick in the memory, like the quotation I gave you. I admit that I have very little interest in Religion on a personal basis; I make no claim to piety. I suppose I ought to think about the place of Religion in Society and ask myself whether it does any good. Frankly, I have no idea. From what you say about the Communists, they are a bad thing, and therefore if they are against Religion, I ought to be for it.'

'That's as good a reason as any. Too much Theology can cloud the mind.'

* * *

During the Autumn, Stefan made two visits to Cambridge, spending the afternoon with Beth. In between they exchanged letters. Both of them were very busy with their studies and as a rule the letters were short, though Beth wrote at greater length one day in November:

> ...I am just a bit down at the moment. Might be a mild dose of something. I woke up this morning, went to my desk and found it almost impossible to open a book. I have been working on Anglo-Saxon poetry, *Beowulf* and all that, and my head is starting to spin. The thought occurs to me that I am spending time on something that I find un-congenial, and all for nothing. Because of the University statutes, I cannot take a degree, since I am a woman. I will sit the papers and be awarded a class (a first is most un-

likely, and I am not being modest) but there will be no letters after my name. In your wisdom you will no doubt say that such letters are fripperies and that the important thing is to have been educated. I agree with that, but with extreme reluctance. Can I come over next Saturday? I need a change of scene and a shoulder to cry on…

It rained most of the day. They had lunch at a café and went to the cinema in the afternoon, to see three films, *The Moonstone*, *The Mummy*, *Trilby and Svengali* and cartoons. Over tea Beth sat back in her chair and lit a cigarette.

'That was just what I needed, Stefan. *Beowulf* hasn't crossed my mind all day. You have been very kind. We haven't put the world to rights, you haven't tried to convert me and we have had a good laugh.'

'All part of Dr Haase's therapy.'

'What are you doing over the vac.?'

'I must go back to Germany to see my brother and his family and spend Christmas with them. I haven't seen them for some time, and my nephew and niece will have grown up a lot since then. They are eight and six. Uncle Stefan forgot their birthdays, so he owes them an extra large present. I should be back by the middle of January. What about you?'

'Oh, home, I expect. I must call on some aged aunts and assure them I am behaving myself and not falling into bad habits. I will not smoke in their presence. If they ask, as I am sure they will, about young men, I will say that I have had tea with a priest.'

'I am not priested quite yet, but you can stretch a point.'

'I won't mention that you are a German priest. That might give them the vapours.'

'Why so?'

'Well, anything foreign is suspect to them. But I enjoy chatting them up. As girls they were taken to the Great Exhibition and they watched the Duke of Wellington's funeral.'

'Do they have any family of their own?'

'One of them married and he died of wounds in South Africa during the Zulu War. They had had a child but it died of diphtheria. Very sad. So she wears widow's weeds and has a modest pension. She has lived with her sister for the last thirty years. It's funny. Their voices sound exactly the same, they look the same, and sometimes I find it hard to tell which of them is opening the door when I visit.'

'They must be older than your father by some years.'

'Daddy was the product of a second marriage, so they are his half-sisters.'

She looked at her watch. 'I must visit the facilities before I catch the train.'

While she was away, Stefan found a copy of the evening paper left on the next table. The headline announced that a secret deal had been made between France and Germany over Morocco. The article quoted a rumour that Germany, forced by the recent financial crisis which had been engineered, it was said, by the French, had given up claims to Morocco in return for large areas of the Congo (now Kamerun) and the assurance that German economic interests in Morocco would be preserved. The paper commented: 'The Kaiser's bluff has been called and he has backed down in the face of a firm French response.'

He was still reading when Beth returned.

'Forgive me. But it seemed quite important.' He showed her the headline.

She nodded. 'One day you must tell me about it, but, Stefan, I must go straightaway if I am to catch the train. I'll take the paper with me.'

'I'll come with you. If we see a taxi, we will take it. Besides, it's raining again.'

There was no taxi to hand, but Stefan had a large umbrella, which necessitated Beth taking his arm to have some shelter. They made what speed they could and arrived with five minutes to go before the train was due to leave. Stefan bought a platform ticket and handed her into the compartment. She stayed at the door and pulled down the window.

'Thank you, Stefan. Today has done me a lot of good.'

She leant forward and put her arm round his neck and kissed him.

The whistle blew and the train started to move. They waved to each other until they were out of sight.

Chapter Three

❄

As soon as term ended, Stefan took the ferry from Harwich to Hamburg and from there travelled by train to Bremen, where he was met by his brother Dietrich. They had a late dinner at home. Hannah, Dietrich's wife, had gone to bed. The brothers had never been intimate, but maintained a cordial relationship which they resumed without effort whenever they were together. Dietrich, though not a religious man, was keen to hear about the progress of Stefan's work. In return Stefan began to ask him about the business, but Dietrich said that they had things to discuss which could wait until the next day.

'Time for bed. You must be exhausted.'

'The sea was choppy and I didn't get much sleep.'

'I'll tell the children not to come and bounce on you first thing in the morning.'

'I am so looking forward to seeing them again.'

Stefan slept very well and it was past nine o'clock before Hannah came in and opened the curtains.

'Welcome back, Stefan. Come down as soon as you can. The children are waiting for you.'

'I have some birthday presents for them, things I should have sent a long time ago.'

'They will appreciate them all the more for having waited.'

When he arrived in the lounge the children were suddenly shy, and he picked them up, Annelore first, then Heinz.

'My goodness, you have grown. Soon I won't be able to carry you.'

He sat down so that their eyes were level with his, though Heinz was considerably taller than his sister.

'Are you good children?'

They nodded enthusiastically.

'Are you obedient to Papa and Mutti?'

More nods.

'Well. I have something for each of you. This is not a Christmas present, but a late birthday present. You see, I have been away in England.'

He went to the sideboard where he had put the parcels last night.

'Here you are. With my love. I hope you like them.'

Annelore undid the string and tore open the wrapping paper.

'Oh, Uncle Stefan. This is just what I wanted.'

She held up a large doll, an English milkmaid.

'I shall call her Blümchen, and she will be my best friend.'

Heinz unwrapped his present.

'What is this, Uncle?'

'It is a cricket bat and there is a ball to go with it, upstairs in my suitcase.' He went up to fetch it.

'Here we are. Now you mustn't play with this in the house, otherwise you will break the windows. We will have a game outside when it stops raining.'

Stefan had watched games in the Parks on his walks and had asked James to explain the mysteries of Cricket to him. The rain eased off midmorning and he and Heinz went outside into the yard. He showed Heinz how to hold the bat and marked off a wicket with chalk on the wall. He threw the ball at him underarm and very quickly the boy was hitting the ball cleanly.

'Well done, Heinz. I have a good friend called James and he plays Cricket for Oxford University. He would be proud of you.'

Annelore came out and insisted on having a go. Heinz objected, saying that she wouldn't like him playing with her doll.

'No, I wouldn't. She's my friend,' was the reply.

Heinz was about to protest further but Stefan urged him to let her have a go. The bat was too big for her and she missed the ball most times.

'Silly game,' she declared and went back inside.

Just then, they were called for lunch. Hands were washed. Hannah asked the children if they had thanked their uncle for the presents.

Stefan nodded. A guilty look crossed their faces.

'Thank you, Uncle,' they said in unison.

After lunch, the maid took the children away for a rest on their beds.

'They will be having supper with us tonight, so they will be staying up a little later than usual.'

Hannah poured coffee and they sat in front of the fire.

'They children seem to be blooming,' he said. 'How are you?'

'I'm fine,' she said. 'Same as ever. I am a bit worried about Dietrich. He has had trouble in the factory to deal with – he will no doubt tell you all about it. Your visit will do him a lot of good. Take him for long walks. He needs the exercise. And yourself? You are getting thin on top, I see, but apart from that?'

'Being immersed in books the whole time can, as they say in England, get on top of you. But I go for long walks in the afternoons, whatever the weather. A trouble is that few people are working on the same topics as myself, so I don't have many contacts to share ideas with, and then only by letter.'

'Have you made some friends?'

'The College has been very helpful. I am the first Rhodes Scholar they have had. The undergraduates look on me as a strange creature; I am rather older than most of them. But my English is good enough to keep up with them at dinner.'

'But what about personal friends? You have been there over a year.'

'Well...' He told her about the Millward family and his Scottish holiday.

'There is the daughter. Her name is Beth. She is at Cambridge but I go to see her and she has visited me. We write regularly.'

'That's good news. Have you... are you engaged to her?'

'Oh no. We have never even hinted at it. She is a good companion and we talk about everything. She wants women to have the vote; there is a big movement in England. I would like to see more of her but there are two reasons why I should not get too fond to her. She is English and I am German and about to be a priest. She is not a believer. If we were serious about each other there could be difficulties.'

'I don't see why, if you really love each other.'

'In an ideal world, I would agree. But both of us have other responsibilities. I must finish my thesis and be ordained; she has to finish her degree and... she doesn't know what she wants to do, but she certainly doesn't want to settle into cosy domesticity just yet.'

'So settle for loving friendship, then.'

'And who's to say what the future will bring? These are very uncertain times.'

Dietrich returned from the office early and he and Stefan went out for a stroll before it got dark. Stefan prompted him with a question about the business.

'Huh. You may well ask. Things are getting tighter. Wages have gone up significantly in the last few years, which, to be fair, is reasonable, but productivity hasn't, not because of the workforce, but because the market is weakening. We have had several good contracts with English firms, but they are coming to an end and will not be renewed.'

'Why?'

'Politics, theirs and ours.'

'I see.'

'The stock market difficulties this summer have not helped, either. They should have made us more competitive for foreign buyers. The Trades Unions are split. The Liberals are generally cooperative, but the Socialists – there are not many of them but they make a lot of noise – want compulsory union membership, free collective bargaining, and worker representatives on the board, for Heaven's sake! I hold consultations, but I will make the final decisions about what wages to pay, since I know what our market will bear. Any other way will bring chaos, which is in no one's interest. The Socialists have threatened to strike, but the men turned them down at a mass meeting. I didn't interfere. Just let them get on with it. But I fear that will not always be the case. The SPD are gaining ground.'

'I can see that you have a lot of problems to face, all at once.'

'There is one glimmer of hope. Government spending on armaments and ships has increased markedly in the last few years, so I am trying to find a niche for our machine tools. Krupps has shown much more interest recently now they have ended their association with Vickers in England. I am going down to Essen the day after tomorrow with two of our managers to make our pitch.'

'Does it worry you that your products are being used for guns?'

'Should it? We have had a line in weapons manufacture for a time, and if we get a good contract with Krupps it will keep our men in work for the foreseeable future. The politics I leave to others. I suppose you could rationalise it and say that guns are needed for defence of our country. What was it that our Latin teacher used to say? *Salus populi suprema lex.** I justify the making of armaments by quoting the old Roman saying: "Let him who desires peace, prepare for war." The danger of that, of course, is that those in power will feel they need to use those armaments, since the country has spent so much on them.'

'I'm not trying to be holier than thou. It is a very complex question. I have started to think about it. As a priest, I must be against war, as war is always destructive not only to the losers but also to the winners, in terms of lives lost or ruined, lives which could otherwise have been fruitful and happy. But that attitude is not much help if others are making war on us.'

'So how would you see your role as a priest in wartime? Is it "Praise God and pass the ammunition"?'

'As a priest, I have to be with my flock, wherever they may be, to minister to their immortal souls, giving comfort and teaching them of God's love, whether it is in the pulpit of the Christuskirche, or down a mine, or on a battlefield.'

'I can see your point. So how do your scriptural studies come into it? What is the use of Biblical Hebrew in that context?'

* The safety of the people is the highest law.

'An English friend of mine made exactly the same point. I replied that my studies into the origins of our faith will help me to proclaim it. That sounds very grandiose, but it has merit. It is up to me to put it into practice.'

They walked on for a few minutes in silence. Then Stefan asked: 'Do you think there will be war? Being over there, I have been rather out of touch with things here.'

'There is a lot of talk about Germany claiming its rightful position at the head of Europe, whatever that means. Naturally the French and the Russians don't like that. England, well, you would know more than me.'

'People don't talk to me very much about it. Maybe they are embarrassed to raise the subject. But I have heard that the aristocracy rather admire Germany, and no one is too keen on the French. There are close personal connections with England, the Kaiser being King George's cousin, and, as I believe, so is the Tsar.'

'I fear that our masters have egg on their faces after the ham-fisted business over Agadir. And for what? A large area of tropical rainforest, of no strategic interest whatsoever. And they have added to the suspicions France and England have of them. Bismarck would have been much more canny.'

'But the new Chancellor, Bethmann Hollweg, he's a moderate, surely?'

'He can't seem to get a grip on the Reichstag. The Navy League has been pressing for a more aggressive foreign policy, which involves more battleships. Admiral Tirpitz and the Great General Staff under von Moltke carry on in their own sweet way and ignore the legislature. Army estimates have not been debated for some years. I'm not a political theorist, Stefan, but it does not seem right in the long term. Sooner or later the people will start to murmur, to use your biblical phrase. Judging by what some of the Socialists say, there could be revolution.'

* * *

Beth had returned to Cambridge in a cheerful mood. Time with

Stefan had banished her blues, and she opened her books again with enthusiasm. But before everything else, she dashed off a letter to Stefan. For a few days she visited her pigeon hole frequently looking for a reply, but none came. She told herself that he must be very busy and she should be patient. Nevertheless, he was always at the back of her mind, and whenever she saw a man in the street who looked like him she quickened her pace. At last, when term was nearly over and she was preparing to go home, his letter arrived:

My dear Beth,

I should have written earlier but I have been totally immersed in writing an article for a journal summing up what I have been researching so far and I had a deadline to meet. Praise God, that is now finished and sent off. I will have the proofs back in the New Year. I celebrated the completion of the task with a drink with James in our favourite pub. He seemed a bit down, what with the gloomy weather here at the moment and the magnitude of the revision he is facing. Please encourage him to stick at his books over the vacation; there are only a few months to go. And you have your own work to do; you can share the load. I remember one vacation at Heidelberg I went on a reading party in the mountains. We all sat round a table and worked for eight hours a day, with the afternoon free to walk and refresh oneself. I found that a very helpful discipline. In the evening, to relax, we played silly games, nothing to do with our studies.

I treasure the memory of the days we have spent together. You are always in my thoughts, and will continue to be so while I am in Germany. I start my journey tomorrow. I hope you will have a very happy Christmas with your family, and I look forward very much to seeing you again.

Dein liebevoller Freund,

Stefan

Beth was heartened by his letter and wanted to reply at once, but then she realised that she did not know his address in Germany, and she would have to wait until the new term. She resolved to put Stefan's advice about work methods into effect and twist James's arm if necessary. When she suggested to him that they work together, she did not mention that it was Stefan's idea; she had decided that she would not reveal to the family the extent of her feelings for him. James was reluctant at first, but she persisted and within a couple of days he was hard at it and refusing distractions. She kept her side of the bargain. They allowed themselves a break from Christmas to the New Year.

Beth's mother, not having seen her daughter for some months, was anxious for a tête-à-tête. One dry afternoon she said to Beth: 'Take me for a walk. It will have to be a slow one, what with my poor legs.'

They wrapped up well, and Beth took her for a walk along the lane adjacent to their house.

'Your father takes me out in the car for a jaunt, but it is awfully noisy, and smelly. Otherwise we go shopping in the village or up to town for the day. Much as I love him, it is very nice to have other faces around.'

She leant on Beth's arm. 'Sometimes I feel I have been neglectful of my children, sending them away to boarding school at an early age. And when you were with us in India, there were so many servants to look after you.'

'I don't feel neglected, Mother, nor does James. I think that thanks to you both you have given us a good start in life. We have grown up to be reasonably well-balanced individuals, enjoying good health. Compared with many people we have been very fortunate.'

'Well, as I said, it's lovely to have you home. Now tell me, how is your work? I'm glad to see you and James getting your heads down but don't drive yourelves too hard. To overwork is as bad for you as being lazy.'

'Mother, I realise that. But for both of us it will all be over in six months' time. James's future career depends on his results, and I must encourage him by working alongside. Besides, I want a good class for myself, if only for my personal satisfaction. So for both of us the effort will be worth it.'

'And what do you want to do after all your education? You have never mentioned anything.'

'That is because I don't have any clear ideas. I would like to do some more travelling. I suppose I could end up as a teacher, but the prospect doesn't thrill me.'

'Beth, dear, I have to ask this. Do you have a young man in mind? You are twenty-five, and it is about time you settled down. And, dare I say it, you would be a good catch for a professional man.'

Beth took her time to reply, as her thoughts whirled. Did a few meetings with Stefan and an exchange of letters amount to a significant relationship? At last, trying not to sound too sharp, she said: 'Mother, this is the twentieth century. I know that women still have legal handicaps, but they will be done away with eventually, I'm sure of it. I can make a good career without marriage. But I do want to marry at some time and have a family as you did.'

Mrs Millward nodded. 'Well, I hope you don't leave it too late, not just for your health but for my own sentimental reasons. I long to have a grandchild, and I am ashamed to say I feel jealous when my friends boast about their grandchildren.'

'You may have aches and pains, Mother, but you are not that old. You have many years ahead of you.'

'I wish that were true.'

They walked on slowly. Beth noticed that her mother was limping more obviously and sometimes wincing with pain.

'Is it your knees, Mother? Are you going to see a doctor?'

'What can a doctor do? It's a family failing. My mother suffered from arthritis too, and she had it in her hands as well. It caused her a lot of pain and was very frustrating for her. She was a skilled needlewoman. The thing to do, I have been told, is to keep moving, however slowly, and not sit down all day.'

'I'm sure that must be right.'

'Anyway, enough of my health, or lack of it. That young man who came with us to Scotland. He wrote us a nice letter, excellent English, though perhaps a little formal.'

Beth wondered what was coming next.

'Interesting man,' Mrs Millward went on, 'very academic but he had a sense of humour. James tells me that they meet in Oxford from time to time when he has time to spare from his researches. What is he working on?'

'Biblical studies, I believe,' said Beth.

'James also told me that he is proficient in ancient langauges, Hebrew as well as Latin and Greek.'

'He would have to be, wouldn't he, for the Old Testament.'

'I suppose he will be a Herr Doktor or Herr Professor back in Germany.'

'Probably.'

'Maybe he will come to Scotland with us another year. I will tell James to invite him.'

Beth's father, despite being retired, seemed to be busy with matters in London and went up for a day most weeks, and stayed the night at his club. While at home, he discussed the latest news over dinner, which usually resulted in a monologue, because James and Beth were too busy to read the papers. One evening, however, when his wife had left the table, he offered James a cigar and poured him a glass of port. Then, noticing that Beth was still at table, he poured her a glass as well. Beth lit a cigarette.

'Now your mother doesn't like you smoking.'

'Too bad, Father. I bet she doesn't like you or James smoking either, but she doesn't say so, because she loves you.'

There being no direct response he could make, Mr Millward changed the subject.

'That German fellow who came with us to Scotland – nice chap – what is he doing over the vac.?'

'He has gone back to Germany to see his family,' said James, 'for the first time in over a year.'

'I'd wondered if we ought to have invited him for Christmas.

It would have been useful to have a German perspective on things.'

'What do you think is going to happen, Father?' Beth asked.

'They say that the Kaiser is a bit of a loose cannon. His latest sally is to call himself Admiral of the Atlantic. I ask you! Think about it. What does Germany want a deep-sea navy for? Against whom? How would she use it? She has few overseas colonies and none of them are in a strategic position. If she attempted to challenge the Royal Navy, we could block the Channel and the North Sea, and the Russians, I suppose, could keep her out of the Baltic. Geography is against her.'

'But she has a powerful army,' said James. 'It has successfully fought recent wars against Austria, Denmark and France. All in the last fifty years.'

'That is a problem for Europe, not us. We would only intervene if Germany came to dominate Europe militarily. Our policy has always been to ensure as best we can that no state has total supremacy in Europe. That was true in Marlborough's day, Wellington's too, and it holds true today.'

'We are allies of both France and Russia.'

'Agreed. But those alliances are flexible. We are not committed to jump in at the first sound of gunfire. And, to put it bluntly, so long as we have the Navy to control the sea, we can resist invasion. We don't really need to put British soldiers on the Continent. We haven't done so since Waterloo.'

'So, Father,' said Beth, 'you think that alliances and ententes are not worth the paper they are written on?'

'We have no more necessity to join in a European war than Sweden or Norway.'

'But if, as you say, Britain controls the seas, then we can easily transport our troops to Europe.'

'Listen, Beth. Indulge your father in a history lesson. Since Waterloo, the British Army has fought most of its wars outside Europe, using colonial troops. Ever since Cromwell, we have distrusted the idea of having a large standing army at home. At

Culloden, many of the soldiers were German mercenaries. Our professional army, such as it is, is mostly stationed abroad. The last time it was used in an European context was in the Crimea sixty years ago, and we didn't do very well. I fear that if we engage in a European war today, we will have to conscript thousands, perhaps millions. Heaven knows what that would do to the country.'

'Well,' said Beth, 'in that case, women will have to take over work usually done by men. In return, women will demand the vote, quite justifiably.'

Chapter Four

❄

A week after her return to Cambridge, Beth slipped away from her studies to attend a Suffragist Rally in London. After an early lunch at the Lyons Corner House in Coventry Street, as it was raining she took a bus to the Albert Hall and joined the long queue of women waiting outside. By the time she came to the door, it appeared that there were only a few seats left, but she found a place next to a woman whom she judged to be about her age. She was dressed in a dark coat. Beth took off her damp hat and some of the rain drops fell onto the woman's lap. Beth apologised.

'Why does it always rain when I come to London?' she said.

'Have you come far?' the woman asked.

'Cambridge. And yourself?'

'Oh, just from Wimbledon. Are you at the university?'

'Yes. Newnham. One of the reasons why I wanted to come was to hear Mrs Fawcett again. She founded our college, you know.'

'I thought about Cambridge, but in the end I went to Royal Holloway. And I am now teaching, for my sins.'

'I am in my last year. Beth Millward.'

'Frances Stevenson.'

'Have you been to many rallies, supporting the cause?'

'I heard Mrs Pankhurst several times. She is a very inspiring speaker but I find her tactics distasteful.'

'I too have heard her. I was standing not far from her at a rally and I was nearly arrested. Actually, it was quite frightening. The women round about me were screaming at the Police, and three of them were carried off and put in a black van. I beat a hasty retreat before the Police came back for more.'

'I want to hear Mrs Fawcett. She is a very important woman, and would have been a member of Parliament, and a very distinguished one, if the Law had allowed it. She speaks out on many issues besides Suffrage.'

Beth was about to continue the conversation when the audience suddenly hushed. From the side of the stage, under a huge banner proclaiming the 'National Union of Women's Suffragist Societies', came a procession of ladies, and at the end the diminutive figure of Millicent Fawcett herself. The organ struck up and everyone sang the National Anthem before settling back in their seats. The Chairman called the meeting to order and introduced the first speaker:

'Mrs Garrett Anderson is one of the most distinguished women of our generation. You will probably know of her achievements, but they are worth repeating. She was the first woman to qualify as a medical practioner, and surgeon. She founded her own hospital for women. She is the first woman to be Mayor of a borough, her home town of Aldeburgh. And yet this lady, who has made such a significant contribution to our national life, is not able to vote in a Parliamentary, or indeed, any other election.'

Cries of 'shame'.

'Mrs Anderson.'

The Chairman sat down and Mrs Anderson rose to speak. Despite her seventy-six years she spoke with a clear, firm voice, outlining the difficulties she had experienced in her career, and how lonely she had felt in her struggles. 'Not only has it been the fault of the system, but also our fault, ladies. We have been too ready to accept meekly the position that society has decreed for us. I am too old to take the campaign for women's rights to the streets, and I am not altogether happy with some of the antics of our younger sisters. My own daughter, for example, a qualified doctor, has been arrested at a rally. Yet holding up a banner does not deserve being manhandled by a burly policeman. My appeal today is to all of you, young and old, to press peacefully for the enfranchisement of women by argument and persuasion, not least among your own menfolk. Spread the word, ladies, spread the word, keep up the pressure, and be assured we will achieve our aim.'

She sat down to much applause. Other speakers followed, who spoke to similar effect. Finally it was the turn of Mrs Fawcett.

'Ladies, we have heard today many fine words, persuasive arguments and many instances of discrimination against women. I will add one from my own family. My daughter Philippa, who, it must be said, did not inherit her ability in Mathematics from me, was the first woman to obtain the top score in the Cambridge Maths Tripos and yet she could not be awarded the title of Senior Wrangler, which is open only to men.'

More cries of 'shame'.

'But enough of that. Our movement is primarily directed at obtaining votes for women, but there are other issues that must be faced as well, some of them very distressing. I mean the abuse of childen, which can be prevented to a certain extent by raising the age of consent, and general cruelty to children even within the family. I want to stamp out the so-called white slave trade. I want the repeal of the Contagious Diseases Act. This is an unpleasant topic, ladies, but it too must be faced. Our fallen sisters, prostitutes, can be imprisoned for passing on sexually transmitted diseases, and can be imprisoned also for refusing an examination that is intrusive and painful. Men infect women, but they are not subject to the law. Double standards indeed. And when sexual offences are considered in court, women are excluded, so that they cannot speak for themselves. These issues will not hit the headlines, but they are pressing and need to be considered by Parliament. They can only be considered in all their implications if women are allowed to take part in the debates.

'Now I have to tell you, ladies, that in March of this year a bill is being laid before Parliament, the Parliamentary Franchise (Women) Bill. This is a significant move, in that it is a bill devoted specifically to our cause, not just an amendment tacked onto other legislation. I know Mr Lloyd George had endorsed that procedure, as a means of getting the matter more easily through Parliament, but in my view it was not good enough. This new bill will indeed open the vote to women of some property, in line with legisation for men.

'At the moment there is little chance of any bill for the enfrenchisement of all women passing, but it is a step in the right direction. We have to be patient…'

At that point several rows in the audience stood up and, unfurling a banner with purple, white and green stripes which read 'Women's Social and Political Union', started chanting 'Deeds not words, deeds not words'. Other women in different parts of the audience stood up and joined in the shouting. One woman waved a policeman's helmet on a stick. Mrs Fawcett tried to calm things down, but the volume increased as more women pitched in. Most of the audience remained seated but some took their umbrellas and tried to force the hecklers to sit down. When Mrs Fawcett saw that exchanges were becoming angrier and there was a risk of violence, she led a procession from the stage. Afterwards a woman jumped up and tried to pull down the banner but was restrained by two stewards. Meanwhile, the doors were opened and the audience was invited to leave. Within a few minutes only the protestors were still in the hall. They took over the stage and started to hold a rally of their own. Outside, a line of policemen stood at a discreet distance but did not intervene.

Beth and her new friend Frances made their way to a café nearby.

'My goodness, what a carry-on,' said Beth. 'It was lucky it didn't turn really violent. I think that Mrs Fawcett was right to leave the platform. There is no point in arguing with people who won't listen.'

'The trouble with the Pankhursts,' said Frances, 'is that they make a lot of noise, as you heard, but also they refuse to join forces with our organisation, and they make Women's Suffrage something to be feared because they create disorder, and in other quarters they become a laughing stock. I hate to think what the papers will say tomorrow.'

'Do you think Mrs Fawcett was right to be content with limited female suffrage in the first instance? I am not sure myself.'

'We have to be practical, Beth. I know that the Prime Minister is against us, and his wife virulently so. Other members of the Cabinet are supportive, up to a point.'

'We have an ally in Mr Lloyd George. As Chancellor of the Exchequer he must surely carry some weight.'

'He has so much else on his mind just now, and he can only devote so much time to the cause. He is a marvellous speaker, and he is pulling the Liberals in the right direction, pensions, reform of the House of Lords and so on. I think he is the coming man.'

'I have never seen him, but I have read about him.'

'Believe me, you will find him very impressive in person.'

'Have you met him?'

'Oh yes. I was recommended to be a tutor to his daughter Megan over the last summer holidays. I was interviewed by him in Downing Street. I went up to stay with them in Criccieth. It was quite an experience.'

'It must have been fascinating.'

'He talked quite freely about his colleagues, and I learnt things that I must not divulge.'

'Well, although I am naturally curious, I wouldn't dream of asking.'

Beth smiled and Frances gave a broad grin. 'Seeing our leaders face to face,' she said, 'makes a great difference. The public persona is quite different from the man you meet in his home.'

'Mr Lloyd George can be quite abrasive in his speeches. He likes to pour scorn on his opponents.'

'With me, he has been kindness itself. And as someone said to me, "When you talk to Lloyd George you think you are the most important person in the world." He has a keen sense of humour and likes to tell jokes against himself. And he tells stories wonderfully.'

Beth noticed the animation in Frances as she spoke; Beth could see that she had considerable attractiveness. A wicked thought entered her mind, which she hastily suppressed.

'I have a friend who is German and I have talked to him about Female Suffrage in Germany. He is in favour in a vague way. So is the Social Democratic Party but it actually does very little. He told me that there was a bill two years ago to extend the vote to all adult males in Prussia, but there was no reference to votes for women. The Socialists are very keen, of course, but only as a way of attracting attention and disrupting Capitalism. They do not see Female Suffrage as an end in itself. And the general feeling is that full Female Suffrage can only come when all men have the vote. The Trades Unions are afraid that Female Suffrage will encourage women to steal men's jobs because they are usually paid less than men.'

'Trades Unions over here think the same. Mr Lloyd George has said that dealing with them is like leading a reluctant horse to water. The Trades Unions and the Directors deserve each other. He has spent quite a lot of time in the last few years banging their heads together. Your German friend, what does he think about England?'

'He is studying at Oxford. There are times when he is regarded with suspicion, but fortunately his accent is very good and he does not sound obviously German. He is worried about the way things are going there. The Kaiser is very envious of the British Empire and wants to build up a navy to match ours.'

'And Zeppelins. If they can't get across the Channel by sea, they will try by air. Mr Lloyd George told me this story. He was in Stuttgart and watched a demonstration of the Zeppelin. It crashed. There was no loss of life but the reaction of the crowd was interesting. They were aghast and wept. Then they began to sing *Deutschland über alles* vociferously. It was as though a national icon had been besmirched. I don't think the British would have reacted in the same way.'

'Does Mr Lloyd George think that there will be war?'

'He says that Germany feels herself hemmed in by France and Russia on land, and by Britain at sea. He has met Bethmann Hollweg the Chancellor, who told him that there is a plot. The reason why Britain is in alliance with France and Russia is not because, to use his own words, "You love each other. It is because you hate Germany".'

'That is nonsense. No one who knows ordinary Germans could possibly hate them. They are modern Europeans, not barbarians. I may be naïve, but there is no reason why we should be at enmity, still less at war. There is so much we share. For a start, King George and the Kaiser are both grandsons of Victoria. And our interests complement each other; they don't clash. It's only the hotheads and some politicians like Churchill who like to stir things up. Think what a difference it would make if women were in charge, Frances.'

* * *

With the New Year out of the way, James Millward settled back to work. His parents tiptoed around trying not to disturb him. Occasionally his father would ask how it was going but James merely replied 'as well as could be expected', as though he was recovering from an operation. Mr Millward once tried to probe further, citing his own experience at a similar stage and offering sympathy; this was not warmly received.

'You were bound to get a first, Pater. But I am not.'

Mrs Millward did not press him to break his isolation by visiting friends, but insisted on fresh air in the afternoons.

'A good walk can put things into perspective. You smoke too much. Leave your pipe at home when you go out.'

As a dutiful son, he did.

When he returned to Oxford, he had a long talk with his tutor.

'Sometimes I feel as though I am bashing my head against a brick wall. I am afraid I am not a natural philosopher. I know what I am supposed to be doing with language, literature and history. But how do I study Philosophy? I have been ploughing my way through Plato and a little Aristotle – I treat them as set texts, but the moderns… I have been through the reading list. I make notes but what do I do with them? I have covered pages and pages but how do I separate the wheat from the chaff? It seems that philosophers devote whole books to a single idea which could be stated in a paragraph. I may as well read a summary and have done with it.'

'I quite understand,' said his tutor. 'You are a man of action, witness your prowess on the cricket field.'

'I am not playing again till after Finals.'

'Well, that is up to you. However, I do advise some serious recreation. As for Philosophy, you are not the only man who has found himself with this problem. There are summaries available; concentrate on them. Take a limited number of problems and work at those…'

'And hope that they come up in Finals.'

'Quite. The pragmatic justification. We all have to make compromises in life. I think your Classics will come up to scratch, but don't try to be too clever in your answers.'

'There's no danger of that.'

'I won't predict a grade for you. All I would say is that examiners are not trying to catch you out, but to put you on your mettle. And don't compare yourself with others. Be satisfied with what you get and move on. There are so many worthwhile things in life besides poring over ancient texts. Do you have plans beyond Oxford?'

'Only vague ideas, mostly negative. I don't want to be ICS like my father and I feel I will have had enough formal education in my life ever since the age of five. The Law would involve further study and does not appeal anyway.'

'Cricket?'

'I might try it for a year or so – I have the means – but what's the Biblical phrase? Many are called but few are chosen. I will go for a county trial this summer and see what happens. And as for the traditional careers, Church and Army, they don't ring bells. I once said I might try for the Colonial Service, but…'

James broke off. His tutor remained silent.

'The thing is,' he went on, 'niggling at the back of my mind is the feeling that as a gilded youth with more advantages in life than ninety-nine per cent of the population I should make good use of them and not footle around.'

'Your father, can he not open doors for you?'

'He would, I think, if I asked him. But he would have to be convinced that I was set on a particular career and not just playing for time.'

His tutor sighed. 'Again, you are not the first young man to find himself in this predicament. Do you want my advice?'

'Yes, please.'

'In a way it is better just now to limit your horizons to Finals. When they are over by all means enjoy a holiday and have a go at a county. If you don't, you will always regret not having tried. And somewhere along the line you will meet someone or experience something that will make your mind up for you. You have time on your side. Is that a help?'

'Well, I certainly feel less guilty now about not having a chosen career mapped out, like a few of my chums.'

Despite his determination not to be deflected from his work, he applied to Middlesex for a county trial and was accepted for a second eleven match in June. He set aside an evening in the week away from his books and usually ended up in the Lamb and Flag or the White Horse in the Broad. When he went to the Lamb and Flag he noticed that Stefan was in deep conversation with a group from St John's, which pleased him.

One evening Stefan was standing at the bar alone, and James went over.

'I should have got hold of you earlier, but I have been trying to stick to my books and ration my visits to the pub. I am glad to see that you have made contact with some other chaps.'

'Yes, we have had some good chats, and not all about the iniquities of the Kaiser. How is your revision?'

'I have become a hermit, quite unlike me. I am not sure how much more I can take of it. I have even made a chart, like the chart we made at prep school, counting the days till the exams. Sometimes I want to chuck it all up and shake the dust of Oxford from my feet, and then I pull myself together and tell myself that a couple of months is nothing compared to a lifetime.'

'That's interesting. Your sister has said much the same sort of thing.'

'She never said anything to me. We did work at our books together over the Christmas vac. I love her dearly, but she is not very communicative. Never has been. Have you been in touch?'

'We write and visit each other on occasion.'

'Why, you crafty old thing!'

'She has become a good friend. Thank you for introducing us.'

'And I never really noticed. I don't know what to say, but... well... I'm glad for your sake that you have found an English girl you like, and... glad that she likes you. You don't have... er... an arrangment, do you?'

Stefan shook his head. 'We are good friends, but nothing more, especially at this present time and with our possible careers – she is agnostic, by the way.'

'I have never asked about her views. We don't normally talk about things like that at home – too buttoned up, too British.'

'When my thesis is finished I must go back to Germany and complete my ordination. After her degree she could do anything she puts her mind to and any formal arrangement between us would only get in her way.'

'That's very honourable of you, Stefan.'

'Practical as well as honourable.'

'When are you seeing her next?'

'I told her I would come up to London during the Easter vac.'

'You must come to see us at home. The Mater and Pater would be delighted to see you. I will be there for just a few days then it's nose to the grindstone for the final straight. I am afraid I might peak too early.'

'English idiom is wonderful. Why nose? What is the final straight? I think I understand peak too early.'

'I don't know about nose. The final straight is the last furlong of a racecourse, usually straight towards the finish.'

'I have never seen a horserace.'

'Ah. Before you go home, this is an English experience you must not miss. I will speak to the Pater and get us into the Epsom Derby. Beginning of June, and not far from us. You must stay for that.'

* * *

James and Beth applied themselves to their books but took a short break over Easter. Beth and Stefan continued to exchange letters and met on Easter Saturday afternoon in London. They met on the steps of the National Gallery. This was the first time they had seen each other since the previous November. Stefan was uncertain how to greet her. After considerable thought he decided that a handshake was the most appropriate salutation. He was sitting on the steps and in the warm sun he had taken his hat off. As he saw her approaching he got up, straightened his tie and went down. Holding his hat in both hands in front of him like a nervous city clerk he went up to her.

'Hello, Beth. It's lovely to see you again.'

'*Schön, Sie auch zu sehen, Stefan.*'

He held out his hand and she took it in both hands. They both laughed.

'I have been practising that sentence all the way here,' she said.

'Well, you said it very nicely. How are you?'

'In good heart, thank you. Where shall we go?'

'Would you like to see the pictures, now we are here?'

She shook her head. 'I can go any time. I had much rather chat to you.'

She took his arm and weaving their way through other couples they went down to St James Park and sat on a bench looking over the lake and the ducks. Beth took her hat off.

'So nice to feel the sun on one's face. Easter is pretty early this year and it has been so drab recently.'

They sat in silence for a moment. Then they both spoke at once.

'You first, Beth.'

'I wanted to ask you about your Christmas in Germany, or should I say *Weihnachten*?'

Stefan told her about his nephew and niece and the conversations he had had with his brother.

'He has to run a business, find a market for his production and pay his workforce. He has won a contract with Krupps to provide machine tools which will be used in the manufacture of weapons. We talked about the morality of it. I am torn. A priest is a man of peace. The profits the business makes supports my academic career. Should I have a conscience about that?'

'Oh dear. A big question. You need money to provide for your training to be a priest. It has to come from somewhere. I dare say that the Lutheran Church has all sorts of investments. I think the end justifies the means. The spiritual guidance that you will impart to your flock can't be measured in financial terms, but it will be all the better for your training.'

'Thank you for that. I have been praying about it.'

'What do you pray for?'

'Er... when I am faced with a difficult decision and I can't see which way to go, I ask for guidance from the Lord, basically a push in the right direction. I have trust that the outcome will be the right one.'

'I wish I had your faith.'

'It doesn't necessarily make life any easier. But enough of me. I want to hear about you. By the way, I have told James about us. He called me a crafty old thing.'

'Typical James. Did he approve?'

'On the whole. He was rather taken aback.'

'I will have to explain to him. Sisters often have to point things out to unobservant brothers.'

'I don't have a sister, but my sister-in-law does that for me.'

Beth told him about her Christmas vacation.

'I think I told you in my letter about my mother's arthritis. She has got worse since Christmas. She walks around the house with two sticks or pushes a trolley in front of her if she has to carry anything. Father has bought her a bath chair so that she can go out with someone, usually me or one of the servants, pushing her. She takes pills for the pain, but tries to do without as much as she can. More than the actual pain is the frustration at not being able to get about under her own steam.'

'Poor woman.'

'At least her hands are unaffected, so that she can dress herself and use a pen.'

'And how is your work? You are not peaking too soon, I hope. I am using James's phrase.'

'Sometimes I think it would be good to peak at any time, not just before the exams.'

'Don't let it get you down. I know how keen you are to do well, but have confidence in yourself. I have confidence in you.'

'Kind of you to say so. Perhaps you could say a prayer for me; I need all the help I can get. And your work?'

'If all continues as at present, I will be nearly finished by this time next year. I will spend the Trinity Term not topping and tailing, as you say, but enjoying the delights of Oxford which I have shunned so far.'

'Well, good luck with that. Oxford had better look out.'

'And where will you be, dear Beth?'

'No plans so far. I know I ought to have plans. I don't want to rest on my laurels, such as they will be. It also depends on how well my mother is.'

'I shall say a prayer for her, too.'

'Will you come to us when Trinity ends? I don't know what James's plans are.'

'He did mention something about the Derby. But that seemed a throwaway remark.'

'Of course you must come with us for that. We have been in past years, and it is great fun. Apart from everything else it will be another British experience for you to savour.'

Chapter Five

❋

On Wednesday 4th June 1913, Mr Millward drove to Epsom Downs in his Wolseley tourer; he was very proud of his new machine and was nervous about allowing James to drive it. So James sat beside him with Beth and Stefan in the back. It was a sunny day and the hood was down. They set out early because of the heavy traffic. It was just as well as the field set aside for vehicles was nearly full. Most of the spectators came by special trains laid on for the day. It was later estimated that half a million people had attended the races.

After a picnic lunch prepared by Beth they made their way to the course just in time to watch the King and Queen being driven past the Grandstand amid the cheers of the spectators. Then Mr Millward bumped into a former colleague and together they went up into the stand. James and Stefan joined the queue at a bookmaker's, leaving Beth to guard their place by the rail.

'Come on, Stefan. Have a flutter. It is the British thing to do on Derby Day. Part of the fun.'

'I'm not sure that it is right for a priest to have a wager.'

'Nonsense. Leave your clerical collar behind. If you have scruples donate your winnings to a good cause.'

'Oh well. Why not? How do I go about it?'

'Look at the race card and choose a horse and put five shillings on it. I'll show you.'

Stefan scanned the card.

'I don't know anything about horses. So I will bet on the first one, Aboyeur.'

'The odds are not very good, 100 to 1. But never mind. I am a loyal Briton, so I will bet on the King's horse, Amner.'

Having placed their bets, they rejoined Beth near Tattenham Corner.

'Now Stefan, this is a flat race, unlike the Grand National

where they have to go over jumps. In effect it is a sprint for three year-olds over one and half miles. The start goes uphill but from halfway they start the descent and by the time the horses go past us they will be travelling at well over thirty miles an hour. It will be over pretty quickly, about two minutes.'

'So much effort, and money expended all for two minutes. It's irrational.'

'But historic. It was first run in 1780. And the prize money is enormous, and the bookmakers rake it in unless there is a great upset in the odds.'

They watched some early races. As the time of the Derby drew closer the crush of spectators grew. James and Stefan being tall could look over the ladies' hats, but Beth could only see in front of her. At ten past three there came a cry of 'They're off' and though the horses were still out of sight the cheering and shouts of exhortation started.

'Come on, Amner,' shouted James.

'It can't hear you,' said Beth.

'But it makes me feel better.'

After a few moments the cheering around them increased and the leading horses came into view.

James raised his binoculars.

'That looks like yours, Stefan, just ahead of the pack.'

Aboyeur came to the corner first with Craganour very close behind and other horses within half a length.

'Damn. Can't see Amner. Ah yes, there he is. Just my luck. He won't be placed... Good God!'

* * *

When they got home, Beth described the incident to her mother; she had had a clear view just opposite.

'The whole thing was over in a flash. The King's horse was coming round Tattenham Corner, when a lady ducked out under the guardrail and ran onto the track. The woman tried to seize the horse's reins and was trampled underneath. The horse fell trapping the jockey's leg in the stirrup, but he succeeded in wriggling away. I don't think he was hurt badly. The woman lay quite still. The remaining horses went on their way.'

'That must have been awful to watch, dear.'

'I felt quite helpless, shocked. Some stewards ran onto the track and gathered around the body. Within a few minutes men appeared with a stretcher and she was lifted onto it and carried away.'

'Poor woman. Do we know who she is, or perhaps was?'

'When we were in the car park, I heard a rumour that it was Emily Wilding Davison. I know of her and I may well have seen her at demonstrations. She was a member of WSPU.'

'Why on earth did she do something so stupid?'

'Well, she was not just crossing the track to get to the other side, thinking that all the horses had gone past. She had something in her hand; it looked like a banner. Perhaps she was trying to put it on the horse, or just to bring the horse down. After all, it was the King's horse, so I suppose she wanted to create a scene and be a martyr for the Suffrage Movement. Who knows? Probably we will never know.'

Mrs Millward sighed.

'What a terrible waste.'

'Coming home in the car, I kept on thinking about what had happened and I burst into tears. Stefan comforted me. Father and James didn't say anything.'

They had not stayed long after the race. People were making their way to the exit now the big event was over. Mr Millward was waiting for them near the bookmakers' booths. James explained what had happened. Mr Millward nodded grimly, then asked: 'Did any of you put a bet on Aboyeur?'

'I did,' said Stefan.

'Well, you are in luck. Craganour passed the finishing post first a head clear of Aboyeur, but there was a Stewards' Enquiry. Apparently in the home straight Craganour jostled Aboyeur and was wandering all over the place. I could see it quite clearly from where I was sitting. The jockey's actions were quite deliberate. So Craganour was disqualified, which made Aboyeur the winner, a rank outsider at 100 to 1. You'll be a rich man, Stefan.'

'I am not sure I should claim my winnings. It is such a lot of money. I have done nothing to deserve it.'

'Well,' said James, 'as I told you before, put it to a good cause.'

Stefan found his betting slip and took it to the bookmaker. He inspected it and reached into his bag and produced five white five pound notes.

After tea, James popped out to buy an evening paper.

'Yes. Here it is. Aboyeur declared the winner after a Stewards' Enquiry.'

He ran his eye down the page.

'A bit lower down. "Emily Davison, aged forty, was carried unconscious to hospital with serious injuries. Further bulletins will be issued in due course." Hm. What could have possessed her to behave like that? I can't see the point. What do you think, Beth?'

'It is one thing to go to prison for protesting but quite another to sacrifice oneself.'

Stefan nodded. 'I was watching closely at the time. I think that it was a protest that went wrong. I pray that she recovers but it must be admitted that if she dies she will become known for her death rather than her life.'

'I just hope,' said Beth, 'that others will not be tempted to follow her example. I know she was very passionate about Women's Suffrage. She organised protest marches and she was imprisoned several times. She was an educated woman. But...'

'Is Women's Suffrage worth dying for?' asked James. 'Stefan?'

'There have been Christian martyrs down the ages, witnessing to the Faith. I suppose that if she really wanted to be a martyr she must have thought that there was an equivalence.'

'I was going to say,' Beth replied, 'I think that she would have done more good by living and working for the cause than throwing herself away. I would be very interested to hear what her colleagues in WSPU have to say about her.'

'Stunts like this one,' said James, 'and previous law-breaking activities merely show that she had become obsessed with the idea. No sense of proportion. There are other things in life.'

'Spoken just like a man. You have no idea how strongly a lot of women feel about Suffrage. You may just dismiss them as cranks...'

'I'm sure you're not a crank, Beth.'

'Thank you, kind sir, but it is time you woke up to the fact that Women's Suffrage will not go away. Sooner or later, when you have finished bashing a leather ball about the place and start to earn an honest penny, you might consider marriage, and that involves a woman, a woman who might well have her own opinions, and want to be a person in her own right.'

'But votes for women will change the complexion of British politics drastically. It is too big a step to take just now. And besides, not every woman will want to vote. You will simply steamroller them into a position they have never desired.'

'James, you are impossible.' Beth made to get up but Stefan laid a hand on her arm.

'*Pax vobiscum.* We promise to listen in a humble spirit to what you have to say. I have come to a decision. I will donate my winnings in the Derby to Suffragism, and Beth will tell me how to go about it.'

'That's very generous of you, Stefan.'

'I don't need it, and you are converting me to the cause.'

James raised an eyebrow and was about to make a comment when a glare from his older sister deterred him.

There was a certain froideur between Beth and James that evening. Stefan handed over £25 to Beth for the cause. The next day he returned to Oxford, where there was a month or more's work ahead of him before he could consider taking a break. Three days later he was walking along the Broad and saw the newspaper headline, that Emily Davison had died without recovering consciousness.

'So we will never know why she did it,' he thought after he had said a prayer for those affected by her death.

* * *

James and Beth were both waiting for the results of their Finals. James was not good at idling at home; every day he was first to the morning and afternoon mail and unwilling to go out in case he missed the postman. In between he would settle down to the papers or walk round the garden. Beth was calmer and tried to busy herself around the house helping her mother, and writing letters to friends she had ignored during the past few months of revision. One morning she picked up the morning post and found a letter from Newnham. She took it to her room and, taking a deep breath, opened it. An official letter told her that she had obtained a second class. Inside the envelope was a note from her tutor:

Dear Beth,
I hope you are not upset that you did not get a first. But I can tell you that you were within a whisker. Only a certain number of candidates can get a first, and most of them this year were men. You always impressed me as a sensible girl, with a realistic appreciation of your abilities. I am sure that you will not repine at the result. You have many gifts and you can live a full and worthwhile life. Please let me know in due course what you are up to.
With very best wishes,
Your sincerely,
Caroline Edmonds

She stared out of her window for a while, her brain whirling. Then she opened the window and lit a cigarette. She was not unfamiliar with introspection, as her teenage diaries revealed (they still lay in a drawer, though she had never looked at them again). She took a long pull. Yes, she was disappointed not to have obtained a first. But on reflection she reckoned that she had tried her hardest in revision and had not acquitted herself at all badly in the papers. She had brains, but she was not an intellectual. Thank God for that, for she had come across one or two of her colleagues who were extremely bright but hopeless in managing their emotional life and in day-to-day encounters with the world outside academia.

'No repining,' she said to herself. At last she could begin the next chapter of her life, whatever it was to be, without looking back with regrets. She thought about writing a note to Stefan, but reckoned that she should wait until James had had his results. She went downstairs taking the notice and her tutor's letter and showed it to her parents who were still sitting over their breakfast coffee. James was smoking his pipe in the garden.

'I have got a very good second, for what it's worth.'

Mr Millward read the letter from her tutor.

'Never mind the close shave, Beth. We are very proud of you. Come here.'

He got up and kissed her forehead, something he almost never did. Her mother did not get up but held out her arms to hug her.

'Shall I call James in?' she said.

'No,' said Beth. 'I will go out to him. And please don't ask me just now what I am going to do after university, because I really don't know.'

'We won't, dear.'

Beth took the letter and went out into the garden, where James was pacing up and down. She took his arm and they sat down on a bench.

'Have you had news, Beth?'

She handed over the letter. He read it through twice and handed it back. Then he turned to face her, with a broad grin.

'You deserve the biggest of brotherly hugs.' He embraced her with some awkwardness, since he, like his father, was not given to overt expressions of feeling.

'Let's hope,' said Beth, 'that you have good news soon.'

'Oh, never mind me. This is your day. Are you happy with the result?'

'Do you mean, sorry that I didn't get a first? A first would have been nice, but it wouldn't be me. I am happy that I acquitted myself as well as I could, and that the whole business is over. Now I can concentrate on the future.'

'Which is…'

'Whatever may be in store. I'll think about it tomorrow.'

James was silent for a moment. 'Never mind my previous expectations,' he said. 'If I can get as good a Second as you, I will be well and truly satisfied. I think we must celebrate your success. I'll tell the Pater to open a bottle of fizz this evening. I know he has some in the cellar.'

With that he relit his pipe, got up and walked into the house. Beth was left sitting in the garden, already formulating in her mind the letter she would send to Stefan.

A letter for James arrived by the afternoon post. He took it up to his room, counted to three and opened it.

Dear Millward,

You did very well in your History and Literature papers, but fell down somewhat in Philosophy. In view of our discussion recently that will not be a surprise to you – 'know thyself'. I think you will agree that a Second is a fair judgment on you and your performance. Nevertheless you have the ability to make a success of any profession you choose. Please come back to me if you feel in need of advice or a reference.

With best wishes,

Yours sincerely,

Charles Brooks

Short and to the point, as always, he thought. He told himself not to be disappointed; after all he had his Blue, and no one can have everything.

Thus fortified by Philosophy, he went downstairs to break the news.

* * *

Dear Stefan,

Once again, thank you for the most generous donation to the NUWSS. I have handed it in at their office.

We have news. James has got a Second, which he admits is a fair result, though he did work very hard in the last months. I too have a Second and honour has been satisfied for both of us. We are not cut out for academia like you, but I hope we can make a useful contribution to society all the same. Our parents are pleased, and Father brought out some champagne he had had in the cellar for some years. Both of them have refused to question us on what our plans for the future are. Just as well in my case, because I haven't any. In a way, I feel somewhat deflated now the excitement is over, though I have no reason to complain. James will spend the summer playing cricket; he has a county trial coming up, and some minor counties have expressed interest in him. I don't really understand these matters.

I hope your work is going well. I don't know how you measure progress in studies such as yours, or indeed in your approach to the Ministry. Will the end be in sight soon? Sooner or later you must go back to Germany.

Dein liebevoller Freund,

Beth

After several days, Stefan replied:

My dear Beth,

My usual apologies for not replying sooner. In answer to your question, my studies are going well and I am in what you call the home straight. I think I will be finished before the end of the Michaelmas. And then I will be Herr Doktor Haase.

Congratulations to you, and to James, on your degrees. I know you worked very hard and you can be proud of your achievement. Academic distinction is not everything; I too have known one or two first class idiots! Strength of character and purpose is much more important, and you have these qualities in abundance.

I won't ask what you are going to do in the future. These are unsettling times, and who knows what will happen?

I must go back to Germany in August for a month to prepare for my ordination. I have a proposition for you. I can well understand if you think this is impossible, but I have nothing to lose by asking. Will you come back with me to Germany for a few days? Your family has been very hospitable towards me, and it would give me, and my brother and his family, I'm sure, much pleasure to return the compliment. In that way I feel that we will get to know each other better, something I much desire.

There, I have said it.

I am coming to London on Tuesday. Can I see you?

Mit viel Liebe,

Stefan

They met for lunch. Stefan had come up by an early train as he had to look at a document in the British Museum Library. He had only a hour to spare over lunchtime, so they agreed to meet outside the main entrance. They found a café not far away on New Oxford Street and ordered a light meal.

'If I eat too much I will feel sleepy over my books.'

'All I read just now are trashy novels and magazines. My brain can't take any heavy stuff at the moment.'

'I understand.' He paused. 'Germany? Do you think you might be able to come?'

'Yes, of course I'll come. I have my passport. I will have to mug up my German…'

'Both my brother and sister-in-law can speak English fairly

well, and you can teach my nephew and niece some words. Children at that age are very quick to learn, even out of curiosity. You will get to know them better that way.'

'But I must try to speak. Perhaps as we go, we could speak German, so that I get used to it. You speak English in England and I must try to return the compliment.'

'I must ask. Will your parents approve of your visit?'

'It doesn't really matter if they don't. I have my own bank account. But I am sure they would not mind. They think highly of you. My father is not really aware of the depth of our friendship. I have never told my mother about my true feelings, but I am sure she knows – woman's intuition. The fact that you are going to be a priest makes you very respectable.'

They laughed.

'One thing, though. You will be busy and I don't want to get in the way.'

'I am treating myself to a few days off, and then I must see my bishop. But a week together will be a joy.'

'A week it is.'

Stefan told her about their journey.

'It will be twenty hours and overnight. My brother will meet us off the train at Bremen, which will help. You can have a doze on the way.'

'I shall want to see everything. And tell me about your home.'

The hour passed very quickly. After fond farewells Stefan returned to the Library and Beth, with a spring in her step, walked down towards Waterloo Bridge. On the way she passed the offices of the NUWSS. On an impulse she went in.

'Can I help you?' asked the woman behind the desk in the hall.

'Um… yes, please. I was wondering… Well, I have just come down from Cambridge and I am at rather a loose end at the moment. I was wondering if I could be of use. I am a great admirer of Mrs Fawcett…'

'Can you type?'

'Well… no.'

'Can you drive?'

'Drive? No. I'm afraid not... but I could learn.'

The woman thought for a moment.

'Let me put it another way. What can you do?'

'Anything I am asked to do, however mundane.'

She looked at Beth again.

'What is your name?'

'Beth Millward.'

'Are you the lady who came in a little while ago with £25 for the cause?'

'Yes.'

'That was very generous of you, Miss Millward.'

'It wasn't actually my money. It was contributed by a friend who asked me to pass it on to your organisation.'

'I remember you now. Can you wait a moment?'

She got up and went into a back room. Beth could hear a muffled conversation. Then she returned.

'Come through, Miss Millward.'

Beth followed her and saw a young woman sitting at a table, folding letters into envelopes.

'Ellen, this is Beth Millward.'

'Oh. Hello.' She spoke with a northern accent. 'I'm Ellen Wilkinson.'

Beth repeated what she had told the woman at the desk.

'Cambridge, eh? I have just come down from Manchester. History.'

'English.'

'Good degree?'

'Second.'

'Like me.' She looked at Beth. 'If I may say so, we come from very different backgrounds. Your accent is different. I grew up in a suburb of Manchester, all smoke and grime. You grew up in leafy Surrey, I would imagine.'

'Actually, no. India. And in case you are wondering, yes I did have lots of servants to pick up the clothes I dropped on the floor.

And I went to boarding schools in England, which were not exactly beds of roses.'

'An imperialist, then.'

'Look, I am not any sort of –ist. I am me, Beth Millward, willing to help the cause as best I can. I don't have any commitments just now, though I am going away at the beginning of August for a few days. Use me now where I can be of use.'

While she was saying this, Ellen continued to put letters into envelopes.

'I can even put stamps on envelopes,' Beth said sharply, rather put out by Northern bluntness. 'If you ask me nicely.'

Ellen put down the envelopes and smiled. 'I'm sorry. Pull up that chair. These last few days have been frantic. I've been at it twelve hours a day.' She smiled again, more warmly than before.

'I am a socialist and a member of the Labour Party since I was sixteen, which, come to think of it, is not so long ago. But our cause just now transcends political parties and needs women of every class. We have a big project on hand. A Pilgrimage from all over the country ending with a mass rally in Hyde Park on 25th July. That's just over three weeks away.'

'I have seen some reports in the papers.'

'It will be very exciting. Women from four hundred local societies are coming together to show the Prime Minister that we mean business. Mr Asquith says that he insists on being shown that women really want the vote. Well, fifty thousand women in Hyde Park from all over is pretty good evidence of that.'

'Indeed. Who will be speaking?'

'Mrs Fawcett, of course. We have twenty lined up including the Australian lady, Miss Matters. She is a very powerful speaker. She has been arrested and has spent time in prison.'

'I remember now. She chained herself to the grille in the Women's Gallery in the House of Commons, and was sent to Holloway.'

'She has been going round with a caravan speaking all over

the country, even Scotland. She will be leading the contingent from Sussex, Surrey and Kent. She is quite a character.'

'So, what can I do, apart from coming to express my support?'

'Well, you can help with these envelopes, for a start. The address book is over there. Can you come to this office fairly regularly and help me with the clerical work?'

'I can't type.'

'We have a tame typist. We have a telephone, but Mabel out front can only come in at certain times. We can't pay you anything, I'm afraid.'

'That will not matter.'

'Good. And on the day, can you be a steward, pointing people in the right direction? You will be carrying a placard. I have quite a number of women doing that.'

'What about the Police?'

'They have been fully informed of our arrangements. They will keep a discreet distance. We have to police ourselves. We must have a law-abiding protest and show the public that most suffrage supporters are not violent militants.'

Chapter Six

❋

Nearly every day Beth went to the office. She attended to the post, made telephone calls and busied herself with whatever Ellen required of her. Within a few days she was able to take the initiative in making arrangements for the Big Day, to Ellen's relief. Two days before the Rally, the office was visited by Millicent Fawcett, the founder of NUWSS. Beth had heard her speak in the Albert Hall and revered her as the founder of Newnham Hall. She was now looking her age at seventy-five, but was still as lively as she had ever been. Beth sat in while Ellen briefed her on the arrangements for the Rally. Mrs Fawcett listened carefully and nodded approval, then turned to Beth.

'Miss Millward. Thank you for giving so much of your time to this venture.'

'Well, I was at a loose end.' She explained how she had just finished her finals.

'And what will you do with your degree, or rather non-degree?'

'I have told myself that I will give myself a few months before looking for a career. Who knows what fate has in store for me. But I don't want to just be a housewife. I want to travel again.' She explained about her childhood in India and time as a lady's companion.

'You have many life experiences to draw on. I am sure you will find something that will fulfil your aspirations. By the way, which college were you at Cambridge? Girton?'

'No, Mrs Fawcett. Your college.'

'Ah.'

'My tutor was Miss Edmonds.'

'A good scholar and a close friend to me.' Mrs Fawcett thought for as moment. 'How are your languages?'

'I have a smattering of French and Italian, but my best language, and it is not very good, I must admit, is German. I have a German friend who is very patient with my attempts.'

'Well, I keep in touch with Women's Movements overseas, and I am always a little embarrassed when they write excellent English, and I cannot reply in their own tongue. Not just now, but when this Rally is over and you have had some time to reflect, perhaps you might consider joining the movement, as it were professionally.'

Beth could not find a suitable answer on the spot.

'Never mind,' said Mrs Fawcett. 'Let's get the Rally over and done with first.'

Early on the day Beth opened her curtains and saw that the sun was shining. She greeted it with relief but then the saying came to mind: 'Sun before seven, rain before eleven.' She caught an early train and met Ellen outside the Underground station at Marble Arch. Other stewards were waiting there, and Beth was handed a placard, a loud-hailer and a map of Hyde Park.

Ellen called the women together and carried out a roll call. 'All here. Good. We have workmen putting up the platforms. There are twenty of them. I want you to stand by your allotted platform and check that the speakers are happy with the arrangements. Some of them may not wish to use the loud-hailers.'

'What if there is any trouble?' someone asked.

'We cannot prevent people from interrupting. Our speakers are experienced and are used to putting down hecklers. But if there is any physical violence there will be police in the background. We can call on them if necessary.'

She looked around.

'All set then, girls?'

They nodded enthusiastically.

Beth's platform was Number Eighteen and the speaker was Miss Muriel Matters. Beth had read about her exploits in the House of Commons and the balloon flight to drop pamphlets over Whitehall at the State Opening of Parliament. She looked forward to hearing her.

There was an hour to go before the Pilgrims were expected to arrive. Beth put down her placard and went round the other platforms to check if the stewards were in place. She had the list of names. At Number Seven she found two ladies. The second one, evidently supernumerary, came forward.

'Beth Millward? I'm Frances Stevenson. We met at the Albert Hall in the winter.'

'Oh, yes. How are you?'

'Very well, thank you. And you?'

Beth told her briefly about Cambridge and her recent work for the NUWSS.

'Good for you,' Frances replied. 'You remember I told you about Mr Lloyd George? Well, now I am working for him.'

'That must be interesting.'

'He is a very busy man and wants things done by yesterday.'

'Does he support our cause?'

'Oh, rather, but he has been heckled by militants.'

'Why, for heaven's sake?'

'Because he does not speak as earnestly as they would want. He has to speak on all sorts of subjects as Chancellor, not just women's suffrage. And because he is a prominent member of the Cabinet, he is accused of being lukewarm on the subject and takes the blame for Cabinet indifference.'

'I suppose that is the penalty people in the limelight have to pay, being blamed for things you are not responsible for.'

'He just shrugs it off. Let us hope that with this rally today we can prevail on Mr Asquith to change his mind; it will be ammunition for David to bring to bear on him.'

Beth noted the use of the Christian name.

'When you see him next,' she said, 'give him a full report of today's proceedings. Nice to meet you, Frances. I'm sure we will come across each other again.'

After her round of the platforms she returned to Number Eighteen. People were beginning to enter Hyde Park as individuals, men as well as women, and soon the band in the centre of the

Park struck up. From four gates to the Park came the columns of Pilgrims, following the scarlet, green and white banners of the movement, and made their way to their allotted stations.

Beth looked at her watch. Nearly eleven o'clock, and no sign of rain.

Hyde Park was filling up. According to Ellen, fifty thousand were expected, but later estimates suggested twice that number were present.

The contingent from the south east, with Miss Matters at its head, came to Number Eighteen. As the ground was dry, the ladies sat down on the grass to rest. Miss Matters shunned the chair that had been provided for her and went up to Beth to introduce herself.

Muriel Matters was a head shorter than Beth, but what she lacked in height she made up for in vitality. Her eyes sparkled and her smile revealed a gleaming set of teeth.

'Here we are, just in time.'

Beth noticed a slight Australian accent.

'Has the march gone well?' asked Beth.

'We had some rain the other day, but that didn't stop us. We are made of sterner stuff.'

'Is there anything you want before we start?'

'No. I'm all set.'

The band finished playing. Beth saw that the other speakers were getting ready. She held the chair as Miss Matters climbed onto the platform. The ladies sitting on the ground and spectators fell silent. Beth, who had been standing for some time, sat on the chair. She noticed that Miss Matters did not use any notes. Her voice, though not forced, was clear enough to reach the back of the crowd, and her articulation was very precise. Beth recalled that she had been trained as an actress and had taught elocution in Adelaide.

'To those who have not taken part in our March but are here today, I wish you a very good morning. Today is the culmination of three months on the road, from all parts of the Kingdom, to show that the women of Britain are deadly serious in their demands for the vote. There can be no excuse any more for our elected representatives to deny us a hearing. Men elected them, but until we women have the right to vote and be elected ourselves, women's voices will not be heard as they should be.

'Now hear what these elected representatives have to say about us. A distinguished legal gentleman, distinguished by his own reckoning but not by mine, has recently said and I quote:

"In order to keep these unsexed hyenas in petticoats disturbing the deliberations of this most majestic assembly in the world, we have packed them off to the Police Court."

'I too bear that badge of honour. He goes on: "My former opinion is confirmed that females are something less than human."

'I am quoting his remarks selectively, I admit, but the general trend is obvious. Here is another member of the aforesaid majestic assembly, a military man:

"We all admire women, but, after all, I like to see them on a pedestal and not on the footing of equality. If you bring them down off the pedestal and put them on an equality with men, you will kill the best spirit of chivalry which exists today and put the government of the country into the hands of women who are not fitted for it by nature and temperament. It would be the most destructive and dangerous thing ever done by the House of Commons."

'His condescension has no limits. I admit that some women are foolish, but that's only because God made us to match the men.'

A ripple of laughter.

'Mr Chamberlain has told us that Nature has made men and women different and Parliament can never make them the same. That is a great joy to us.'

More laughter.

'Here is another example of male condescension, from no less an eminence than Lord Cromer. He told us that women should remain disenfranchised because we are not capable of bearing arms. This coming, forsooth, from a man who is lame in one leg and has a squint in one eye. I ask you!'

Laughter and cries of 'What about Boadicea? Good Queen Bess?'

'These men,' she went on, 'have no idea how silly they appear to all sensible people. Just think about it. We women are classed with criminals, lunatics, paupers, aliens and children as regards the franchise. Yet when it comes down to paying rents and taxes, our money is as good as any man's.'

She paused and took a step forward to the very front of the stage.

'Quite apart from the franchise, there are other very serious matters that must be our concern, and which we must highlight. Temperance and social purity. If we are to remedy the evils of drunkeness and prostitution we must go to the roots of the matter. If you look at it dispassionately, prostitution is more a question of economics than morals. If women had an equal chance, that is, if they received equal pay for equal work, and they were taught at their mother's knee to regard a woman's life as equal to a man's life, it would be less likely that they would sell their bodies. But at the moment women work for a pittance. Recently a widow was charged with attempting suicide. She was sewing uniforms for a penny an hour and could not earn enough to feed herself let alone any dependants. Others toil in stinking factories, carefully stitching shirts and embroidering handkerchiefs and tea towels that sell for twenty times what they have been paid.

'Let me tell you a story. You may have heard it before. A teenage girl was raped. She hid her pregnancy and delivered her child, a daughter, alone. In her despair she killed the newborn child. She was sentenced to hang, even though no woman had been executed for infanticide in sixty years. Fortunately her sentence was commuted, but still she had to spend time in prison and had to bear the stigma for the rest of her life. At present, in such cases, the fathers usually escape both in reputation and pocket. The girl-mothers, with a blasted name, have almost no means of honest livelihood. Only when women are valued equally will it be possible to find a solution to the problems of modern life.

'To sum up the issue. In private households, men do not attempt to run them without some woman – wife, mother, sister or daughter. I believe, with all my heart, that if a woman brings her weight, her knowledge and her womanly instincts to bear, she will bring about as good a result in Parliament as she does in the private home.

'So ladies, and gentlemen – I'm very glad to see you here as well – I could go on for hours on the subject in all its ramifications. You have heard all the arguments for women's enfranchisement. We have been campaigning for a very long time, but now I feel that we are on the cusp of victory. One more push is all we need.

'I will end by quoting a poem that someone passed to me. In its simple way it is a statement of the obvious and gives us great confidence in our campaign:

"Where is the man who has the power and skill

To stem the torrent of a woman's will?

For if she will, she will, depend on't,

And if she won't, she won't, and that's an end on't".'

Beth had never heard Miss Matters before and she was enthalled by the performance. She tried to speak to her and offer her congratulations but Miss Matters had been whisked away by her entourage. Beth watched the crowd as it drifted off. Some went to hear other speakers who were still on their feet. She was just about to do the same when Ellen Wilkinson came up.

'How did it go?'

'She was most impressive. If someone was not convinced before, they would be having heard her.'

'What are you going to do now?'

'I was thinking about going home. My mother is not in the best of health and I haven't seen much of her these last few days. Unless there is something you want me to do.'

'No. Go home. Can you come in tomorrow, just for a couple of hours in the morning? There are letters to be sent off and one or two other things.'

* * *

Beth found her mother still in bed.

'Your father's gone to the shops. I just feel… well, a little low today.'

'Are you in pain, Mother?'

'No more than usual. It's just that getting up and moving seemed to be too much like hard work. I know I should make the effort, and now that you are here I must try.' She shook her head. 'I have never been like this before. I am rather ashamed.'

'Don't be, Mother. It's probably because you did not have a good night. There is no reason for you to get up if you don't feel like it. Father and I can look after things.'

'I'm sure you are right. What is the weather like?'

'It is warm and dry and not much wind.'

'Take me out in my bath chair. And I would like to walk a little. It will cheer me up. Wait for me downstairs.'

Mr Millward returned with some medicine. He took Beth aside before her mother came down.

'What do you think, Beth?'

'Difficult to say, Father. Pain can be very wearing, however brave a face one puts upon it. What's the medicine?'

'A concoction that the pharmacist recommended. I suspect it's just an analgesic. She doesn't like to take stuff for the pain. She thinks it is being feeble.'

'That's nonsense. There is no virtue in suffering.'

'I know. But try and persuade her.'

Mrs Millward came down the stairs slowly, wincing occasionally as she took a step. Her husband and daughter watched anxiously.

'Now don't fuss me. Beth, is my chariot ready?'

'When you have taken this medicine, Mother.'

'Do you insist, Beth?'

'I do.'

'Oh, very well.' She sat down while Beth fetched a spoon and uncorked the bottle.

'Why is it, Mildred,' said Mr Millward, 'that you take the medicine from Beth and not from me?'

'I know you mean well, dear, but women have a way of doing things.'

Mr Millward laughed. 'You have always been stubborn, Mildred, but I am glad you're taking the stuff. I just want to see you enjoying life a little bit more.'

Beth pushed her mother up the lane. When they reached the village green, Mrs Millward insisted on getting out and they walked around it. Beth told her about the events of that morning and how inspired she had been by Miss Matters.

'She makes so much sense.'

'I'm sure she does. But would you give over the whole of your life to the cause? There are other important things…'

'Of course. And I haven't forgotten them. But women's suffrage is the way forward. As Miss Matters said, we are nearly there. One more push is needed.'

'Well, It's your generation, not mine. I am not long for this world, I suspect. But your happiness, and James's, is what I wish for.'

Beth took a deep breath.

'Mother, would you mind very much if I went to Germany for a few days, to stay with Stefan and his family? I am hoping to go over with him fairly soon. I am just worried about your health.'

Mrs Millward stopped and looked directly at her.

'Is it serious, Beth?'

'Well, he has been to us and he wants me to get to know his family. We are fond of each other but we have made no commitment so far. Besides, after Cambridge I do need a holiday. A change of scene.'

'Of course you must go. We liked Stefan. Sometimes he seemed a little stiff... er... Germanic.'

'He has a keen sense of humour and can laugh at himself. But he is very serious about his vocation.'

'Vocation?'

'Yes. Didn't you gather that? He is hoping to be ordained.'

'I knew he was working on something to do with the history of Religion. But ordination will mean he cannot marry.'

'No, Mother, he is a Lutheran. They have married priests and bishops too, just like us.'

'But, Beth, you are not minded that way. You don't go to church very often. Won't you find it difficult to support him in his ministry?'

'Mother, just because a man and a woman are friends doesn't mean that they have to be married.'

'Dear God! You're not thinking of living with him outside of marriage? We would be most upset.'

'Certainly not. And as a priest he wouldn't even dream of it. I am going to Germany to stay with his family - his brother and his wife and their two children. They are most respectable. I will be there for a few days. Then Stefan has to see his bishop and I suppose undertake a retreat. But he will be back in Oxford in September. He will finish off his thesis, have it approved and be awarded his degree. After that... who knows? Maybe he, or I, will feel that we have to move on. I will be sad, but it will not be the end of the world.'

Mrs Millward shook her head. 'It's all so different these days. You will do what you want. I just hope that you will not be hurt.'

After dinner that evening, Mrs Millward retired to bed with a book. Mr Millward poured a glass of port and lit a cigar. Beth pushed a glass towards him and he gave her a half-measure. She lit a cigarette.

'What's this I hear about Germany?'

Beth repeated what she had said to her mother. He listened without interrupting. When she finished he tapped the ash off his cigar.

'Hm. I may be a paterfamilias, but that doesn't count for much these days. You will go whether I like it or not; you are old enough to make your own decisions. One thing, though. There is a strong current of anti-English feeling being whipped up over there. Just watch what you say. It is courteous not to comment on the politics of other countries when you are a visitor.'

'Don't worry. I will be a model guest.'

He puffed away and Beth lit another cigarette.

'Have you seen the evening paper?' he asked. 'There is a full report of your rally. It all seems to have gone off peacefully. Whether Mr Asquith will take cognizance of it is another matter.'

'What do you really think, Father? You haven't said very much about women's suffrage. Was that just being polite to me?'

'Polite? No. I have come to the conclusion that there are many things in life today that I do not understand well enough to make comments about them. Suffrage will mean great change. Whether it will be a good thing remains to be seen. But if it means that sensible people like you and your mother can express their opinion, then it can't be bad. Of course, there are many people, both men and women, whose understanding of politics is minimal, or who are just plain stupid. Should they be allowed to vote? In an ideal world, as far as I remember my Plato, probably not. They should be ruled by the best people. But when the best go bad, then we are in trouble: *corruptio optimi pessima*. So we have Democracy, however messy it is, to decide who governs us. *Vox populi, vox dei.** That means nearly everyone having the opportunity to vote.'

'Who would you exclude?'

'Lunatics; Peers – they're not quite the same thing; children; foreigners. Just so long as the process of enfranchisement is taken systematically, step by step. *Festina lente*.'

'You are full of Latin tonight.'

'Well, a glass of port helps.'

* The voice of the people is the voice of God.

* * *

The next morning Beth went into the office and found Ellen Wilkinson surrounded by piles of paper.

'Please put these letters into the envelopes. It's a chore, but it must be done.'

'Did you see the evening papers?'

'Yes. They were very complimentary. I think yesterday did us a lot of good. The arguments were clearly set out and there were reporters everywhere scribbling away. There were no arrests. No one collapsed and had to be carried off. The sun shone.'

'All because of your superb organisation. Including the weather.'

'Including the weather. Mrs Fawcett was on the phone first thing this morning and she was very pleased. She is organising a deputation to Downing Street, with some MPs to support her.'

When the envelopes were addressed and stamped, Beth said she would go to the post.

'And when are you off to Germany?' Ellen asked.

'In the next few days.'

'If you feel like it, give me a call when you get back, even if it's just for a chat. And if I haven't said it before, thank you for all your efforts.'

After dealing with the letters Beth wandered down Charing Cross Road on the lookout for a new outfit she might take to Germany. There was nothing that appealed to her and so she continued down towards Trafalgar Square intending to spend a few minutes in the National Gallery. She noticed that there were more policemen around than usual. When she turned the corner she saw a sea of hats and figures standing on a platform in front of Nelson's Column. There were banners of the Women's Social and Political Union. She went up the steps by the Gallery, and identified Sylvia Pankhurst addressing the crowd. She had been speaking for some time and had reached her peroration:

'The time for argument is past. What is our motto?'

'Deeds not words,' came the response from the crowd, fortissimo.

'Deeds not words, it is,' she shouted. 'Off to Downing Street. We will beard the Prime Minister in his lair. Follow me.'

She stepped down from the platform and with a male bodyguard (Beth later read that they were East London dockers) she led the march down Whitehall.

Beth watched the procession. It had got only so far when the Police closed ranks and prevented the crowd from following. Sylvia Pankhurst and her immediate entourage were surrounded and a fight broke out. A couple of police helmets flew through the air. She was arrested along with twenty-four other people of both sexes. This was her fourth arrest this year.

The evening papers were scathing.

Chapter Seven

❄

Beth and Stefan met on the platform at Liverpool Street just in time for the afternoon train to Harwich. The carriages were crowded but fortunately they found a compartment with two spare seats. An elderly gentleman moved up so that they could sit opposite. The guard blew his whistle and the train set off. Beth and Stefan said nothing for the first few minutes, while Beth recovered her breath after the rush to the train.

'You know, Stefan,' she said, 'this will be my first time out of Britain for four years. I'm excited. Fresh fields and pastures new for Millward.'

'I am glad to have a companion for my journey. When the train rattles and the sea gets rough, it is difficult to concentrate on one's book, or sleep. And it will be good to show you a new part of the world. I will be looking at my *heimat* in a new light.'

'Can I tell you about my suffragist meeting? I will try in German.'

She was determined to speak as much as she could, and so had rehearsed the first paragraph of what she might say. Stefan listened carefully, prompting her if she stumbled. When she had run out of steam, he asked her some simple questions and she was able to answer with some fluency.

'Very good, Beth,' he continued in German. 'Let me tell you about my family.'

Beth knew the names of his nephew and niece, but not much more, so she was eager to ask questions in return.

After a while they fell silent and contemplated the countryside. The sun had come out after a shower. The old gentleman put down his paper and spoke to her.

'We badly need rain. Look how parched the grass is.'

Beth nodded.

'Forgive my asking,' he went on, 'but I couldn't help listening to your conversation. It's some years since I spoke German, and I would like to try my hand again.'

'How did you come to speak German?' Stefan asked.

The old man was a little hesistant at first, but soon warmed up. 'As a young man I became a journalist for *The Times* and I was sent abroad to cover the Austro-Prussian war in the eighteen sixties. I was accredited to the Prussian Army, hanging around the rear of von Moltke's staff. Occasionally we were admitted to a sit-rep by an officer, and any dispatches had to be cleared by the Army. So I compiled a parallel narrative which I intended to show to the Editor on my return. And the war didn't last long – only seven weeks as far as I remember.'

'Why was that?' asked Beth.

'All sorts of reasons. The Prussian infantry was highly trained and was equipped with modern rifles, which could be loaded and fired from the prone position, whereas most of the Austrian forces, which included many Germans from the south, Bavarians, Württembergers and so on... where was I?'

'Superior weapons, sir,' said Stefan.

'Oh, yes. The Austrians still had muzzle loaders. You had to stand up to load them. And the Austrian Army had many nationalities, conscripts who didn't feel particularly loyal, whereas the Prussians felt they were fighting for their country.'

He reverted to English and said to Beth: 'Are you following, my dear?'

'I am getting the gist, and Stefan will help me out.'

The old man continued: 'And the Prussians were superior also in the... how do I say it?' He asked Stefan in English: 'The sinews of war.'

'*Die Sehnen von Krieg.*'

'Ach, so. Supplies of food and ammunition, reserves of personnel, medical services and of course railways. For rapidity of movement. And the Prussian economy was growing. Herr Krupp's factories were working full time.'

'Did you see any action, sir?' Stefan asked.

'I visited the battlefield of Königgrätz, or what is called over here Sadowa. A melancholy sight. The Austrian losses were huge and thousands were taken prisoner. The battlefield was strewn with abandoned equipment, dead horses and men. The most pitiful sight of all was the wounded. The Austrians had withdrawn from the field leaving their wounded behind. Naturally the Prussians tended their own wounded first, and only later ministered to the Austrians. We have to glorify our warriors, but the reality of war is terrible.'

'I understand that well, sir,' said Stefan.

Beth had been formulating a question.

'Did you actually see a battle in progress? What was it like?'

'Only a skirmish. After Königgrätz, the Prussians were hurrying on to capture Frankfurt, a very important city of the River Main. Ten days after the big battle they came to Aschaffenburg which stood in their way. I found myself standing immediately behind the Prussian troops as they raked the Austrians with their rapid fire, then chased them across the fields to the east of the town. There was a fierce hand-to-hand fight at the Herstaller Tor but the Prussians broke the defenders and pushed them back into the town. Street fighting is a dangerous business, yet we correspondents were encouraged to follow the troops in. I watched them systematically clear the narrow streets. At the River Main the far side of the bridge was already in Prussian hands and most of the Austrians surrendered.'

'How many died?' Beth asked.

'We were given the official figures at the end of the day. I remember them clearly. The Prussians lost twenty-seven dead and over a hundred wounded. The Austrians lost over two hundred dead and nearly five hundred wounded; over two thousand were taken prisoner. It was a small battle in comparison with some others, but it hastened the cease-fire a week later.'

'Were you frightened?' asked Beth. 'There must have been bullets flying around.'

'I had developed a professional interest in the fighting and I was anxious to see as much as I could. I was young and thought I was invulnerable.'

'Did you follow the Franco-Prussian War?' Stefan asked.

'No. I became engaged to be married and my wife-to-be forbade me to go. For a war correspondent, it was the opportunity of a lifetime, but not for me. The Editor gave me other duties.'

The old man looked out of the window. He reverted to English. 'I see we are nearly at Colchester where I must get off. Thank you for listening to my reminiscences of nearly fifty years ago. I hope my German was not too ungrammatical.'

'You were very fluent, sir,' said Stefan.

'Good. So I am not entirely senile.'

The train drew into the station. Stefan helped the old man down with his case and onto the platform. They shook hands.

Stefan got back in and the train moved off.

'I learned so much today,' he said in English. 'German history is very complicated, especially before 1871. Then we were united under the Hohenzollerns. All the modern history I was taught at school was the triumph over France and the power of the Prussian elite, Bismarck and so forth.'

'Was Bremen part of Prussia?'

'No. It is still a free city state, but joined the Federation in 1868. A trading city has to live with the victors.'

* * *

The crossing had been smooth. The connecting train from Hamburg had been on time. Yet it was nearly midnight before Stefan's brother picked them up from the station. When they arrived, Hannah was still up. She offered Beth some coffee but she refused.

'I am so tired I just want to sleep.'

'Of course. I will show you to your room.'

The bed was comfortable. Beth was not used to an eiderdown instead of sheets and blankets but within minutes she was fast asleep.

The next morning, Hannah came in and drew back the curtains. It was sunny outside. Beth looked at her travel clock.

'Nine o'clock. Sorry to be so lazy.'

'You needed to sleep,' said Hannah in English.

'I haven't slept like that for years. It will set me up for the day. Er... I must try to speak German.'

'There's coffee and rolls downstairs when you are ready,' said Hannah in German.

Washed and dressed, she came down to the breakfast room. Stefan was not around. Hannah brought in a pot of coffee.

'Help yourself. I have one or two things to attend to. We'll have a chat later.'

Beth was quite happy to be left alone. Yesterday had been a whirl and she felt the need of a quiet time.

But it was not to be. A little girl crept into the room, carrying a doll, and sat down opposite her.

'Oh. Hello. You must be Annelore.'

'Yes. And you are Beth and you are going to teach us English.'

'I am very happy to do that, but in return you must teach me German. Can you do that? If either of us makes a mistake, we will correct each other. Is that a deal?'

'Yes.'

There was a moment's silence while Annelore fiddled with her doll. Then she asked: 'Are you Uncle Stefan's friend? He is very religious, you know, unlike my Daddy. We don't go to church often.'

'I like your uncle very much, ever since he came to stay with my family in Scotland. So I am looking forward to getting to know his family.'

Annelore nodded.

'What is the name of your doll?'

'She is an English doll, but I call her Blümchen.'

'Ah. Little flower. She is very beautiful.'

"Little flower," the girl repeated. Then she pointed to her head. 'What is that, in English?'

Beth told her. They went through limbs and then clothes. After a few minutes, Annelore sighed.

'I shall never remember all that.'

'Never mind, just keep trying, as I do with German.'

'Can I go now?'

'Of course.'

Beth poured herself another cup of coffee.

Stefan came in to join her.

'Sorry I wasn't here before. Dietrich wanted a word, and then Heinz wanted a game of cricket.'

'Did you know that I once played cricket, at boarding school? I used to bowl at James when he was young.'

'You are a girl with many talents. We will have a game, all of us, this afternoon.'

'I have met Annelore, but not Heinz.'

'You will. Did you sleep well?'

'Like a log.'

'Good.' He pointed to the window. 'You bring the sunshine with you.'

'Of course I do.'

She took a gulp of coffee.

'Apart from cricket, what have you in mind for today?'

'I suggest we will go for a walk this morning, just to show you the countryside. Then a light lunch. Hannah is preparing a feast for tonight. Dietrich is coming back from the office early. He has been very busy recently but he has promised me to relax tonight.'

'I look forward to meeting him properly.'

Stefan was about to say something, but got up and patted her on the shoulder.

'Shall we say half an hour?'

'I'll be ready.'

On the way to her room Beth stuck her head out of the front door. It was warm outside. She changed into a summer skirt. She was tempted to leave her hat behind, but decided to wear it; she had to look respectable for Stefan's sake.

While she was waiting in the hall, Heinz appeared. He was tall for his age. He came forward nervously. Beth held out her hand and he took it.

'I am Heinz,' he said in English, speaking slowly.

'And I am Beth, your uncle's friend,' she replied.

'Un...cle?'

'Onkel.' She spoke in German. 'It's nearly the same.'

'Yes.'

'Your uncle tells me that we are to play cricket this afternoon. I can play cricket.'

'Girls can't play cricket.'

'Why not? This girl can.'

Heinz was nonplussed. 'But...' He struggled to reply.

Just then Stefan came down the stairs. 'Heinz, are you looking after Beth?'

Heinz blushed.

'He has been very polite,' said Beth and smiled at him.

There was a pause, then Heinz turned and fled.

'He is very shy with strangers,' said Stefan.

'I will do my best to put him at his ease. Cricket will help.'

'Beth... do you mind the children using your Christian name? Miss Millward is a bit of mouthful for them.'

'Not at all. I hope we can be friends.'

They went outside, down the drive to the gate. In the fields beside the road, men and women were cutting the corn and bringing it to a threshing machine.

'They have to make the best of this good weather.'

'Does your family own this land?'

'Heavens, no. The estate belongs to the Oldenbergs, a very aristocratic family. They have a large house not far away but seldom use it.'

'How far is the village?'

'Not far, maybe a kilometre. But we will take a little detour.'

They left the road and crossed a stubble field towards a stand of trees on a knoll. From the top they could see over the flat countryside to the factory chimneys of Bremen. In the other direction there was a low range of hills, covered in woods.

They sat down on a fallen trunk.

'This was my secret place,' said Stefan. 'I used to come up here to read and ponder. It was up here that I finally resolved to be a priest.'

'And you haven't had any doubts since then?'

'Of course I have, but I regard doubt as a test of faith. Faith is not the same as certainty. I realise that we cannot understand everything. It is best to recognise one's limitations and carry on the best one can. I am always suspicious of those who proclaim certainty.'

'Very wise. I dislike people who are dogmatic.'

'The church has had too much of dogmatism down the centuries.'

They fell silent.

'Will I spoil the moment if I have a cigarette?' asked Beth.

'Not at all. You can offer me one as well.'

They puffed contently.

'I have to see my bishop very soon. Something has come up. I haven't told Dietrich or Hannah yet.'

'Go on.'

'Both Dietrich and I, like all men of our age, have had to undergo basic military training and as reservists we are supposed to refresh it from time to time. Dietrich is in a reserved occupation, so he will not be called on in the event of war, but I am eligible. I have not done my reservist training as I have been in England but I have had a letter requiring me to attend camp for a fortnight, starting next week.'

'Surely you as a priest should not have to practise firearms drill.'

'I am undecided. As a priest I should not have to kill anyone, but as a priest I also have to understand those I minister to and that means being with them at times of stress and doubt. It would help if I underwent the training.'

'I can see that. But surely you don't have to be a priest in uniform. What about a civilian ministry?'

'I think that the Bishop will recommend me for chaplaincy, as I am young and fit.'

Beth thought for a moment, then said: 'If you can't shoot, and you have no particular medical skills, what use will you be in the front line? I don't mean to be rude.'

'A very good question. The last thing a section commander would want is a passenger along for the ride and getting in the way. I will conduct services in the rear, minister to the dying after the battle, visit hospitals and be a good listener. The one thing I must avoid is descending on a group of men who are tired, hungry and frightened, and spouting platitudes at them. If they see me as well-fed, with shiny boots and spotless uniform, they will quite rightly scorn me and tell me to – what do you say in English? – bugger off. Sorry.'

'I've heard worse.'

'Somehow chaplains have to understand and share the hardships of soldiering, not be judgmental but sympathetic, and above all not be a stooge of the officer class.'

'And Hebrew and Aramaic will help you in this?'

'Yes, curiously enough. I will seem eccentric to most people in my line of study.'

Beth was about to comment but Stefan forestalled her.

'All right, I am middle class, well-educated and don't have to worry where the next meal is coming from. But if you can be yourself and not be seen as a representative of a particular class, then you can gain the respect of the men.'

'Yes. I see all that. But if the men are atheists, or have lost their faith because God does not seem to look after his own, what then?'

'Even atheists love their families and want to write to them. Some cannot write or read well and need help. And when confronted with extreme danger or imminent death, men often feel the need of God. I can be his vessel in bringing comfort.'

Beth said nothing.

'That sounds awfully pretentious,' Stefan went on. 'I discussed my mission briefly with Dietrich some time ago. At first he dismissed it and said it was "Praise God and pass the ammunition", but I think he now has a better idea. I'm sorry to have burdened you with all this, but I wanted you to understand what may be in store for me.'

He started to get up but Beth put her hand on his arm.

'Whatever you do, Stefan, please don't get yourself killed.'

'I'll do my best.'

'Where now?' asked Beth.

'Down to the village and back to the house.'

* * *

After lunch they played cricket on the lawn. Stefan had chosen a flat bit for the wicket and had asked the gardener to mow the grass for a strip. The outfield was rougher. Three sticks acted as the wicket and there was a wooden box at the bowler's end. Hannah and a reluctant Annelore were recruited as fielders. Stefan kept wicket and Beth bowled. Heinz was the first in. Beth bowled him a gentle underarm which he missed and it hit the wicket. He was about to burst into tears, when Beth said that was a warm-up. She bowled again on the off and Heinz put his foot forward and hit it hard towards Hannah. Heinz set off for the other end and completed three runs before Hannah caught up with the ball.

'What do I do now?' she asked.

'Throw it to Beth,' Stefan called out.

Hannah returned the ball and Beth touched the box with it.

Heinz resumed his stance. Beth bowled him a straight ball which he despatched smartly towards Annelore, who watched it go past her. Meanwhile Heinz ran up and down the wicket.

'That's enough, Heinz,' said Stefan, after six runs.

'Come on, Annelore, pick the ball up and throw it to Beth.'

The child attempted a throw but it didn't go far and in the wrong direction. She picked it up and carried it to Beth.

After a couple of overs, Heinz had made a good score, though no one was really counting.

Stefan asked Annelore if she would like a go. At first she shook her head but then was persuaded. Beth bowled to her but she took a wild swipe and missed every time. She was about to dissolve into tears but Beth called to Stefan to bowl and went to stand behind Annelore. Holding her hands she showed her how to make a straight hit. Stefan bowled and the ball was smartly returned.

'Again,' said Beth.

This time the ball was on the off side and was hit towards Hannah. Beth and Annelore started down the wicket holding hands.

'Run, Mutti,' Heinz shouted.

Hannah attempted to stop the ball and fell over, amid general mirth. Beth and Annelore took two more runs.

'Come on, Beth,' said Stefan. 'Your turn. And I will bowl.'

Beth took the bat. Stefan positioned the fielders, and Heinz kept wicket. Stefan whirled his arm around as a warm-up, which Annelore found very funny. With his right foot he pawed the ground like a horse. More laughter.

'Ready, Beth?'

He commenced his run-up. Just before he got to the wicket, Beth stood back. He stopped short.

'You did that deliberately.'

'So I did,' she replied with a grin.

'What's going on?' Hannah asked.

'She's playing tricks on me. Right, Beth, this is it.' He bowled overarm rather faster than he intended, straight at Beth's waist. Beth rocked back and chopped the ball firmly past Hannah. It hit a tree trunk and rebounded.

'Good shot!' called Heinz.

Stefan looked abashed. 'I didn't mean to…'

'One of James' favourite shots. Bowl me another, Stefan, but remember I am not wearing pads.'

Stefan sent down a gentler ball, this time on the off. Beth made to play forward, but it hit a bump and turned sharply and trickled down the leg side. Beth started to run.

'Come on, Annelore, pick it up,' shouted Heinz.

Annelore looked at it. Beth had reached the bowler's end and started to walk back for another run.

'Annelore, here.'

She picked the ball up and threw it towards Heinz. It didn't quite reach him, but he ran out and retrieved it. Beth started to run but Heinz was too quick. By the time she got to the other end, the wicket was down.

'Out, out,' he shouted gleefully.

Stefan stood impassively at the other end, then raised a forefinger.

Beth laughed. 'Now it's your turn, Stefan.' She handed the bat to him. Heinz rebuilt the wicket. Beth was about to take the ball, but Heinz insisted on bowling. She kept wicket.

The first two balls were wide and Stefan didn't chase them. The next was straight. Stefan swung at it and missed. The wicket went down.

'Out, out,' shouted Heinz and Annelore.

'Give your Uncle another chance,' Beth called.

Heinz, who was hoping for another innings, made a face. However, he took the ball and paced out a long run up. His arms whirled and the ball hit Stefan in the midriff. He rubbed the afflicted part and took his stance again.

'Just play the ball down the line,' whispered Beth.

Again the ball came down fast and straight. Stefan followed Beth's advice and played a straight bat. The ball flew up into the air and was caught by Heinz. The boy grinned and held up a finger.

'Out, out,' he shouted.

'Good catch, Heinz,' said Beth, 'but you mustn't shout like that. It's not cricket. Cricket is a polite game.'

'But he was out,' he protested. He threw the ball up in the air in celebration and caught it. He did it again but this time it slipped through his hands and hit him on the face. He howled.

'Time for some juice,' said Hannah. 'Let's go in.'

Chapter Eight

After the children had been taken away by the Nanny, Hannah and Beth went to her sitting room. Stefan had retired to his room to write letters and Dietrich was still at the factory.

'Have you been ever been to England?' Beth asked.

'I have been with Dietrich on business trips, usually to Barrow-in-Furness. While he was negotiating, I was given a driver and taken on a trip to the Lake District. Much more interesting than machine tools and steel specifications.'

'I'm sure. I must confess I have never been there. We usually go up to Scotland for part of the summer.'

'One time, I was allowed to stay in London. I'm afraid I spent a lot of money in Oxford Street, on summer dresses and a good tweed coat. I only had two days, so I didn't see the sights. I managed to get lost on the Undergound, so confusing. But I loved London and I keep pestering Dietrich to spend some time with me there, if he can get away from his work. But I fear that we Germans are not very popular at the moment. His business with Vickers has come to an end. What of your travels? Stefan has told me a little.'

'I suppose I am child of Empire, brought up in India and sent home to boarding school at an early age. I have forgotten all the Urdu I spoke quite fluently. We were largely brought up by our amah, you see, and only saw our parents at tea time, on a normal day. After school, I was given the opportunity to go abroad as a lady's companion, which was an education in itself. We, that is, Lady Valentine and I and a string of servants, went round Europe, then to Egypt, Palestine, Transjordan. I have photographs of me on the Acropolis at Athens, on a camel by the Pyramids, at Petra.'

'How exciting. I have never ridden even a horse.'

'Camels take a bit of practice and they can be temperamental.

I acquired a smattering of several languages, but since I met Stefan, I have tried to improve the German I learnt at school.'

'You are doing well, though still a little British in accent, too stiff upper lip.'

'I still find German consonants difficult. Well, after my travels I went to Cambridge as a mature student, if twenty-two is being mature. I finished my course early this summer, though women are still not allowed to take degrees. Were you at university?'

'Alas, no. My parents sent one of my brothers to Berlin and another to a military academy. I was sent to Paris for a finishing school. When I came back I was expected to look out for a husband... and Dietrich found me. I have no regrets but I would like to get beyond the domestic round. I do good works locally but I think I am capable of more.'

'I understand. I found myself involved in rights for women.'

'But you don't have the vote in England.'

'No, not yet anyway, but it can't be long. I am a keen, er... suffragist. I don't know the word in German.'

'*Wahlrecht* is suffrage. We don't have the vote, but I would join the movement if I didn't have a family to look after. I read that some of the women in England have been violent and have gone to prison.'

'Not me. I believe in peaceful demonstrations. Violence, throwing stones at politicans, chaining yourself to railings, setting fire to postboxes, breaking windows, just makes men less sympathetic to the cause.'

She told Hannah about the meeting in Hyde Park. 'We had a huge turn-out and a favourable press report. I felt that we made real progress that day. What does Dietrich think of female suffrage?'

'He doesn't really think about it at all. I did mention it to him once and he replied "Well, perhaps, sometime".'

'Rather like my father and James.Typical men.'

Hannah laughed. 'It's the same all over the world.'

'Not New Zealand.'

'That's rather a long way to go for a vote. Look, James went to Oxford, didn't he? I would like to visit Oxford, but I don't think I will have the opportunity while Stefan is still there. He has always said that he is very happy there. And very glad he met your brother and you.'

'And vice versa. We don't see each other very often, but we write and when we do meet, it is as though we had never parted.'

Hannah smiled.

'I have to say that I am not very religious,' Beth went on. 'We have talked about it but Stefan does not try to convert me. I admire his faith, but I cannot share it, at least, at the moment.'

'I can't say that we do, either. I should take the children to church, hear their prayers – Nanny does that – but too many things get in the way.'

'Does Stefan teach them Bible stories?'

'No. He prefers to be a benevolent uncle. He says it is up to us as parents to guide them.'

'Do they go to school nearby?'

'Oh, yes. The village school. Annelore will be starting soon, and Heinz enjoys it because he can play football with the boys. He doesn't seem to have any trouble with the lessons. We had thought about engaging a governess for Annelore, but she wants to join her brother. The school has a good reputation. We shall see. I think it important that they mix with other children, even if they are not of the same class. We do have to check Heinz for headlice. I refuse to crop their hair. Annelore has lovely curls.'

'She does, indeed. I know nothing about bringing up children, except what I have observed in other families. I suppose you have to rely on your instincts. I hope that when my time comes I can be patient and loving.'

'Don't get too idealistic. It can be hard work.'

Hannah looked at the clock.

'Time for the children's bedtime story. Will you come?'

As they went upstairs, a fleeting thought crossed Beth's mind, that Hannah was sizing her up as a possible sister-in-law.

* * *

After kissing the children goodnight, at their request, Beth went to her room, washed and changed for the evening. She wrote a note to her parents to say that she had arrived safely and took it downstairs for the post the next day. Stefan was sitting in the parlour, flicking through a magazine.

'I'm sorry to have abandoned you to my sister-in-law,' he said, 'but I had to write a... er, delicate letter to my Bishop.'

'I don't feel abandoned. We had a good chat, woman to woman. Am I allowed to ask about the delicacy of the letter?'

'It's all bureaucracy. I have to report for training next week, but the military authorities have not accepted my request to be posted to the Chaplains' Department. If I were, my basic training would be reduced to a single week per annum, and the other week to specifically pastoral instruction. However, because I have not been ordained yet, I do not qualify prima facie, unless the Bishop can certify that I will be receiving ordination in due course. He has proposed a date when I am back in Oxford.'

'Can't he stretch a point, ordain you sooner? I am sure you are ready for it.'

'If only I were. But the Bishop has never been very enthusiastic about my Oxford studies, and he thinks I should have been doing more pastoral work. I have had to persuade him to certify me and that my studies are worthwhile, advancing the Kingdom of God, or some such phrase. I do realise that I have been more concerned with my academic pursuits recently.'

'Perhaps he is worried that you are more learned than him. Sorry, an unworthy remark.'

'I wouldn't entertain the thought – at least, I shouldn't. Sometimes, being humble and obedient is difficult.'

'But there cannot be many like you, with your academic background and spiritual gifts.'

Stefan raised an eyebrow.

'I don't know what spiritual gifts are exactly,' Beth went on, 'but I am sure you have them.'

'I wish I knew, too. But I do know that I have a calling, and I have to accept wherever I am called.'

'Even if it means route marches with rifle and pack?'

'I'm afraid so. The other thing is that I don't think I would be very good at it. And as for shooting, my brief experience convinces me that I couldn't hit a barn door at ten metres. And if I weren't to be a priest, I could apply to be declared a conscientious objector. Yet I might be sent to prison.'

'You could serve as a medical orderly, which would be part of your ministry.'

'I hate the sight of blood. Honestly, Beth,' said Stefan, 'the more I think about it the more muddled I become.'

'You can't anticipate every outcome. Just send the letter, and… and leave it to God.'

Stefan sighed. 'Wise words, as usual.'

He got up.

'Let's have a drink. I wonder what Dietrich has in the cupboard. Ah. A Scotch?'

'A little one, please, with water.'

'Cheers.'

Just then Dietrich bustled in.

'Pour me a big one, Stefan. It's been a tough day.'

He turned to Beth. 'Sorry. I should have said hello.'

He took her hand. 'I hope you have been looked after.'

'Very well, thank you.'

Beth had met Dietrich only briefly the previous night, when she was very tired. He was a taller and fatter version of his brother, with a trim moustache. He lit a cigar.

'What's up at the factory?' Stefan asked.

Dietrich grunted. 'Let's leave that till another time. Beth, what would you like to do during your stay?'

Beth was a little taken aback.

'Well, everything is new to me here. I am in your hands.'

'Hm. Why not come in with me tomorrow, you and Stefan, and my driver can take you to the coast? It's not far and the weather looks fine.'

'Yes, please. I would like that. Tell me, Dietrich, just as a matter of interest, do you employ many women on the shop-floor?'

He thought for a moment. 'We have some as cleaners, and secretaries in the offices, including Miss Seiffert, my personal secretary. She is a formidable woman. She was my father's, and I think she was secretly in love with him. She treats me as a poor substitute.'

'But do any women operate machinery?'

'Heavens, no! Far too dangerous, and most of my men are skilled operators with years of training and experience behind them.'

'But is the work heavy?'

'Not necessarily.'

'So women, if trained, could operate the machines?'

'Er…'

'Forgive me, Dietrich, I shouldn't be quizzing you like this on my first day. But I am a keen suffragist, as Stefan knows, and I am sure women can do most things just as well as men, outside the home environment.'

There was silence. Beth was afraid she had gone too far, but Dietrich smiled.

'Very well. I will arrange a short tour of the factory tomorrow, and you can see for yourself.'

* * *

After an early breakfast, Dietrich drove them into Bremen to the factory compound. A foreman was waiting for them outside Dietrich's office; he took them to a store and fitted them out with overalls.

'We will visit the machine shops and the foundry, but I can't take you to the Design offices, because the work is secret.'

'I understand,' said Beth, 'but do any women work there?'

'Oh, no. The men have to sign a pledge of secrecy.'

Beth wondered why women should not able to work on designs, and be less reliable in keeping secrets than men. But she did not press the point.

As they walked across the yard towards a long low building, the noise of clattering increased. The foreman led them in through a small door onto the shop floor. There were rows of lathes and other machines, powered by belts from the ceiling. The men worked in leather aprons, with shirt sleeves tied at the wrist so that nothing could catch in the machines. They all had short hair, and there was not a beard in sight. The noise was deafening. One machine was punching a preset arrangement of holes in small metal plates. The workman took one from a basket, put it onto the machine, clamped it down, pulled a lever and dropped the perforated plate into another basket. The operation took about half a minute. Beth watched him, then asked the foreman how many he could do in a day. The foreman pointed to his ears and shook his head.

Further down the building were lathes on which metal castings were being turned. The foreman led them to one particular machine. A workman wearing goggles stood beside it. He was watching the process and every now and then poured coolant over the casting; it drained into a tray below. While Beth was watching he stopped the machine and brushed away the swarf onto another tray. Then he took off his gloves and measured the work done with calipers and compared it to the specification clipped to a board beside him. He was not satisfied, and took out a micrometer and made another measurement.

The foreman spoke in Beth's ear.

'It has to be accurate to a fraction of a millimetre.'

They left the machine shop and emerged into the open air.

'That man,' Beth asked, 'that man with the hole-punching machine, does he do that every day for nine hours? He must be bored stiff.'

'He has been working that machine for five years. He works fast because he is on piece rates. He gets paid by how many plates he does. There is some skill involved, but not as much as the lathe operator.'

'I can understand that, but why does the man on the lathe wear goggles?'

'Because if he gets swarf in his eye, either from the machine or from his gloves, he could lose his sight.'

'Oh. But how can men work in such noisy surroundings? It must make them deaf.'

'I don't know if you noticed but they communicate by hand signals. If they have to speak they get up really close. Some of them wear ear plugs; others can't be bothered, and they do suffer from deafness.'

They walked across to the foundry, a large building with two tall chimneys. Beth tripped on the step and Stefan caught her hand. She did not let it go.

Inside the foundry the noise level was lower but the heat was overpowering. The men were wearing light clothing, aprons, goggles and thick gloves up to their elbows. Overhead was a crane lifting a tub of molten metal run off from the furnace. It was manoeuvred over a line of moulds, and a workman turned a wheel which tilted the tub over to pour the metal into the moulds. It was a delicate operation but no metal was spilt on the ground, apart from a few droplets.

Beth was fascinated. The foreman took her closer to the door of the furnace. The heat was blistering. Two workmen came up with large shovels full of scrap metal and threw it into the furnace. Another man came forward with a pole, which he poked through the furnace door. After a few seconds he took it out and looked at the gauge on the handle.

'What's he doing?' Beth asked.

'Taking the temperature. It needs to be no lower than 1300 degees Celsius. But an experienced man does not need a thermometer. He simply looks at the colour of the floating metal and can tell within a few degrees when it is ready. But it has to be checked with an instrument.'

Beth took a long look inside the furnace and felt her eyes getting sore. The foreman saw this and led her away.

When they were outside, she asked Stefan if he had seen this before.

'Only once, when I was a boy, and it frightened me, the ferocity of the heat. I don't envy the men who have to work there. But they get paid well.'

Beth turned to the foreman. 'Are there many accidents in the foundry? It seems such a dangerous place.'

'The foreman of the foundry is very strict with them. Anyone who arrives apparently drunk is instantly dismissed. And there are very strict rules about working practices.'

They went back to Dietrich's offices. He left a meeting and came out to them.

Beth thanked the foreman, who touched his cap.

'Well, Beth,' said Dietrich. 'Did you find it interesting?'

'It has given me much to think about.'

He went to a table and handed Stefan a hamper.

'Something for your picnic. Enjoy the sea and sunshine.'

They were driven for over an hour alongside the River Weser. The land was low-lying and the fields were separated by dykes. Opposite Bremerhaven was the small town of Nordenham, where Beth asked the driver to stop so that she could buy some cigarettes. They turned left and followed the coast past Burhave to Langwarden. Just beyond the village, Stefan told the driver to stop. It was midday and the sun, which had been reticent, now came out. There was little wind. Stefan carried the hamper and Beth the rug. The driver brought two camp chairs. They went through the sand dunes and found a spot looking out over the mudflats. The driver then went off to a café; Stefan had given him some money for his lunch.

'I thought we were going to the seaside.'

'This is the Wattenmeer. The tide will come in this afternoon. It comes in very fast and it is dangerous to walk out onto the mud unless you know the times of the tide. Here, look through these while I get lunch ready.'

He handed her a pair of binoculars.

'Just look at the foreshore.'

Beth adjusted the binoculars. There were large numbers of small birds pottering on the mud.

'I wish I knew more about birds. What am I looking at?'

Stefan took the binoculars. 'I'm not an expert but I think there are dunlin, godwit, ruff, and maybe an avocet. Oh yes, and over there are group of oystercatchers, bigger birds, black and white and with a large orange beak.'

Beth scanned the shore. 'They all look much the same, all with pointed beaks. There's one with a really long beak, a rather dumpy looking bird.'

'Probably a redshank. What colour are its legs?'

'Can't see. Ah. It's standing up. You're right. Red.'

Beth watched the small birds, some scurrying about, others balancing on one leg and others taking off and landing on an unoccupied patch of mud.

'The mud is not very scenic,' said Stefan, 'but it is full of nutrients. There is a different population in the winter. Birds come down from the Arctic to breed. Ornithologists migrate here too and set up camps along the shore. Time for lunch, don't you think?'

Hannah had prepared cold chicken with salad, cheese, fruit and a flask of coffee. Stefan laid these out on the rug. Beth took off her hat.

'It's nice to feel the sun on my face. Let me fill your plate. Some of everything?'

'Please.'

They ate in companionable silence. Beth took the binoculars again.

'Look. The tide is coming in. There was a rock or some such thing out there and now it is covered.'

Stefan poured the coffee and they smoked cigarettes.

'It's a bad habit,' said Beth, 'but on a day like this it just adds to the contentment.'

'Get thee behind me, Satan.'

'You haven't brought me all this way just to preach at me?'

'I wouldn't dare. I enjoy bad habits just as much as you.'

'You know, Stefan, our factory visit this morning has changed my mind, up to a point.'

'Yes?'

'In my ignorance, I reckoned that women could do everything a man does, and indeed, better. But seeing those men at work, I am beginning to wonder. You cannot change biology. Men are stronger physically, as Nature made them, but men can't bear children, which is demanding in all sorts of other ways. But anything that involves the brain rather than the hand, women can surely do just as well.'

Stefan thought for a moment. 'Do you know of any female composers, or artists?'

'Not offhand, but I am sure there are some.'

'Well, I can think of Fanny Mendelssohn, Clara Schumann and your own Ethel Smyth, and she is a suffragist.'

'I've heard of her but I didn't know she was a composer.'

'And there are female scientists: Marie Curie; she has won two Nobel Prizes; female artists: I can't think of any just now, but I am sure there are, and lots of female poets and novelists. They all prove your point.'

'Yes, but there aren't any female politicians, judges, financiers, people that matter in the world. That world is the world of men.'

'I agree. Female talent is being wasted. Before I met you, female suffrage did not cross my mind, but now I have become converted to the cause. That is your doing.'

'There is more joy in Heaven over one sinner that repenteth.'

'Luke fifteen seven. Very good, Beth.'

'You can't study English Literature, especially Milton, without the Bible and Prayer Book. Oh, and Vergil, but I had to have some coaching for my Latin.'

'Are you going to do more for the Cause when you get home?'

'If there is something useful I could do. After my degree that is not a degree, I decided that I would take time over my future, not jump into something. But I can't be idle for long. I hate wasting time.'

'So do I. Perhaps I am afraid of being idle. I must always have some project in view. But as of this afternoon, the future is far away and I couldn't care less.'

Beth looked at him, and stood up.

'Come on, let's walk. Besides, I can't kiss you sitting in a chair.'

Stefan got up and took her arm. They walked along the shore a little way and came to a secluded hollow.

Beth put her arms round his neck and kissed him. He held her waist.

'Stefan, is this a fleeting moment?'

'I hope it will bring more joys.'

'Amen to that, as you might say.'

They laughed and kissed again. Then they heard a shout. It was the driver.

Beth heaved a sigh.

'Time to go? It was fleeting, after all.'

'There will be other times, if you want, Beth.'

'I do. But we must be patient.'

They went back to the picnic. The driver was waiting. They gathered up their things and went back to the car. Nothing much was said on the way home, but they held hands. Back at the factory, Dietrich came out to meet them.

'Had a good time?'

'Very good, thank you,' said Beth. 'Nothing like sea air for bucking one up and improving the complexion.'

'Let's go home. It has been a tiresome day, and enough is enough. Things can take care of themselves till tomorrow morning.'

He drove them home. Beth went upstairs for a bath and fell asleep afterwards with a gentle smile on her face.

Chapter Nine

❄

The following morning, Dietrich left early as usual for the factory. The car returned to take Stefan into Bremen for a mid-morning interview with the Bishop.

'Come into town with me. I shouldn't be more than an hour. It will give you a chance to explore.'

They passed through the suburbs which used to be villages surrounding the medieval city. There were factories with chimney stacks and a pall of smoke hung over the city in the still air. The driver negotiated his way through pedestrians, horse-drawn wagons, lorries and buses and crossed the river by the Kaiserbrücke into the Old Town. He parked along the embankment. Stefan took Beth through narrow streets till they reached the Marktplatz. On one side was the Rathaus, and on another the twin towers of St Peter's Cathedral.

'It is basically very old,' explained Stefan, 'but over the centuries bits collapsed, and it was extensively renovated at the end of the last century.'

'It certainly looks like how what I imagined a continental cathedral should look.'

'A nineteenth century version of Late Gothic. But fine, all the same.'

He looked at his watch. 'I will meet you in an hour beside the statue over there. The Bishop's office is just round the corner. When I have finished with him, we will go and find some lunch.'

This was the first time during her visit that Beth had had to herself. She went over to the Rathaus and lingered looking at its imposing frontage. She thought how dull most municipal architecture was in England by comparison. Clearly the good burghers of Bremen had devoted some of their considerable wealth to civic pride. She walked slowly around the square looking at the buildings and the people; they all looked well-dressed and there were no beggars. She stopped in front of the statue. It towered above the pedestrians. On the plinth was an equestrian statue and the inscription said simply *Bismarck.*

'Must ask Stefan about him.'

The Cathedral was open and she went in and picked up a guide. She sat down in the nave and began to read. After ten minutes she was about to get up when the organ started to play. It had been a long time since she had heard an organ without a choir. She put aside the guide and settled down to listen. She recognised that it must be Bach. There was a long and slow introduction with much elaborate fingerwork and there were times when Beth could not work out where it was leading. There was a pause. She had made up her mind to get up and follow the guide around the cathedral, when the fugue started. Within a few seconds Beth was gripped. She banished all other thoughts from her mind and concentrated on the themes as they entered in various registers. The last chord in the major key was held for what seemed an age, and the echo reverberated for longer.

She plucked up courage and asked the man sitting two seats away what the piece was.

'*Fantasie und Fugue in G moll.*'

'*Danke.*'

'Are you English?' he asked.

'Oh dear, is my accent that bad?'

The man smiled. 'Not at all. But I have the chance to speak a little English. Our organist is very accomplished, but he needs to practice for a recital tomorrow afternoon. Will you be able to come?'

'Alas, no. I am staying with a family in the countryside... and I have to help with the children.'

'Ach. A pity. Is this your first time in our city?'

'Yes. But it is only a short visit and I have to go back to England soon. I am meeting someone in half an hour. I thought I would come in here to pass the time and it has been a unexpected delight.'

'There is a lot more for the visitor to see in Bremen. The Kunsthalle, for instance. Perhaps if your friend has time.'

He sighed.

'I don't, however. I must get back to my office. I escaped just to hear the Bach. I hope you have a good day.'

He got up and strode down the aisle.

Beth too got up and wandered around the Cathedral, guide in hand, but was conscious of filling in time rather than taking an active interest. She was thinking about Stefan and his interview with the Bishop.

On the hour she returned to Bismarck's statue and there he was waiting.

'Am I late?' she asked.

'I have only just got here. Let's go and eat.'

There was a café at one end of the Rathaus on the ground floor.

'You order for me, some local produce.'

Stefan looked through the menu.

'Nothing wildly exciting today, I'm afraid. How about *wurst* and *sauerkraut*, with a roll? And a glass of wine?'

'Sounds good to me. I am hungry.'

Stefan placed the order with a waiter and asked: 'How was your morning?'

'Fine. But your morning was more important.'

'I will tell you in due course, but I want to hear about you.'

'Well, first tell me about Bismarck and why he has such a huge statue.'

'You will know that he was called the Iron Chancellor and he was the man who united Germany under the Kaiser. So he deserves a statue even though he was a Prussian. We Bremeners have never been too fond of Prussia, but History has overtaken us. We accept the fact and get on with our business.'

'Which is?'

'Making money. Has been since medieval times.'

'Was Bismarck a great general?'

'No. His uniform is purely symbolic. He never went near a battlefield, I believe.'

Beth thought for a moment. 'The statue must be quite recent.'

'Three years ago. There was a certain amount of resistance to the project but other cities had statues of him, so we had to have one.'

Beth told him about listening to the organ in the Cathedral.

'It must be thrilling to play like that, to be able to create a huge sound and make the building vibrate. I wish I knew more about music. We didn't have pianos in India; apparently they can't stay in tune because of the heat, and bugs eat away at them. I sang hymns at boarding school but never in a choir; choir practice always coincided with extra hockey. You must take up my musical education.'

'Well, I am not an expert. We could learn together.'

The food arrived.

'This helping looks enormous, too much for me.'

'You are in Germany, remember. Eat what you can.'

Stefan finished his plate, Beth had half. He ordered coffee.

'Now, the Bishop,' said Beth.

'Yes, the Bishop. He will ordain me but after my military training. So I will have to do the full two weeks this summer.'

'Disappointing, but it will be good for your soul.'

'It will mean rubbing up against men of other classes, which is part of my pastoral training, I suppose. I am not very good with physical discomfort, because I have never had to endure it. As you say, it will be good for my soul.'

'And ordination? When is that likely to be?'

'I am coming back to Oxford straight after military training, so it will be towards Christmas.'

He called for the bill.

'Let's take a walk down to the River. See if the driver has come back.'

'What about the Kunsthalle? Is that worth seeing?'

'Very much so. I haven't been in for some while. Do you want to go in?'

The sun had come out.

'I think I would rather spend the time with you. I prefer my culture in small doses. Let's just wander and find a bench for a smoke.'

She took his arm as they strolled across the Square.

Most of the river traffic now used Bremerhaven nearer the sea, though some small steamers, mostly for tourists, still used the pontoons. The old warehouses had been demolished and a wide embankment created, with maple and lime trees planted at intervals. They found a bench in the shade. Beth delved into her handbag for cigarettes. Stefan took one as well and they lit up.

'Now, if I were a pastor I would not be able to light up in public. We are expected to behave better than most people. But I am allowed one or two secret vices.'

'Of course you are. Unless you are a sinner yourself, you can't understand other sinners. That is a good reason for pastors to sin.'

'I'm not sure the Bishop would agree with your argument.'

'Didn't St Augustine have something to say on the subject: "Lord, make me pure, but not just yet"?'

'Well, let me quote one of your hymns:

And if I tempted am to sin
And outward things are strong,
Do Thou, O Lord, keep watch within
And save my soul from wrong.

Do you recall singing that at school?'

'I do. We discussed it and thought it was rather spoilsporting. We were sixteen with no knowledge of the real world. But seriously, Stefan, does it worry you that you have the feelings and desires of ordinary men?'

He took a long draw of his cigarette.

'It worries me if I yield to sinful thoughts. I have to try harder.'

'So do you have a list of commandments, and tick off those you have obeyed and put a cross against those you have broken?'

She looked at his face and saw that he was frowning.

'Sorry, Stefan. I mustn't make fun of your calling. You are so committed to it and I find it... admirable... no, wonderful.'

She put her hand on his arm.

'I don't share your faith, at least, not yet, but I hope I can share some of your spiritual journey. But before that, there is something I must do.'

She dropped her cigarette, took the cigarette from his hand and put her arms around him. They kissed deeply.

'Let's not pretend,' she said when they emerged from the embrace. 'We have strong feelings for each other – well, I have for you. I will miss you terribly when I have to go home. And that is not an unworthy feeling.'

Stefan said nothing. Beth wondered if she had gone too far. After a moment he got to his feet.

'If I had a ring, it would be on your finger this instant. I haven't. But the thought is there. And I don't feel unworthy in my desire for you. It is one of God's many gifts.'

* * *

The driver came for them in a few minutes, and they were taken home. Stefan went up to his room to write more letters. Beth sat with Hannah while the children played in the garden.

'How did your day go?' she asked.

'Very well, thank you. I listened to the organ in the cathedral and Stefan bought me some lunch. Then we walked along the river bank.'

'Poor Stefan. He is very worried about this military training.'

'He told me what the Bishop had said. It seems that he has to do the full course, but, all being well, he should be ordained over the Christmas period. He has to juggle so many other things in his mind when he needs a clear head to finish his thesis. And he has articles to write for learned journals.'

'Can you really see him as a pastor? He is surely too much of an academic.'

'That is another thing that worries him: has he got the common touch to be a pastor to ordinary folk?'

'What do you think?'

'I don't share his faith and these matters are rather out of my depth.'

'Has he tried to convert you?'

'Gracious, no. But we have talked about it. He has said sensible things, practical advice, not vague theology. So he has the basis of ministry. I think he will learn fast.'

Hannah called for some tea and cake.

When she had poured and given Beth a slice, she sat back.

'Stefan is uncertain about his future. From what you have said, you are unsure what you are going to do with your life. And I... well, I feel that there is something in the air. Of course, as a woman, I am not supposed to concern myself with such matters. Dietrich has his business but also he has his worries, and they are not just about strikes or workers' rights or production targets. Occasionally, he lets slip a remark about the political situation. He is worried about the direction the government is taking. That sounds odd coming from an arms manufacturer. But Wilhelmstrasse is becoming more and more aggressive, looking for an enemy to challenge. Have you met anyone who is anti-English?'

'A man in the cathedral, when I asked him about the piece being played, was very friendly. And he recognised me as English and spoke in English.'

'A lot of educated Germans admire England... Shakespeare, the Navy, Queen Victoria. Not your music, though. As someone called it: *Das Land ohne musik.*'

'Perhaps it is. I think we spent too much time inventing sports to be composers. There's always Handel, of course, and Mendelssohn. The Queen was fond of him.'

'Both of them were German.'

The children came in and demanded juice and cake.

'Come and sit down with Beth, while I go inside.'

Juice and cake disappeared in a trice. Then Heinz said: 'Annelore won't play football with me.'

'Girls don't play football,' said Annelore.

'Well, this girl might,' said Beth, 'if you ask me nicely, Heinz.'

'Oh. Will you? Please.'

'Very well. But you are not to kick the ball too hard at me.'

'I promise.'

He took her out into the garden where a small goal had been chalked on a wall.

'You go in goal first,' said Beth.

She put the ball down in front of the goal.

'This the right distance?' she asked.

'A bit further away.'

'Right. I will have six kicks and then you have six. And we will add up the score.'

Beth stood back a little, took a run at the ball and it was sliced off her foot into the flower bed.

'Does that count, Heinz?'

'Yes, yes.'

Next time she took more care. The ball bumped along the ground towards the goal, but Heinz stopped it easily. She didn't get one past him.

'Perhaps Annelore was right,' she said.

'My turn now.'

Heinz took the ball and put it quite close to the goal.

'Hey, that's not fair,' she called out but he had already taken the kick. She bent down to stop it but was too late.

'Goal! Goal!' he shouted.

The ball had bounced off the wall. Heinz stopped it with his foot and took another kick. It sped past Beth's hand.

The next three Beth stopped with her feet. The last was kicked hard and hit her in the stomach.

They changed places.

'Right, Heinz, it's my turn now. So look out.'

Heinz stopped the first three easily. The fourth one got up in the air, bounced on a bump and caught Heinz in the face.

He started to cry. She offered him a handkerchief. 'Come on, Heinz. You're a tough guy. And you are winning. I have two more shots so I can only draw. Let's see if you can stop the last two.'

She took a gentle kick which he stopped easily. The last one rose in the air, but he caught it deftly.

'I've won!'

'You have. Shake hands.'

They solemnly shook hands. Heinz picked up the ball and ran inside to tell his mother. Annelore was still sitting at the tea table with her doll.

'Beth, when are you going to teach us more English?'

'I have been so busy these last few days with your uncle. How about after breakfast tomorrow?'

Annelore was satisfied with this and went into the house.

She sat for a few minutes, replaying in her head the conversations with Stefan that day. She had no doubts about her own feelings, but she was worried that she had forced Stefan into a declaration. They were not formally engaged but they had an understanding. She had never felt for anyone so strongly before and, as far as she could tell, he hadn't either. But they had never used the word 'love'. If they did formalise their relationship, the implications for her, a new country, a new family, a language she as yet spoke imperfectly, were considerable. She trembled at the prospect. But would she have it any other way?

Enough musing. She got up and went upstairs to wash.

She wrote a quick note to her parents and put it on the table to go to the post the next morning. Stefan's letters were ready to go as well; she recognised his angular handwriting. She went into the parlour and picked up a newspaper, the previous day's *Norddeutscher Zeitung*. She tried to read the main article but her brain baulked at the effort of translation. Instead she glanced at a magazine. She idly turned the pages; it seemed that German women had the same pre-occupations as English women. Stefan came in and picked up the newspaper.

'Anything of interest?' she asked him, after a while.

'Well, yes, actually. Here.' He showed her an article which someone, presumably Dietrich, had ringed in red ink.

'It mentions Sheffield.' He read on and then explained. 'It concerns a British metallurgist who has discovered an alloy which he called 'rustless steel', to counter corrosion in gun barrels.

Krupps also has been working on a similar alloy of steel, nickel and chrome. An anti-corrosive can be used for all sorts of purposes; the problem is to ensure that the alloy is strong enough to resist the tremendous forces released in firing a large gun.'

'Bigger and better weapons to kill people with.'

'I'm afraid so. Dietrich has said something to me about it. He doesn't make gun barrels but all the other bits and pieces that they need. Recently he won a contract with Krupps to supply them.'

They were called up to say good night to the children. Dietrich came back from the office, hurried upstairs to change, came down and poured himself a large drink.

'This is a bad habit,' he said, 'but needs must.'

'More problems?' Stefan asked.

'There are always problems.'

'What are they, this time?'

'I want to leave them back in the office.' He spoke with some asperity. 'They can wait till tomorrow.' He turned to Beth.

'Sorry I have been so busy. These last two days – all well? I hope Stefan has been a good guide to the charms of Lower Saxony.'

'Um...I couldn't have asked for a better guide.'

Dietrich looked at Stefan, who was blushing, and then at Beth who was smiling.

'I see. And what are your plans for tomorrow, Stefan?'

'Can we borrow your driver to go to Wildeshausen? There are some good walks round there. Once he has taken you to the factory.'

'I don't see why not. Fresh country air and no factory chimneys.'

'Can we take Hannah and the children as well?'

'Good idea. Beth?'

'Yes. A family outing will be fun.'

They were just sitting down to dinner when the front door bell rang.

'What on earth?' exclaimed Dietrich.

He went to the front door himself. A courier stood there waiting with a brown envelope.

Dietrich looked at it and felt in his pocket for some coins to tip the courier, who saluted and went back to his van. It was a telegram addressed to Miss Beth Millward. He came back to the dining room and handed the envelope to Beth.

'Do you want to take it away and open it?' Hannah asked, after seeing the look on Beth's face.

'I will. Thank you.'

Nothing was said after she left. Hannah looked at Stefan and nodded slightly. He got up and went to find Beth. She was in her room, sitting on the bed, her face glistening with tears.

'Beth, *Schatz*, what is it?'

She handed him the telegram. Beth's mother had had a bad fall, was unconscious and sinking fast.

He put his arm round her.

Beth took a deep breath.

'She hasn't been well for some time. The pain of arthritis... I must go home.'

'Of course. It will be arranged. I will go and speak to Dietrich.'

Stefan went downstairs and passed Hannah on the stairs.

Hannah went in to Beth with a supply of handkerchiefs. She was now weeping openly. Hannah sat with her until the sobbing subsided.

'I'm sorry. Such a shock. I must go back. My father will not cope very well and I don't know where my brother is.'

'We will do everything we can to get you home as soon as possible.'

'You have been very kind to me... welcomed me into your family. I have been happy here. I am sorry to go, but I have to.'

'We quite understand. Now we have to be practical. You must have some supper before a long journey. I'll have it sent up.'

'No. I will come down. Much better than brooding alone.'

She dried her eyes and went back to the dining room. Dietrich was on the telephone. Beth and the others were still eating when he returned.

'This is the plan. There is an early train to Hamburg. The ferry leaves at ten. I have booked you a cabin and meals in the restaurant. I will drive you to the station. We had better leave at five tomorrow morning.'

'That's very kind. Thank you. Can I repay you for the ticket?'

'Certainly not.'

'I'll come with you to Hamburg,' said Stefan, 'and I will send a telegram to say you are on your way.'

After supper, Beth went upstairs to prepare for the early start. While she was packing, Stefan knocked on her door and entered.

'Am I being punished for being happy?' she said. 'I shall always be afraid of being happy in the future.'

'No, you are not being punished. God doesn't work like that.'

'I know she is dead, Stefan. Say a prayer for us.'

'Let us pray together now.'

They sat on the bed. Stefan took her hands and bowed his head.

'Give strength, O lord, to those who mourn. And take our sister into your everlasting arms. May she rest in peace, and rise in glory.'

Beth wiped her eyes.

'Have you a photograph of yourself? I would like to take it with me.'

He brought her one.

'What a serious young man!' she said.

'I am serious.'

'I shall treasure it.'

Chapter Ten

❄

James Millward spent July playing cricket for various teams. The weather was sunny for the most part and the pitches were hard. He made several fifties and on one occasion scored a century. He impressed with his abilities as a fielder but his slow leg spin was not called upon very often, and then only for short spells, when the captain decided that he had to 'buy a wicket'. A breakthrough having been achieved, he was taken off.

His biggest challenge was in a Minor Counties' match against Staffordshire at the County Ground at Stoke-on-Trent. The openers having been dismissed cheaply, at Number Three he was facing Sydney Barnes. James had watched him on a couple of occasions and his fiercesome reputation was well-known. In 1913 he was forty years old, as fit and single-minded as ever and limbering up for the forthcoming MCC Tour of South Africa. He gave James a sardonic smile; he had seen plenty of 'varsity men before and had disposed of them easily.

'Oh aye, here's another,' he said to Mid Off in his pronounced Midland accent.

James had been told that Barnes could spin the ball both ways; his finger spin was difficult to read. Because of his high action the ball rose sharply off the pitch. He would bowl medium and fast medium, but also slip in a slower ball. Every ball was different from the previous one and had to be played. Barnes employed a circle of fielders to intimidate a new batsman, and the wicketkeeper, well used to keeping for Barnes, always stood up, ready to whip off the bails if the batsman strayed out of his crease.

James took guard, glared round at the fielders, patted the crease and took up his stance. James was tall; his stance looked comfortable. The university coach had praised him for his fluid footwork. 'Get the feet in the right place, Mr Millward, and everything else will follow.' James had developed the practice over several seasons of putting everything else from his mind except the bowler's run up and his hand. He did not move his feet until the ball had left the bowler's hand, but he had the time to play it smoothly. The first three deliveries he covered with a solid defensive stroke. The fourth was wider but nipped back off a patch of rough; James was prepared.

After two overs, he had not scored a run and another wicket had fallen at the other end. Barnes had added another fielder to the ring about him. Two or three balls were well off the stumps, no doubt to tempt James into a rash stroke. He did not rise to the bait, but watched each ball carefully onto the bat. At the end of the over his colleague came to talk to him, but James merely nodded and turned away; he wanted no distraction.

Three overs later, James was still at the crease. He could see that Barnes was giving signs of impatience. For once there was an overpitched ball. Though it was on the wicket, James drove it past Mid On's left hand to the boundary. There was applause from a previously silent stand, but James didn't hear it. Gradually more runs came. James found the other bowlers easier to deal with but he did not let his concentration lapse. At tea, he had scored forty-five runs. He sat by himself, puffing at his pipe. In the three overs after tea, he scored twelve runs and his colleague was getting into his stride. Then Barnes came on again. The flow of runs slowed, but James kept playing every ball on its merits and Barnes was not able to get past his defence. But not long before the close, when he was on ninety-three, Barnes bowled a ball well outside the leg stump into the rough, which turned so sharply that James's defence could not follow it, and it clipped the wicket. James looked at his feet and the wicket. Then he left the crease without delay. As he walked past Barnes on the way to the Pavilion he gave him a respectful nod; Barnes replied with a muttered 'Mr Millward'. James's innings had saved the side from ignominy. He only made thirty in the second innings, but honour had been more than satisfied. As a result, more invitations to play came his way.

James's father, while applauding his successes at the wicket, began to press him to consider his future. James evaded his prodding by saying that he wanted to fulfil his talent as a cricketer while he was young, and a few more months would not matter in the long run.

'That is as may be,' said Mr Millward. 'However, you must try to focus on the years to come. Do you have a young lady in mind?'

'No. I haven't met anyone that interests me.'

'In that case, there is no impediment to you choosing whatever career you want.'

'True.'

James paused; his father said nothing.

'There is one thing, Pater, that I have thought of as a possibility, in the short term, of course. And it wouldn't interfere with other things I might do.'

'Oh?'

'I could join the Territorials. I did well in the OTC at school. I know one end of a rifle from another. I would be doing something useful for society, instead of massaging my own ego. And who knows? If Kaiser Bill keeps rattling his sabre...'

'Hm. I suppose you are right. But soldiering is not all dressing up in peacock uniforms and cocktails before the Mess dinner.'

'I know that, Pater. I've seen enough of the other side out in India. It's...it's that after four years with my nose in books I want to do something practical. Dealing with real people, not ancient characters or philosophical entities.'

'Very well. But you will still be living at home for the time being?'

'Of course.'

'Good. I am becoming increasingly concerned about your mother. She is less and less mobile, and just looks frail.'

'She is always sitting down when I come home and asks me to bring things.'

'I know Beth helps, but she is busy with her suffragist work, and she is going off to Germany soon.'

'Really! She obviously likes Stefan more than she lets on.'

Mr Millward ignored that remark.

'I think we need to engage a nurse. We have a spare room.'

'What does Mother think?'

'Talk to her. She is reluctant of course, but is coming round to the necessity. I will get one from an agency as soon as Beth has gone. So don't tell her, otherwise she might abandon her visit to Germany out of a sense of duty.'

* * *

The next day, James applied to the East Surreys' Territorial Battalion. On the first evening he expected to be shouted at by the Drill Sergeant along with ten other new recruits but the Lieutenant in charge, having learnt that he had been in the OTC, called him out and told him to explain basic drill movements to the men.

'Sir.'

James cast his mind back several years, and recalled his own RSM at school.

'First, standing at attention: chest out, stomach in, feet at an angle of forty-five degrees, thumbs to the seams of the trousers ("That's what the seams of the trousers is for"), feel the collar on the back of the neck.'

He proceeded to demonstrate the position.

'Now saluting,' said the Lieutenant.

James demonstrated: 'Longest way up, shortest way down, with a pause of two/three between each movement.'

The men watched him at first with amusement and then with respect when he showed them standing at ease and left, right and about turns.

'Why do we insist on these postures, Mr Millward?'

'Well, sir, they are really natural positions and movements smartened up. As my old RSM used to say, smartness is a part of discipline and a smart soldier is an efficient soldier.'

'Very well, Mr Millward. Fall in.'

It was shortly after his second attendance at the Drill Hall that Mrs Millward had a bad fall in the house. No bones were broken, only a cut on the forehead. The nurse was able to get her back to bed, but she was clearly very shaken and began complaining of palpitations. Mr Millward was called on the telephone and hurried home. James was in town and did not come back until the late afternoon. The three of them watched at her bedside during the evening. The doctor came, examined her and shook his head.

'Her heart is in a bad way. I have brought something to ease her pain. But I have to say that it will be touch and go.' He gave her an injection. 'I will come back tomorrow morning, but call me sooner if necessary.'

She slept for most of the night and for a moment appeared to rally. She spoke to James and his father, saying that she was sorry to cause so much trouble; when she had had a good rest she was sure she would feel better. By midday she had lapsed into unconsciousness again and Mr Millward sent the telegram to Beth. She died that evening.

The next morning Stefan's telegram arrived and James said he would go to Harwich to meet her.

* * *

'She's gone, hasn't she?'

'Yes, Beth. She has. Just faded away in the last few hours, quite peacefully.'

'Were you there?'

'Yes. And Father. And the nurse.'

Beth sighed deeply. 'Stefan's family were very kind. I had a lovely time with Stefan, and the children. But if only I had known she was going to die…'

'Don't blame yourself. None of us could have known. She was suffering from the pain of arthritis, but apparently her heart was also affected. I suppose if she had survived she would have been an invalid for the rest of her life. And she couldn't have borne that.'

'You are saying it was a merciful release?'

'Yes, Beth.'

Beth said nothing. She wiped away tears, but they kept coming. James brought out handkerchiefs for her. The other people in the compartment watched sympathetically. Soon she relapsed into dry-eyed silence.

When they reached London, they had to change stations. At Paddington there was an hour to wait before the next train.

'I'm starving, James. I couldn't face breakfast on the boat. Can we have something to eat?'

There was a café just outside the station and Beth tucked into eggs and bacon. James had a cup of tea.

'I have been talking about myself. Sorry, James. How are you feeling?'

'Well, it was the first time I have seen someone die, and, if I think about it, that would be the way I would want to go when my time comes. Not lingering. Easy to say now, but it is something we all have to face.'

'Never mind philosophy, James. What do you really feel?'

'I... I don't know what I feel. It has just happened, and we must get on with it. I'll tell you next year, or whenever.'

'And Father?'

'He hasn't said much. Just went into his study after the arrangements had been made. When I was about to leave, he called me to her bedroom and we just looked at her in silence for a few minutes. I left him there.'

'I wish I had seen her, to say goodbye.'

They arrived at home in the afternoon. Mr Millward greeted Beth with a hug and asked after her journey.

'Never mind that, Father. I'm here. Has she gone?'

'She is at the undertakers. Do you want to see her? I asked them to wait for you. We must go now.'

They drove in silence.

'Go in by yourself, Beth.'

She was led into a room at the back, where her mother was laid out in a coffin, dressed in one of her gowns. Her hair had been tidied, her eyes were closed and her hands were clasped across her stomach.

Beth stared at her motionless, as her thoughts whirled around in her head. The face in the coffin was very dear, but locked into a fixed expression, so unlike her in life.

Beth felt awkward, even though she was alone. She remembered James's words: 'We must get on with it'. She touched her mother's forehead, then kissed it. The action served as a release and she turned away to join the other two. She thanked the undertaker and led the way out to the car.

Back at home they sat together in the drawing room. Mr Millward poured them a drink.

'I have arranged the funeral for next week. A notice has been put in the paper. James, I want you to ring round people who would want to know in person. That is something I would rather not undertake myself.'

'Right, Pater.'

'I will write letters where appropriate. Beth, I know you have only just got back, but could you take over household matters in the short term? I have asked the cook and maids to carry on as before, but there may have to be changes in due course. And when you have the time, could you please look through your mother's things, not throw anything away but see what's there?'

Beth nodded.

'It's barely two days since she died,' Mr Millward went on, 'but I feel I want to get on with the practical things. It will help to divert my er... dark thoughts. I will be seeing the solicitor tomorrow.'

'Father, where will she be buried?'

'The church. I bought a plot when we moved here. So it will be easy to visit her.'

Beth felt tears coming on again, so she hurriedly went to her room, saying that she must change after her journey.

Over dinner, Mr Millward asked Beth about her time in Germany. She told him about the family and the visit that she and Stefan had made to the factory.

'I don't know about factories, but Dietrich seems to work very hard and the factory is well-run. All male workers, of course, but some of it is heavy and dangerous work, especially in the Foundry.'

'Is he the owner?'

'I think so. He supplies the Government with parts for munitions, like guns. Stefan tells me that he has to do that to keep his men in work. But he admits that if the Government spends all that money on munitions, they might be tempted to use them.'

'Germany is not the only country to spend money like that. We have to ensure that our own navy is bigger and better than anyone else's. For defence of our interests, of course. And how is your German?'

Beth thought for a moment, then replied in German. 'With Stefan's help I am becoming much more fluent. I hope I don't lose it, now I am back.'

'Very good, Beth,' said James. 'It sounds just right, not that I would know if it wasn't.'

'I am going to read more German,' she went on in English. 'Quite apart from sharing the language with Stefan, who knows whether it might be useful in the future?'

'Are you going to see Stefan again?' Mr Millward asked.

'He should be back in Oxford, once his military training is over. I hope I can visit him soon.'

The telephone rang in the Hall. James got up to answer it.

When he was out of the room, Mr Millward said: 'We liked Stefan when he was with us. He seemed a very respectable young man, and destined for the Ministry. But... but this is nothing personal. From what I read, relations between us and Germany are getting increasingly fraught. I can envisage a situation where your friendship could bring trouble for both of you. I don't want you to be hurt.'

'He is a man of peace, Father. Not everyone in Germany is a warmonger. I don't have a crystal ball, but I do know that we were genuinely happy together in those few days. Surely that must count for something.'

'Well, do you have an arrangement?'

'Nothing specific, if that's what you mean. Time will tell.'

James came back into the room. 'You will be pleased to hear that I am now a member of the MCC.'

'Congratulations, James.'

'What does that mean?' Beth asked.

'Oh, I can represent the MCC in matches, and I can sit in the Members' Pavilion at Lords.'

'Could you take me to watch a Test Match?'

'Good heavens, no. Sorry. Men only.'

Beth laughed. 'I thought you would say that. When we women rule the world, we will be sitting in the Pavilion watching a women's Test.'

James looked abashed.

'I said it to tease you.'

'Good,' said Mr Millward. 'We can't be solemn all the time, even now. Any other news, James?'

'I have been asked to play against Sussex next Thursday, a three-day match.'

'Again, congratulations. But that is the day after the funeral.'

'I will wear a black armband, Pater.'

Beth was starting to yawn. 'I didn't sleep much last night. I must go to bed.' She kissed her father, and then James, who was not expecting it.

When she had gone, Mr Millward remarked that she was bearing up well.

'She is tough, Pater. We will need her. And she has a mind of her own.'

* * *

Beth was so busy over the next few days that she had no time to write to Stefan, even though he was never far from her thoughts. To her surprise, she found her father and brother becoming dependent on her in household matters; she arranged catering, laundry, paid the maids, and booked a hotel for the gathering after the funeral. They sought her advice where she would not have expected it. Mr Millward asked her to look over the eulogy he would pronounce at the funeral. James asked her whether he should really play cricket so soon afterwards.

'We are not Victorians any more, James. The important thing is to mourn her in your own way, not by some public display. I am sure Father would agree.'

She wrote to her own friends with her news. Apart from a reference personal to each friend, the text was much the same and ended thus:

> …I now have to look after two men and I feel very responsible. I am beginning to find out what being a *hausfrau* is. It makes me realise what a wise mother she was. I hope that when and if I come to it I will be worthy of her.

Her mother's clothes did not fit Beth, who was considerably taller than her, nor were they appropriate to current fashion. However, she did keep some shawls. Mr Millward told her to have most of the jewellery if she wanted it, but there were some items he intended for James's bride, if there was one, and a granddaughter likewise. In her will, she had left all her chattels to her husband to deal with as he sought fit. There were some legacies for servants but the remainder was left to her children, in trust till they reached the age of twenty-five. Beth could claim hers as soon as probate was settled; James would have to wait.

As the cricket season was coming to an end, James was at home more often, doing nothing very much apart from the Territorials. For a fortnight he was away on a course for potential officers. Mr Millward went up to London two days a week for meetings at the India Office, where he had been co-opted onto a committee; he stayed overnight at his club. Beth was thinking about returning to the Suffragist fold but she was not sure whether she wanted to be directly involved any more. No other activity beckoned. After the turmoil of her mother's death and the aftermath, she now found time on her hands. As a result, she began to fret that she had not heard from Stefan.

When the letter did arrive, by the afternoon post, she resisted temptation to tear open the envelope but carried it upstairs to her room and put it on the dressing table while she finished some chores.

Liebe Beth,

I thought about writing to you in German, but I must write in the language of your country. When you write to me, try a bit in German; it will be hard work, but I know you can do it.

Now I am a pickelhaube-wearing *gefreite*, yes, Lance Corporal in your army. Why? Because I am older and more educated than the other recruits. I can march, though my boots rub, and I can present arms, after a fashion. But when it comes to shooting, I have yet to hit a target at a hundred metres. It might be something to do with my eyes, or the rifle. I also now know how to fold my bed-clothes in the approved Army fashion. Thank goodness it is still warm. The blankets are so thin that I would shiver in winter. And they are not very clean. I have learnt to like Army stew, because one gets very hungry at the end of the day and there is nothing else to eat.

My colleagues have started calling me *Onkel Haase*, which I suppose is a term of respect, though I can't be quite sure. When we go to the *Lokal* near the camp, I have one beer, while they have several. We do not talk about religion, and I have not let on that I am destined for the priesthood.

On that front, the bishop has accelerated my ordination. When my military commitment ends in a few days' time, I have to go on a retreat, which will be good for the soul, and then be ordained. It means, dear Beth, that I will not be back in Oxford till the beginning of November.

So much for me. I have been thinking about you a great

deal and praying for you, even when I am polishing my boots. Actually, that is one of the few times in the day when I have a quiet moment to myself. How are you getting on? Life goes on even after a great bereavement. You are a very practical person and I am sure you will cope. There will be times when waves of sadness seem overwhelming but they will pass and be replaced by sweet memories of your Mother. Forgive my preaching, but that is what pastors are supposed to do.

When we were in Bremen, we said things to each other, not making a commitment yet but simply expressing the warmth of our feelings towards each other. My feelings have not changed in any way. If you are having second thoughts, please don't feel constrained by me. I will fully understand. There is so much outside our control that could come between us. A book is going the rounds here, *Weltmacht oder Untergang*, World Dominion or Decline. It outlines a plan for the subjugation of the whole of Europe. There is resentment at the British attitude, in that the British brought about the encirclement of Germany to stifle rightful German ambitions. It is dangerous nonsense, of course. But it is seen as gospel and the government has not disclaimed it.

Enough gloom. Just to say that I miss you very much and, as you say over there, roll on the day when we can meet again. Please write when you can.

Ever yours,
Stefan

It took Beth a couple of days to craft a letter, with the help of a German grammar and dictionary.

Dear Stefan,
Thank you for your long letter. Your English is impeccable, as always. Don't mark this letter of mine too harshly.

Somehow I can't imagine the gentle scholar in a spiked helmet, carrying a rifle and polishing his boots. I hope they are more comfortable now. Will you wear uniform as a chaplain, like British padres? I suppose you will be an officer.

Talking of officers, James has signed up for the Territorials. Now that the cricket season is over he had nothing else to do. To be honest, I think he is worth more than soldiering, but nothing else has so far appealed to him. It is one thing to go through school and university when the next event in your career seems inevitable, but when you have to make a decision at the crossroads, that is a different matter.

Father keeps himself busy with something in the India Office and he spends a lot of time in his study. He does not wear his heart on his sleeve (is that a German idiom?) so I can't tell what his feelings are. He seems in good health, thank goodness.

I find myself looking after two men and running the household. A new experience for me. And it has prevented me from brooding. I do have bouts of weeping on occasion, when some memory of her rises in my mind. Christmas will be difficult, but we will manage. Come the New Year, I want to find a new role for myself. In that sense, I am a bit like James.

It may not be seemly to wish you good luck for your ordination, but I hope you will find fulfilment in it. Please tell me all about it when we meet. And, please God, may that be soon.

Give my respects to Hannah, Dietrich and the children. I have been meaning to write, and I will do so, I promise.

Take care of yourself, my love (there, I have said it), and hurry back to England.

Beth

Chapter Eleven

❋

Apart from his activities with the Territorials, James had little to occupy him. He spent the mornings reading the papers or writing letters, on occasion running errands for Beth. In the afternoons he went for walks. His mood was subdued. Mr Millward gently urged him to take more active steps in choosing a career, and Beth made one or two comments to that effect. James made noncommittal answers.

'Well, it's your life,' said Beth.

One morning a letter came for him. He took it to his room. He came down ten minutes later with a broad grin.

'O ye of little faith. I have a job, if I want it.'

'If you want what?'

'My old headmaster is in a jam. One of his Classics teachers has suddenly gone sick and likely to be off for some months. Would I fill in for him? I will go and see him this afternoon.'

He borrowed his father's car for the short journey. He was admitted to the Headmaster's study, where he had had one or two painful encounters in the past.

'Ah, Millward. Thank you so much for coming over. Do sit down.'

The Headmaster pointed to an armchair beside the fire and took the other one opposite.

'We have followed your exploits on the cricket field with interest, but that must be at an end till next season. What else have you been doing with yourself?'

'Well, sir, I have joined the Territorials, the East Surreys. We meet once a week and I have been on a course for potential officers.'

'You rose quite high in the OTC. Cadet Warrant Officer, I believe.'

'The masters had to call me Mr Millward.'

'Yes, of course. Do you have any commitments coming up?'

'None. I admit I am at a loose end.'

'Poor Jackson – did he teach you? – has cancer. I have to keep his place open, but I fear that he is unlikely to return. Therefore you will be employed as a temporary master, until such time as Jackson's position becomes clear, one way or the other. So, what do you feel about joining us?'

'I would be very happy to do it. I hope I can be equal to the challenge.'

'I see no difficulty. You know the place, I am sure you haven't forgotten all your Latin and Greek and as a praeposter you will have had experience in exercising discipline.'

'I will need guidance, though, now I am on the other side of the desk. Will I have any boarding house duties?'

'One evening a week, ending at ten o'clock. You will have accommodation anyway.'

'Games?'

'Rugby and Running, if you want to take part. Jackson did not do games.'

'I would be happy to do cross-country. I am not as fit as I ought to be.'

'Very well. Two afternoons a week.'

'What books will I be teaching?'

The Headmaster consulted a piece of paper.

'This is what Kirkwood, Head of Classics, has written out for you. Have a look.'

James studied the paper.

'Thucydides, Tacitus, Sophocles OT. I will have to do some homework on that. Cicero *In Verrem*. Horace for the Sixth Form, Caesar and Livy for the Fifth and basic grammar lower down. I think I should be able to manage it. My own schooldays were not so long ago.'

'Excellent. Can you start next Monday?'

'Yes.'

There was a knock on the door.

'Mr Kirkwood, sir,' said the Secretary.

'Come in, come in. Kirkwood joined us shortly after you went up to Oxford; he did Mods and Greats like you.'

They shook hands.

'Now go with Kirkwood and he will fill you in.'

Kirkwood was rather older than James and he seemed a little suspicious.

'What college, Millward?'

'Trinity. And you?'

'Hertford.'

'Never came across anyone from Hertford.' James instantly regretted the remark.

'We weren't a very prestigious college. Let me walk you over to the classroom.'

'This list. I haven't read Sophocles since Mods. I read some Horace in Greats, mainly for his connection to Augustus. With the rest I should be very familiar. After all, I only finished at Oxford this last summer.'

'Good.'

'I will need some guidance on the lower forms – how much prep to give them and so forth.'

'Jackson left all his teaching notes in his desk. Here is the key. Go through the notes and you will see what is required. Have you a gown? We usually wear them while teaching.'

'No. I borrowed one for my graduation.'

'Well, use his. It hangs on the door.'

Kirkwood unlocked the classroom door. The room smelt of unwashed bodies.

'I'll leave you to it. Be here on Monday at nine.'

Kirkwood left and headed across the Quad.

James looked around him. Everything was very familiar. He tried on Jackson's gown; it was a bit short and was rather dusty. Evidently he had used the sleeve on occasion to wipe the blackboard.

Underneath the gown a cane was hanging. James took it down

and put it at the back of a cupboard, well out of sight. Then he opened all the windows. There was pile of books on a table – Remove Latin notebooks, neatly marked in red ink. He looked along the bookcase. Most of the texts he would be teaching were there, with commentaries. Jackson's mark book was in the desk, along with his timetable. James took it along with the books he needed for Monday. Three days of solid preparation lay ahead.

The first class he had to face was the Remove. They came in and sat down in silence, contemplating him with undisguised curiosity. He counted heads; all seemed to be present. Although Jackson had kept meticulous records of what had been covered in class, James came round the desk, sat on it, looked the class up and down and told them to stand up. He found the tallest boy and made the rest sit down again.

'Your name?'

'Maxwell, sir.'

'Very well, Maxwell. Tell what you did last week.'

'Nothing much, sir.'

'I see, a joker. I have your book here, Maxwell. It says that you were learning the third declension. You didn't do very well in the test. What did you find difficult?'

'Er… it's the cases, sir.'

'I see. Well, sit down and perhaps someone else can explain them to you. First, everyone put away the grammar books.'

James selected a boy from the back.

'Your name, please.'

'Barnes, sir.'

'How interesting. I'll tell you why later. Explain cases to Maxwell.'

Barnes wore glasses and looked like a swot. He rattled off the case endings of the third declension and also gave the variations in the ablative singular and genitive plural.

'Most impressive, Barnes. I know that it seems complicated but there is no other way of learning them than by reciting them. But first we must write them down.'

He referred to the pile of books and selected one whose handwriting was the neatest.

'Who is Godfrey?'

An arm went up from the front.

'I am, sir.'

'Very well, Godfrey. Come up here, take some chalk, and write down the names of the cases down the board.'

Godfrey got up nervously and went to the blackboard. He had to stretch to reach the top of the board.

'Stand on the chair, if it helps. But don't fall off.'

This brought a giggle from the class.

James went to the back of the class and sat on a windowsill.

'I often sit at the back, because all the troublemakers sit at the back and I like to join them. On you go, Godfrey.'

With the names of the cases on the board, he invited the class to call out the endings. They were hesistant at first.

'Don't be shy. Let's start with the accusative.'

'-em', they shouted.

'Go on.'

'-is, –i, -e, or –i.'

Godfrey wrote them down.

'Now the plural.'

'-es, -es, –es, -um or –ium, -ibus, -ibus.'

'What about the neuter?'

A boy turned round and explained.

'The neuter has the nominative, vocative and accusative all the same, sir.'

'What are they in the plural?'

'-a or –ia.'

'Sir, sir,' another boy called out. 'You have left out the nominative and vocative singular.'

'Dear me, so I have. But with good reason. What do you think that is?'

'Er… because they are all different.'

'And that is why we have to learn the stem of nouns and adjectives

as well. I'm sorry, Maxwell, but it gets more and more complicated. But that is what happens in life as well.'

He went to the front of the class and stood to one side.

'Down you get, Godfrey.'

'Let's recite them, all of us. You lead off, Maxwell.'

There was a mumble from Maxwell and the class.

'Come on, louder.'

Voices rose.

'Still louder.'

By this time the boys were shouting. After three times, James
called a halt.

'Now, when you clean your teeth – I hope you do clean your
teeth – don't stop until you have recited the case endings three
times. I want you all word-perfect.'

'Will there be a big test, sir?' a boy asked. 'Griffiths, sir.'

'Oh yes, Griffiths, a monster test. But have you ever wondered
why you have to learn all these cases, Griffiths?'

'No, sir. We were told just to learn them.'

'No curiosity? No. Well, after our test, I will reveal the reason.
That's something to look forward to, isn't it?'

There were one or two nods from the class.

'Now,' James went on, 'I know Griffiths, Maxwell, Godfrey
and Barnes. I must warn you that it will take me some time to
learn the names of the rest, so you must be patient with me.
Barnes, are you related to Sydney Barnes?'

'No, sir. Who is Sydney Barnes?'

Maxwell intervened: 'He is England's greatest bowler today.
He will be going to South Africa with the test team this winter.'

'Well,' said James, 'I have faced Sydney Barnes.'

The boys sat up.

'He is indeed a great bowler and it is very difficult to read his
deliveries.'

'How many runs did you make, sir?'

James looked at them for a moment then consulted his watch.

'Time for Break.'

'Come on, sir. How many?'

'Ninety-three.'

* * *

The next hour was free and James used the time to plan the next class with the Remove. At eleven o'clock, the Middle Sixth arrived for a class on Thucydides. There were six of them.

James asked them to identify themselves.

'Now, you should have some work for me.'

'We have been preparing chapter twenty-three of Book One.'

'Tricky stuff. Who is going to start the construe?'

With a nudge from James here and there, the boys eventually got to the end of the chapter.

'Well done. I too used to struggle with that passage when I was at school. Can you give me examples of the disasters that occurred during the war?'

'Well, sir, there was the plague at Athens.'

'And the civil war in Corcyra,' another boy volunteered.

'Good. Curiously, Thucydides does not give any examples of the earthquakes, eclipses or famines he mentions. However I can give you a good example of wanton brutality towards civilians, which Thucydides mentions in Book Six – Mycalessus. Look it up. It is truly horrifying and illustrates the pernicious effect on human behaviour which war brings. And that applies just as much today as it did two thousand years ago.'

The boys nodded sagely.

'Let's consider the the relationship of Athens and Sparta. Was war inevitable?'

'There were all these disputes before the war, sir, which Thucydides decribes. I suppose that they did not amount to a casus belli in themselves, but just created suspicion.'

'And then there was Plataea,' someone chimed in.

'Yes, of course,' said James. 'Tell me what went wrong.'

'Um… there was heavy rain which prevented the Theban relief force from crossing the river and getting there in time. The Thebans accused the Plataeans of breaking their oath. The Plataeans denied there was an oath. The Athenians sent a message to the Plataeans, who were their allies, warning them not to take action against the Thebans they had captured, but it arrived too late. The Thebans prisoners had been killed. So the Spartans, the allies of the Thebans, declared war on Athens and prepared to invade.'

'So the whole twenty-seven years' war was caused by a rainstorm?'

'That was not the only reason, sir.'

'What if I said to you that there was no intrinsic reason why Sparta should have gone to war with Athens? Their relations, sphere of influence if you like, were laid down by the Peace of 445, which had lasted fourteen years. It was their allies who prodded Sparta to declare war.'

'But Thucydides says that it was fear of the Athenians which was the real cause of the war.'

'And Sparta used the allies' complaints as an excuse to make war,' added James. 'I have thought a lot about this question. If you consider the respective strengths and weaknesses of Sparta and Athens, they complement each other. The Athenians could not invade Laconia and defeat the Spartans in a set piece battle on land, but the Spartans could not defeat the Athenians at sea. If the Spartans attacked the city of Athens, it was so well fortified that they could not carry it by assault. Supplies could easily come in by sea. So the only way they could capture the city was by treachery or denying it supplies, which could only happen after the destruction of the Athenian fleet.'

There was silence while the boys digested James's conclusion.

'So they should never have gone to war. Does any of this have an application today?' he asked.

Eventually a boy put up his hand. 'You could say that England was like Athens, a sea power, but with a small army. Germany has a very strong army but not much of a navy, like Sparta.'

'So what does Germany want?'

'I suppose every country wants security.'

'So who is likely to attack Germany?'

'France possibly, sir, to avenge 1871.'

'Right. So what should England do?'

'My father says that England should keep out of the Continent. It is called splendid isolation.'

'So why did we intervene in the days of Marlborough and Wellington?'

'My father says it was to prevent one power dominating the Continent, like Louis XIV and Napoleon.'

'Two hundred and one hundred years ago,' said James. 'Are we due for another war, then?'

* * *

The fact that James had scored ninety-three runs against Barnes was soon bruited round the school, and boys, who tend to be unsure of or even hostile to new faces, treated James with awed respect. The Remove responded well to his lively approach. Jackson had taught from behind the desk; James was on his feet most of the time and the gown remained on its hook. He made the boys write on the blackboard and explain what they had written. Even Maxwell became more enthusiastic for grammar. After a week, James gave them a test in their exercise books, which he corrected with cricketing terms: ten out of ten was a six over long on, seven was a good length ball on the off stump; below five was described as a dropped catch in the slips. As the term went on, there were fewer of these.

Recalling his own experience of being taught at school, when he was spoonfed with information, James tried allocate at least ten minutes of every hour to discussion. One day, after a concentrated session on the declension of nouns and adjectives of all declensions, he drew a huge question mark on the board.

'Why?'

'Why what, sir?'

'Why do we spend so much time with declensions and their endings?'

There was silence from the boys.

'Has no one got any idea? Why don't we have declensions in English?'

Still silence. So he wrote on the board: dog/man/bite.

Still no response.

'Who is doing the biting?'

Barnes the swot put up his hand: 'The dog bites the man.'

'How do you know that?'

'A man wouldn't bite a dog.'

'Possibly. Translate it into Latin.'

'*Canis hominem mordet.*'

James wrote it on the board.

'Correct. We could also write this sentence thus: *Canis mordet hominem, Hominem mordet canis.*' He did so. 'They all mean the same. So how do we know which is doing the biting?'

'In English, sir, the subject nearly always comes first in the sentence and the object after the verb.'

'True. But it is the case ending of the noun in Latin that tells us what it is doing in the sentence. Barnes, translate "The man bites the dog".'

'*Homo canem mordet.*'

He wrote it down. 'Word order is important in English but not so much in Latin. Do you understand a little better now, Maxwell?'

'Yes. I suppose so, sir.'

'On which happy note,' he looked at his watch, 'it is time for lunch.'

* * *

Within a few weeks, James felt comfortable in his new role. He was busy with all sorts of activities, from cross-country running to the Debating Society. Some of the older masters, who remembered him from his schooldays, had been initially dismissive of him, but they soon came to recognise his energy and commitment. James had no firm aspiration to make a career of teaching, but it became a possibility. The topic arose over dinner at home during one of his rare visits.

'I don't know, Pater. It is a young man's job, at least at the sharp end. There is nothing worse, as I remember from my days, than being taught by a elderly man who is seeing his time out and has no interest in his pupils. There was a Mr Boyes, who, it was rumoured, after the first lesson of term told his pupils to re-vise, and just sat there reading the newspaper. Just now I am en-joying myself. Not earning much money, I admit, but enough. I don't have any expenses. Whether I will feel the same five years hence is another matter.'

'Well, I am glad you are doing something purposeful.'

'And you, Pater. You disappear up to London. Can I ask what you are up to?'

'Well - and its mustn't go beyond these four walls – there is a committee in the India Office of which I am Chairman. We have to think the unthinkable. Under what circumstances would or should we, the British, give up the Raj? And how would we ac-complish it? And what would be the effect of withdrawal, both for ourselves and for India? We have two years to produce a doc-ument. I expect it will gather dust on the shelves and be taken down only when there is a crisis. It is, for me, an interesting in-tellectual exercise.'

'Do you think that withdrawal is coming?' asked Beth.

Mr Millward took a sip of wine. 'All over Whitehall there are files covering all sorts of eventualities, from an outbreak of plague to war with France.'

'Really?'

'Yes. Really. It's all just in case, so that we are not caught to-tally unprepared.'

'What about another European War?'

'I am sure the General Staff has plans – at least I hope they have - which they keep under their helmets.'

He drained his glass. 'Now I must work. See you at bedtime.'

When he had left, Beth lit a cigarette and James took out his pipe.

'I'm glad things are going well for you, James. You are a changed man.'

'I hope so, Beth. I hated being idle. I am still doing my Territorial stuff, and I help with the OTC at school. I still have no idea where all this will take me.'

'And have you met someone?'

'At this boys' boarding school there are no mistresses, only kitchen maids and a secretary. The Headmaster is a bachelor as are most of the masters, so there are no daughters to brighten the scene. I would like a lady friend, but until I know where I am going or where I will be, I don't have much to offer. I have to wait nearly two years for Mother's legacy but I am in no hurry. On the other hand, if one of your friends is pining for male companionship, I am not too far away. Have you heard from Stefan?'

'Yes. In his last letter he had nearly finished his military training. His return to Oxford is delayed because the Bishop is going to ordain him. It will be lovely to see him again, but I must be patient.'

'So, apart from Stefan, what is on your horizon? You can't be a housekeeper for ever and ever. You would be bored stiff.'

'Quite right. Maybe I will go back to the Suffragists in the New Year. I wish I could use my German more. I am quite fluent now, and I am practising writing it. In a way, like you I am waiting for something to happen. Father seems to be in good health and in good heart, but he does need looking after.'

'Have you talked to him about yourself?'

'I think he does not want to probe or interfere.'

'Well, you need to talk to him, man to man. I am sure he will support you whatever you want to do, because you are clearly a responsible person.'

'Thank you, kind sir.'

'Alright, I am the younger brother, who does not know anything about women, but I don't like to see you marking time, just as you thought I was. We have gone our separate ways in the past. If you won't talk to the Pater, would you now talk to me?'

'I will, James, I will. When I have something to report. Suffice it to say that Stefan and I are very fond of each other, but until he comes back to England we can't see further. And when he goes back to Germany…'

'Will you follow him, Beth?'

'I… I…'

Beth's eyes glistened.

'Sorry. I shouldn't have asked.'

Chapter Twelve

❉

Stefan had been in seclusion until his ordination and only wrote to Beth during the few days with his family before he returned to Oxford. She had begun to fret that he had not written, but out of pride did not write him a gentle remonstrance.

She carried out her domestic duties conscientiously but still had a lot of time on her hands. She persuaded Mr Millward to teach her to drive, but he did not let her go out on her own at first. One day she went up to London to shop and to search for books in German. There were German classics, poets such as Heine and Schiller, but poetry had never been one of her strong interests. She then looked for novels and found Goethe's *The Sorrows of Young Werther*; she bought it because she had heard of it. In another part of the shop she came across Thomas Mann's *Buddenbrooks*. It was a hefty volume, a saga of a family and the fortunes of the family business, but what attracted her was that it was set in the north German town of Lübeck, which in many respects resembled Bremen.

Furthermore, it had been published fairly recently. She devoted her mornings to reading. *Werther* she abandoned because the extravagant language and emotional incontinence disgusted her. *Buddenbrooks* was a linguistic challenge but she could understand the themes; she made notes so that she could discuss them with Stefan.

Out of the blue she received a note from Frances Stevenson:

It is seems such a long time since we last met at the Hyde Park rally. I have been very busy working for D. and I expect you have been busy too.

If you are ever up in town, let's meet to compare notes. I am allowed a long lunch break from the Treasury once in a while…

Beth was already at a table when Frances came in. Without ceremony Frances took off her coat and sat down. A waiter was hovering and they ordered at once.

'Sorry I am bit late. He is involved with so many meetings at the moment.'

'He?'

'Oh, David. It's not a state secret to say that there is a great row going on about the Budget and naval estimates. Churchill wants to build more battleships, David says we can't afford them. It's all over the papers. I have to sit there and pass him information when he needs it.'

'It must be exciting, being so close to the centre of things.'

'The excitement wears off very quickly. In fact it can be quite frustrating when men bicker over details as a way of asserting their virility, when they can't or won't see that there is a clear course to follow, for the benefit of the country.'

'Do you see much of er... David?'

'When I can. He works so hard. Sometimes I have to smooth ruffled feathers. What about you? What have you been up to?'

Beth told her about her mother's death and how she had been living at home for the first time in some years.

'Is that boring?'

'It's a change.'

She told Frances about her brother and her driving lessons.

'And I am trying to improve my German.'

'That's good. Why German?'

Out it all came. Frances listened intently.

'There. Do I follow him when he goes back to Germany? And how will it affect our relationship now he is a priest? I have committed myself to admitting I love him. He has not actually used the word, but he is very tender. And there are times when I wish I hadn't fallen for someone so unattainable, unattainable because of all the circumstances.'

'How soon before you are going to see him again?'

'Not long, I hope.'

'Well, I think that in your heart you will find the answer soon after that meeting.'

'I wish I had your clarity of mind. I am usually a rational person, but I find myself swept away by new emotions.'

'It's easy to give advice. Not so easy to follow it.'

'I am not sure how my family, especially my father, will react if I tell them the full truth about our relationship.'

'My parents strongly disapprove of my knowing David, but I still live with them. They haven't forgiven me but they have not thrown me out of the house. They have more reason to disapprove than your father has.'

'Why is that?'

'Oh, because David has a wife and family.'

Beth thought for a moment. 'I'm sorry. I didn't understand at first.'

'We have shared confidences, Beth. They must remain between ourselves.'

'Of course. You have my word.'

Frances looked at her watch. 'Time I was off. Keep in touch, Beth. Thanks for the chat.'

Frances put her coat on and left. Beth sat a little longer, digesting what had been said. She had no intention of giving herself to Stefan outside marriage. Stefan surely would not agree to it, since it would break one of the tenets of his faith. At least that problem would not arise. But if they were not to marry, how would their relationship survive, and in what form?

And then another thought arose in her mind. Would it be better to end it now? It would be painful, very painful. But in the long run, it would clear the air for them both to make a new start. Stefan was beginning his life as a priest, anyway, a major step if ever there was one. He should not have to have her as an encumbrance.

As for herself, she had many advantages in life and opportunities to use them. Something would crop up.

When she got home, she thought about putting away the German books. But she was not one to give up, she reminded herself. Anyway, a knowledge of German was a useful asset.

The letter from Stefan arrived two days later. Could he see her before going up to Oxford? She replied at once that he must stay with them for a night or two. A week later a telegram arrived from him saying that he would be arriving at the station at 3.15; he would find a taxi.

Beth asked her father and then took the car to drive the short distance to the station. She arrived in good time. She paced up and down as the minutes ticked past. When the train drew up she went into the station building. Her heart was beating. Then she could see his head as he crossed the footbridge. When he reached the platform, she saw that he was struggling with a mound of luggage. She rushed forward. He dropped his bags and held out his arms for her. Without thinking she spoke in German.

'It's lovely to see you again. I have missed you, Stefan.'

'I too. I have been counting the days, like a schoolboy waiting for the end of term.'

They continued to speak German as they gathered up the bags.

'Have you had a good journey?'

'It was long and tedious. I am so glad to be here at last. Thank you for meeting me. I am not sure I would have remembered the way to your house. Did you come by taxi?'

'No. I am your chauffeur. Come along.'

As they walked to the exit, some other passengers overheard them speaking. One said: 'Germans. I expect they are spies.'

'Should we report them?' said another.

'You can't be too careful,' was the reply.

Beth and Stefan were so engrossed in each other that they did not notice. Someone followed them outside and just in case, he made a note of the registration number. He was also surprised to see Beth climbing into the driving seat.

Beth drove home safely and smoothly, without crashing the gears.

'If I learn to drive, I hope I can drive as well as you,' said Stefan.

'Flatterer.' She kissed him. 'Now come inside and say hello to Father.'

Mr Millward was in his study. He heard their arrival but waited until they had carried the cases inside.

'Herr Haase…'

'Stefan, please.'

'Stefan, welcome. I see you survived the journey from the station.'

'Beth is a very good driver.'

'She is, I agree. Come and have some tea. I have asked the maid to bring some as soon as you arrived.'

They sat in the lounge. Mr Millward asked about his journey, and his family.

Stefan duly answered.

'Good, good,' said Mr Millward. 'I'm afraid that you may not see James while you are here. He is teaching now.'

'I let him know you were coming,' said Beth. 'He might manage an hour tomorrow. We could go and see him at the school.'

'We haven't been in touch for some time,' said Stefan. 'He is not the best of correspondents.'

'He never has been.'

Mr Millward got up. 'I must get back to work. Retirement means being almost as busy as before, but at least you are busy with things you want to be busy with.'

When he had gone, Beth took Stefan up to his room and left him to unpack. She went downstairs to supervise the arrangements for the dinner. Then she went to her room and looked at herself in the mirror. She was smiling, a big broad grin, her previous resolution forgotten.

'Let me just enjoy him for himself and never mind the long term,' she said to herself.

At dinner, it was not long before Mr Millward asked Stefan what he would be doing once his thesis was completed.

'Well, sir, I don't know if Beth has told you that I am now a minister in Holy Orders, to give it its official title. I was ordained a fortnight ago. Everyone in Germany of my age has to do two weeks of military training each year as a reservist. Since I have been in Oxford these last few years I was able to postpone my training, but now I have no excuse for avoiding it. I did some this summer, but then I was diverted to the Corps of Chaplains. So I won't have to carry a weapon. Although polishing boots was a chore, it was good for the soul. If I am to be a pastor, I must understand the lives of those I minister to. Soldiers need Religion just as much as anyone else. Actually, I may well be appointed to a civilian ministry. That is up to the Bishop. On the whole he has been very supportive of me, despite my earlier doubts of him.'

'So you will be going back to Germany?'

'Once I have my degree. I want to take it in person, in the Sheldonian. In the meantime I will have to arrange for publication, and I have another article to write. Plenty to keep me occupied until then.'

'And when will "then" be?'

'End of June, possibly.'

Mr Millward appeared satisfied with his answers.

'Beth has suggested to me that you might like to stay with us over Christmas. You would be welcome.'

'Well... that is very kind of you. I hadn't thought that far ahead. But *Weihnachten* can be lonely on your own.'

'We are not great churchgoers but we usually go on Christmas morning. My wife used to insist on it.'

'I am very sorry for your loss.'

'Thank you. We had hoped for a long retirement together... but it was not to be.'

* * *

The next afternoon Beth drove Stefan over to the school. James met them in the Quad.

'I have skipped games this afternoon. Delighted to see you again, Stefan.'

'It's been a long time... much water under the bridge, as you say.'

'Who would have thought, this time last year, I would be a humble pedagogue? And you... are you now a priest?'

Stefan opened his coat, to reveal a small pectoral cross.

'I thought only bishops wore those,' said James. 'Is it a sign of a clerical future?'

'In Lutheranism there is no ruling on that. I wear it to remind myself to behave as a priest. And everyone who sees it will expect me to do so. That sounds pompous, but there it is.'

'I understand. Well, come and have a tour of the School.'

He took them around the Quad, pointing out classrooms, the Library, Big School, and the Chapel.

'Shall we go in? I have to attend every day, for my sins. It can be jolly cold at times.'

The main entrance was under the organ and beside it two impressive stalls for the Headmaster and the Second Master. The stalls were set out facing each other in the traditional fashion, decani and cantoris, with the Choir stalls halfway down the Nave. At the East End there was a large stained-glass window and in front of it the altar, raised some steps above the rest. The ceiling was vaulted stonework. The walls were plain, except for plaques to Old Boys.

Stefan examined them.

'James, has the School a strong military tradition? Most of these men were young when they died - wars in New Zealand, in India, in South Africa. And one or two perished at sea.'

'The OTC was, and still is, compulsory. Now I am a Territorial I have to do my bit. I am an officer, a subaltern, which is the lowest form of commissioned life.'

'You outrank me, then. Technically, in the German army I am a private.'

'But won't you become an officer if you are a chaplain?'

'I suppose so. Like you, James, as a reservist I may be an officer only on annual camp.'

Just then the School Chaplain, a middle-aged man in clerical garb, came up the aisle.

'Millward, showing guests around?'

'Yes, Standish. This is my sister, Beth, and Herr Haase, an old friend from Oxford. Mr Standish.'

They shook hands. James saw the Chaplain glancing at Stefan's cross.

'Are you a Lutheran, Mr Haase?'

'I am now a pastor, but so far I haven't got a flock. I have only been ordained a few weeks.'

He waved an arm. 'A very impressive chapel, Mr Standish.'

'I wish it impressed the boys a little more. Chapel is compulsory, but we don't have many at Holy Communion, even though the Chapel is right in the centre of the School. I feel it is a uphill struggle. The masters are not as supportive as they should be.'

'It is a secular age, Mr Standish. Germany is not much different.'

'The boys sing hymns lustily, but they mutter the psalms. A pity because the psalms have some wonderful words.'

'At Congregational Practice we spent much time rehearsing the psalms,' said James. 'It takes a lot of practice to do them well. And yet when you hear them, you would never know it.'

'*Ars est celare artem*,'* said Stefan.

'I hope my Remove now know what that means,' James replied.

'Do the boys ever come to you about personal problems, Mr Standish? It must be a delicate balance you have to maintain, between being a master with authority and confessor. I ask, because it is likely that I may be a military chaplain at some stage.'

'Hm. An interesting question. I have a large dog, which I walk round the school regularly. The boys can't resist giving it a pat and it provides a topic of conversation. Sometimes they want to carry on talking, and things come out. I try to give a gentle hint

---

* The art lies in the concealing of the art.

and discreet advice. There have been occasions when a further talk is needed and I invite them to the Chapel at a quiet time. Bullying is difficult to deal with and I have to assess whether it merits going to the housemaster, or can be dealt with by a word in the appropriate places. Since I have been here there has been only one occasion when I had to go to the Headmaster directly over a serious matter, and the boy was expelled. It caused me much anguish. All you can do is to pray for wisdom to make the right decision. As in so many other matters.'

'I have been thinking a lot about my future role,' said Stefan. 'I am really an academic. I have to learn to be a pastor of souls.'

'It is a great responsibility. Will you be going back to Germany, Herr Haase?'

'I am afraid so. I will be very sorry to leave my friends here. These last few years have been a great joy.'

'Duty calls, eh. We are all on the treadmill. Well, I must get on,' said Standish. 'A pleasure to meet you.'

They shook hands and he went towards the altar, bowing as he reached the top of the steps. James, Beth and Stefan wandered out into the Quad.

'Standish is after my time,' said James. 'He seems an agreeable old cove. I never thought much about the chaplain when I was at school. To me, he was someone who bored us on Sunday mornings. So long as we maintained a pious exterior. One of my friends used to read a book. He concealed it in the cover of an old bible.'

'Are you sure that wasn't you, James?' said Beth.

'Well…'

Stefan laughed. 'So long as the book wasn't a threepenny novel.'

James looked at his watch. 'I must get back for some marking, one of the trials of a schoolmaster's life. Will we be seeing you again, Stefan, before next summer?'

'I have been invited for Christmas, for which I am very grateful.'

'We can talk more then, over a pint perhaps. I hope you haven't lost your taste for English beer.'

'I think my clerical office will permit me to imbibe. Some in Germany think flat warm beer is a heresy. But I am broad-minded. I might even buy the first round.'

* * *

Christmas Day was rather subdued, since this was the first since Mrs Millward died. Nothing was said openly. They all went to church, as was their custom, for form's sake, but brushed aside sympathetic remarks from the Vicar and other parishioners. Mr Millward spent a lot of time in his room. Beth's efforts at seasonal gaiety were half-hearted and she wept from time to time. Even James was low-spirited. In the evening Mr Millward did not linger over the port. James had several glasses and dozed in the lounge. Stefan helped Beth to clear away, since the maid and cook had gone to their homes.

'We haven't been very good hosts, Stefan. It is the first time we have really been together since she died. We should have made you more welcome, having invited you.'

'Beth, I quite understand your grief.'

'Having suppressed it at the time, being stiff-upper-lipped and British, it has all come back in a rush.'

Her lip quivered. Stefan took her in his arms.

'I'm happy just to be with you, as you are, in good times and bad.'

'I was thinking in church this morning that religion doesn't help much with mourning.'

'Maybe it helps to understand mourning. My faith helped me to come to terms with my parents' deaths.'

'But I haven't got your faith.'

'Faith is not a panacea. It can be very difficult, and painful. Sorry, I must stop preaching. It's a bad habit to get into.'

'You said some warm and comforting things in your letter, which made me feel better at the time. Now I seem to have forgotten them.'

She kissed him and broke away.

'We must get these dishes done. Must you go tomorrow?'

'In the afternoon.'

'Let's take a long walk in the morning.'

Overnight her gloom returned. Whether she was simply tired, physically and emotionally, or she was suddenly faced with the prospect of Stefan leaving, her usual bounce had departed. Once the holiday season was over, her future was uncertain. All she knew was that she could not remain at home, but she had no idea how to escape.

The morning was cold, but dry. As they walked through the woods nearby, they talked of inconsequential things until Beth stopped and faced him, taking his hands.

'Where are we going, Stefan? You are embarking on a new career, in another country. I have no commitments myself, but I want to be more than a housewife like my mother. What I am saying is, our future together is so uncertain and I am afraid to cast my bread on the waters.'

Stefan said nothing.

'And as you said in your letter, there are so many things outside our control that could come between us.'

Beth couldn't look at him as she continued. 'I was wondering... it occurred to me... perhaps it would be better in the long term... if we called a halt. I will be very unhappy but... I don't want to stand in your way... Oh, God, Stefan, say something.'

He kissed her hands. '*Schatz*... I am at fault. Loving you has made me ignore the implications for you. I blithely assumed that all would be well, that we could continue as before. Now I am a pastor, with all it entails. I have been selfish.'

Beth felt in her bag for a handkerchief. He took it and wiped her tears. When she was more composed she said: 'I felt attracted to you the first time we met. I suppose I have led you on since then. I was the first to use the word love.'

'You may have said it first, but I had it in my heart for a long time before that. What do you want to do, Beth? A clean break...'

'Please, not that. I couldn't bear it.'

'Nor could I.'

'Let's keep writing and meeting when we can.'

'Of course. It will give us time to see things in perspective. Will you please come to my graduation in the Sheldonian at the end of May? Then I had better return to Gemany. But I hope you can come up before then.'

On the walk home, Beth clung to his arm. While he brought down his luggage, she brought the car round. They did not say anything during the drive. At the station, Beth did not get out. Stefan unloaded his luggage. Then he leant inside and embraced her. They parted without a word.

* * *

They exchanged letters about their activities and family news. During February Beth was confined to bed with a chest infection that took time to clear. Not until late March did she go up to Oxford for a day. Stefan commented when they met that she looked a little fragile, but she assured him that the prospect of seeing him had cheered her up. Her next visit was for his graduation. She was his sole supporter. Beth had brought a camera and photographed him in his mortar board, white bow tie, subfusc and elaborate gown (hired for the occasion). She promised to send a copy to him. Stefan took her out to lunch and ordered a glass of champagne each.

'Here's to you, Stefan.'

'To you, Beth. And to us, whatever the future may bring.'

'To us.'

Stefan told her that he now had to report for military duties in the middle of June; Annual Camp had been brought forward. Beth said that she had been thinking about nursing or teaching and was making enquiries.

'It's time I did something useful.'

After lunch they walked in the Parks, speaking German at Beth's request.

'I have to keep practising.'

When they came to St John's, Stefan said that he would go to his room and change out of academic dress.

'I'll walk you to the station.'

'No, Stefan. Let me go now. I don't want you to see me crying.'

'Just as well. I would have cried too.'

They smiled and kissed briefly. Then Beth walked away without turning round. Stefan watched her until she crossed St Giles and turned right at the Ashmolean.

Chapter Thirteen

※

After parting from Stefan, Beth had busied herself by sending out applications for teaching posts for the following September, but without enthusiasm. She went to visit old friends. Though enjoying their company she felt envious of their married state. She told them of her ennui and lack of direction, alluding obliquely to a relationship that was over.

'Not like you, Beth, to be at a loose end,' was their response. 'Tell me more about your man.'

Beth took a deep breath to marshal her thoughts.

'If he were to propose tomorrow, I would say yes. But he won't... he can't.'

'Is he already married?'

Beth was indignant. 'Of course not. He's... Drop the subject. I am trying to put him out of my mind. Let's talk about you and your family.'

After an account of the progress of husbands and children, one of her friends asked if she had any positive ideas about her future.

Beth shook her head and then said that she had given a passing thought to nursing.

'You would hate it,' was the reply. 'Tyrannical ward sisters, humanity at its worst, all that dealing with unmentionables and wearing absurd uniforms. You are far too intelligent.'

'Perhaps it would be good for me to get out of my usual milieu, see the world as it really is.'

'Phooey. Do something that you would be good at.'

Nevertheless Beth made some cautious enquiries, but did not commit herself in any way.

Shortly after these conversations a letter arrived from Stefan. Her heart missed a beat when she saw the German stamp and the familiar handwriting.

Mein liebe Beth,

It seems an age since we parted. I hope you are well and in good heart. I am now Chaplain to the Oldenburg Regiment. Our Colonel is the Duke himself, at least on the parade ground. The soldiers are mostly locals, so I can call myself one of them. I don't have much to do apart from Sunday services, which are attended by a faithful few. I therefore have time to deal with some matters arising from the publication of my thesis. Suffice it to say that it has not set the academic world alight, but I have put down a marker for the future.

The last month has seen intensive training: musketry, route marches, section in the attack, and all that. I go along to see what is happening and have done a couple of marches myself, just to show that a man of God can heft a pack with the best of them. This has not gone down very well with my fellow-officers, but it has earned me a bit of respect in the ranks. I have had some good conversations as we march. The soldiers like to sing and often the words would make you blush. They look at me to see if I'm shocked. I laugh and join in the choruses.

Over here there are very mixed feelings. The Socialist parties are deeply hostile to militarism and many ordinary people I have talked to are profoundly suspicious of the government. There have been workers' demonstrations in Berlin, which were put down by mounted police with sabres. Onlookers cheered the police. The majority are proud of their country and want to see it take its rightful place in the comity of nations. Not my phrase. Just a mantra that the newspapers and politicians trot out. Hostility to England is a frequent theme. Which is odd, seeing how many Germans have lived and worked in England, for example a certain Doctor of Philosophy!, and tradesmen as well. And there is the close association of the Royal Houses. But there is also fear of the alliance between France and Russia, which might attack us on two fronts. There is great anxiety and at the same time anticipation. I am very afraid that a spark might ignite something terrible.

Sorry, Beth, to mention all this. It's just that I am very fearful.

When you have time, please write. My brother can forward your letter. I haven't stopped thinking of you and there is a special corner in my heart and prayers for you. So much for my self-denying ordinance!

As ever yours, *Schatz*,

Stefan

Beth resisted the urge to write straightaway in order that her thoughts might settle down. She composed a draft in English, choosing her words carefully, then put it into German.

My dear Stefan,

When we parted in Oxford, I was determined not to forget you, of course, but to put you to the back of my mind. Your letter has made that more difficult, but it has filled me with sweet sorrow, sweet because we are back in contact, and sorrow because we cannot be together. I, too, have foreboding for the future in general, made worse by my own uncertainty. Please, put in a word for me in your prayers on that account, so that I can find the right path for myself.

I have not forgotten the time I spent with your family in Bremen. Please give them my best wishes, and kisses for Annelore and Heinz.

Because of his schoolmastering duties, James has not been able to play as much cricket so far this year, but he has invitations for the summer vacation. He has enjoyed being a pedagogue, but I think it will not turn out to be a career for him. The school may well appoint someone permanently for next September.

My father is slowing up, which is not surprising being seventy-one. He enjoys his forays into London, but he has little else to occupy him. Although he never mentions it, I wonder if he is writing his memoirs; he spends a lot of time in his study. If I leave home, he will have to employ a housekeeper, as he can't look after himself.

Please write when you can. Yes, I am keeping your letters tied up with a pink ribbon. I am an oldfashioned girl, really.

Yours, as ever,

With fondest love,

Beth

PS I have included the photo of you in academic dress; it had slipped my mind. I thought I may as well include a recent photo of myself.

A letter came from Stefan, dated August 1st.

Mein Liebe Beth,

A shooting by gangsters in Sarajevo has led to war in Europe. We are now on the march to Belgium. Can't write much. I am in despair for my country. It has committed a supreme act of folly. Dear Beth, there is no knowing when we will see each other again. So I hope, and pray, that you will in due course find a good man, since all this has come between us.

With my love,

Stefan

Beth wrote back at once.

Dear Stefan,

If your ministry takes you into places of danger, please, please, take care. You will always be in my heart. One day… may it not be too far away… can't say more.

Love you,
Beth

She had no way of knowing if her letter had reached him.

* * *

By the summer term, the novelty of schoolmastering was beginning to wear off. James enjoyed sparring with the Remove but, like them, grew tired of grammar-bashing, as had been prescribed. Instead he talked about Roman history – Hannibal's battles and the Empire. He relished lessons with his Greek pupils in the senior school, exploring Thucydides and explaining the mysteries of the optative. He offered to do some coaching with the First XI, but the master in charge resented his prowess and kept him at arms length. In the annual Masters v. Boys match, he made a sprightly fifty, then dismissed himself by knocking a bail off. He bowled three overs of leg breaks, and took two wickets. He was able to play club cricket at weekends, which kept his hand in, but he could not commit himself to county games.

Teaching at a boarding school was very constricting, even one near London. He had not found a congenial colleague to relax with. However, over the Easter holidays he had come to know Marjory, an acquaintance of Beth from Cheltenham Ladies' College, and they corresponded now and then. He acquired a motor bike and visited her when he had a free afternoon, which was not often. On a couple of occasions she had watched him play cricket. She was attractive and lively, but inclined to do all the talking when they met. James enjoyed her company and looked forward to seeing her, but their relationship remained on a superficial level. He once mentioned her to Beth, who shrugged her shoulders.

'Well, I'm glad for your sake that there is a girl around, but from what I know of her, which is not much, admittedly, I wouldn't say she was likely to be a life-long companion. But don't let me discourage you.'

James was a little dismayed at her frankness and wondered if any girl would come up to her exacting standards. Nevertheless he continued to keep in touch with Marjory, as a relief from the enforced bachelordom of his teaching.

The East Surrey Territorials continued to hold parades once a fortnight, and he attended as often as he could. The School OTC paraded every week. James supervised drill instruction with the help of two senior Cadet NCOs; they taught the boys how to clean their rifles and polish their boots. With the help of the School RSM, he organised a war game he had learned with the Territorials, a platoon attack through light woodland. The platoon was divided into sections under a lance-corporal which leapfrogged each other, giving covering fire while one section advanced from cover to cover. The aim was to reach a chair at the far edge of the wood, a distance of three hundred yards. Halfway along, an adult NCO took up position to watch proceedings and to declare anyone dead if they exposed themselves too much. James himself paced up and down beside the chair as though he were a sentry.

The first two attacks were disorganised and a lot of casualties ensued. The third attempt was much more organised, only a quarter of the boys being declared dead. They enjoyed the game. It was a warm dry afternoon. James congratulated them on their efforts. Then he led them to a field nearby with long grass and scattered small bushes.

'How would you attack across this field?' he asked. 'You have a hundred or so yards to cover.'

'Charge, sir.'

'You mean deploying into a long line?'

'Yes, sir.'

'Well, in that case most of you would be dead within a few seconds of jumping up. Accurate musketry would pick you off easily. Look at the ground.'

The grass was a foot or more high.

'You have to get within a very few yards of the objective and then charge when the order is given. You use the element of surprise. And when you charge you shout as loud as you can, holding your rifle in front of you.'

'But how do we get to charging distance, sir?'

'On your tummies, using elbows and knees to inch yourselves along. You hold your rifle crosswise in front of you, at eye level. It's called the kitten-crawl. Would you like me to demonstrate?'

'Yes, please, sir.'

James took a rifle, got down in position and wriggled his way forward with surprising ease.

'See?' he said when he got up. 'Now get into a line over there where the grass is shorter and lie flat.'

The boys did so.

'Now advance towards me, slowly keeping your line. Mr Hitchcox will follow and give you a prod with his swagger stick if you are too high. I will stand here and if I turn around you must freeze. Try and reach the chair. Think of it as a form of Grandmother's Footsteps. Slowly does it.'

The distance was only twenty yards. Prods from the swagger stick kept their bottoms down. James disqualified those who were going too fast and did not freeze.

He called them together.

'Next week we will do this again. Across the whole field. I will divide you into two teams and there will be a competition. The team which reaches the objective with fewer casualties will be the winner. There will be one difference from today. You will have to camouflage yourselves. Put twigs into your hat and smear your faces with mud. I have asked the CO to excuse you from contingent parade.'

'Thank you, sir.'

'Better than square-bashing, isn't it?'

They agreed enthusiastically.

The exercise went off better than James expected. He had given the boys half an hour to prepare themeselves. The two cadet sergeants in charge of their squads tossed for the first go.

James gave a final instruction. 'Remember the element of surprise. I don't want to hear any talking. Use hand signals. That means watching out for each other.'

The first attack took half an hour. James walked up and down turning to face them occasionally. He was pleased that it was not always possible to pick out where the boys were; he noted those who did not freeze immediately. Then, when the team had reached twenty yards from the chair, he sat down on the ground. The sergeant gave a yell and the boys got up and charged the chair.

'Not bad at all. I'll tell you the score later. Now and go and sit over there.'

He waved to the staff NCO at the start line. The second team got into position and started off. One boy was stung by a nettle and swore. James noted him as a casualty.

The second team had had more time to camouflage themselves, and so they came out winners by a narrow margin.

James called them together and told then that they had all done well.

'Now I want you to imagine that there is a machine gun firing at you at waist level. You therefore keep well down. And silent. I heard you swearing, Stratton. So you are dead.'

'Sorry, sir.'

'No. Easily done. You have to keep your wits about you at all times, and concentrate on the task in hand.'

'I have a question, sir,' said another boy. 'What happens if I... er... want to relieve myself?'

'Quite simple. Lie on your side, open your flies and try not to make too big a splash.'

This amused them.

He looked at his watch. 'Time to march back to school. I have organised something for you from the kitchens. You will have to brush your uniforms before the next parade. And wash your hands and faces for afternoon school. I don't want complaints from your masters that you look like ragamuffins.'

The 'something' turned out to be a dixie of tea and a large tray of biscuits, which disappeared very quickly.

* * *

After the Commemoration Service at the end of term, the OTC entrained for the Annual Camp at Bordon near Liphook. It necessitated an early start to deal with not only the boys' personal kit but also all the equipment and stores. James was detailed to assemble the boys and march them down to the station. They took the train into London for a military train to Liphook, whence there was a three mile march to the camp. James was anxious not to lose any boys in transit, but everyone seemed to regard it as an adventure, and he did not have to reprimand anyone or chase them up. They arrived at Bordon camp in the late afternoon of Sunday August 2nd. The kit was unloaded from the lorries, and the cadets were shown to their quarters. Once they had been fed, the officers and staff NCOs repaired to their messes for drinks and dinner.

The OTC CO bought his officers a round of drinks. James had been on the go since five o'clock that morning and he was hungry and tired. He was very glad of a whisky before dinner and a glass of wine with it. They were halfway through the main course, when the Camp Commandant came up to the CO and led him out of the room. No one took much notice at the time and continued lively conversation.

After fifteen minutes the CO returned, sat down and rapped the table.

'Gentlemen, Germany and France have mobilised. The Germans are concentrated on the border with Belgium. If they cross the border, it is most likely that we will declare war on Germany. Therefore our unit must leave camp at 0500 tomorrow and a train will take us back to London. When we get to Waterloo, the cadets will disperse to their homes with travel warrants. We and the NCOs will have to go back to school and deal with the kit.'

There was consternation around the table.

'Grave news indeed. Who knows what the future will hold for the country? In the meantime, we will pretend to be Sir Francis Drake and finish our meal. I think we all need another glass of wine.'

* * *

The next day Germany declared war on France. When James reached home the following evening there was a telegram waiting for him. He was ordered to report to the East Surreys' Drill Hall at 0800 on Tuesday 5th August.

Beth was very quiet with her own thoughts and did not contribute much to the conversation. Mr Millward was in a sombre mood.

'We are treaty bound to come to the support of Belgium,' he said, 'if, as it looks almost certain, Germany invades Belgium. If they are to get to Paris quickly, they have to cross Belgium in order to avoid the Ardennes Forests. That, I believe, is the grand plan.'

'What are we to do, Pater?' James asked.

'The talk is that we must send a force to Flanders and try to stop the German advance. We owe it to the French. And also for our own defence. We cannot allow a hostile power to control the Channel coastline.'

'So we send a force to the Continent, as we did in past centuries?'

'I'm afraid so. The trouble is most of our forces are overseas, scattered around the Empire. We have only a small standing army at home. I don't know the numbers involved, but someone at the club reckoned about 150,000 all told. We must leave some at home for emergencies, so I would say we could send 100,000. The French can mobilise millions of men, Germans likewise. So our force will be a token one. Unless we have conscription, which will be very unpopular. So it looks as though you will have to go, James, as a Territorial.'

Beth broke in. 'I couldn't bear that.' As she acknowledged to herself, she was thinking not only of James.

'But I will have to go, Beth. I have my orders. I can't resign from the Territorials. I assume we will be sent to France, too. Maybe it will all be over soon and I will be back by Christmas.'

'That surely will not happen,' said Mr Millward. 'The French will not capitulate, as they did in 1871. It could be, James, that you will be fighting over ground well-known to Marlborough and Wellington. That should appeal to you as a historian.'

'Recently, Pater, I read a book about the American Civil War. There was appalling loss of life because they used Napoleonic tactics with modern weapons, rifles instead of muskets; the soldiers were conscripts and the generals mostly amateurs. All the generals could do was to line up the men and shoot from a static position. I have been taught in the Territorials that modern warfare is about movement - mobile artillery giving close infantry support. If you stay in one place for too long, you are dead.'

Beth spoke up again. 'I don't want to hear any more. It's all too awful.'

With that, she got up from the table and left the room.

'I know war is awful, Pater, but for men of my age it is an adventure. How will I react to mortal danger? I have never been in that position but I hope I am not found wanting when it comes.'

'I'm sure you won't be. I have never told you this. When I first went to India, before I married your mother, I was on a hunting expedition in the hills. We went out for buck to supplement our rations. One of my guides, not far ahead of me, was attacked by a tiger which was hiding in the undergrowth. I could easily have left him to die a horrible death – he was screaming – and slunk away. Without thinking, I took my rifle from the bearer and advanced towards the tiger. I had a twin barrel point five. My presence distracted the tiger for a moment. I took aim carefully for the shoulder. It was an accurate shot from fifteen yards. The tiger flinched but came on. This time I fired at the jawline. He fell and writhed on the ground. Someone else finished him off. He was a big brute, eight feet from nose to the tip of his tail.'

'What about your guide?'

'He was badly mauled about the shoulder but he lived.'

'That was very brave of you, Pater.'

'I was shaking like a jelly afterwards and it took several stiff drinks to calm down. But the point is, I had a duty to try and save the poor man. No time for weighing up the situation. You know what has to be done, and you do it.'

'Well, I hope I live up to your example.'

James went to his room to organise himself for his departure. Mr Millward remained at table with a glass of port.

Beth came back into the room. She had been weeping.

'I am sorry that you were upset, Beth, by our talk of war. I am worried for James, too. Come and sit down, Beth. Have a glass of port. No ifs and buts.'

Beth took a long sip.

'I am desperately worried for James, naturally. But there is someone else.'

'Stefan?'

'Yes, Father. He is a chaplain in the Army. His regiment is attacking Belgium. We care for each other very much.'

'Hm. I may be oldfashioned, Beth, but I am not blind. In other circumstances, I could welcome him as a son-in-law.'

'We tried to break it off when I went up to Oxford to see him take his degree. But our feelings were too strong. And we cannot contact each other. I just have to accept the fact. But it is hard.'

'I am not at all happy about my son going off to war. I have to accept that, too.'

'I used not to pray, Father. Now, I can't stop praying.'

'You must find something else to occupy your mind. Have you any idea?'

'Ideas but no conclusion. I have thought about teaching, but only as a last resort. I have read that the Suffragists are abandoning their campaign if war is declared and they will support the government for the duration. They see a new role for women, if all the men are enlisted. With Stefan's help I have been improving my German; I would like to use it somewhere.

'Another idea has crossed my mind – nursing. I have no idea if I would be any good at it. I am going to investigate. My friends think it is a silly idea. I know that I will have to do unpleasant things, and I will be tested. Perhaps it is time for me to have a new challenge.'

'Dear Beth, I understand fully your thinking. Whatever you decide to do, I will support you. These are terrible times and one can't stand idly by.'

* * *

A fortnight later, Beth had an interview with Mrs Furse of the Voluntary Aid Detachment. She expected to meet an elderly lady, but Mrs Furse was a tall woman in her late thirties with an authoritative manner.

'Miss Millward, why do you want to join the VADs?'

'My brother has been called up. I feel I have to do something for the country.'

'I have a note here. You are twenty-six years old. You were brought up in India, you went to Cheltenham Ladies College, then Newnham Hall, Cambridge, to read English. In between school and university you went as a companion to Lady Valentine. Where did you go?'

'All over Europe and some of the Middle East. Lady Valentine was compiling notes for a book on Art Galleries.'

'I see. What skills can you offer?'

'I can drive. I have had some experience in nursing my mother. She died last year.'

'I see that you did some work with the Women's Suffragist Society.'

'I met some of the leading speakers, and I worked in the office for a short time.'

'Hm. You are obviously a woman who is not content to sit about. I have seen quite a number of ladies like you, well-educated, cultured and with a sense of adventure. How do you think you might cope with the dirt and squalor of war, let alone the blood?'

'I have never been tested like that, so I don't know. I hope I can measure up.'

'You are not alone. What other expertise can you offer?'

'I can speak German.'

'Oh? Tell me more.'

Beth had wondered if that topic would come up and had prepared some ideas. Speaking in German, she told Mrs Furse about her visits to Germany with Lady Valentine before the war and her friendship with a German student. She did not elaborate on that point.

'And French?'

'Enough to get by.'

'Interesting.'

At the beginning of September she and a few other women accompanied Mrs Furse to France to work in canteens and as drivers.

Chapter Fourteen

James duly reported to the East Surreys' Drill Hall. His name was checked against a list. He filled in a form with his personal details, including his father and sister as next-of-kin. Then he joined the queue of men being measured for a uniform but he was too tall for those which were in stock.

The Quartermaster looked again at his list.

'I see that you are down for Officer Training, so it will be up to you to provide yourself with a uniform, sir.'

'Very well.'

Just then an officer came out from a back room, clutching James' form. 'Millward?'

'Sir.'

'Come with me.'

James followed the officer into the room and was invited to sit. The Officer introduced himself as Captain Maitland. James reckoned he was just a few years older than himself.

'I see that you have been in the OTC at your school and as a teacher you now have a temporary commission with the school.'

'Yes.'

Maitland consulted a file. 'You have been assigned to the 2/7th East Surreys. You will go forward for Officer Training starting on the 12th of next month at Aldershot. You will receive joining and other instructions in due course. At that point you will receive seven shillings a day, so make arrangements with your bank. Cox's are the Army bankers. Also, get yourself a uniform. Here is a list of military tailors. Any questions?'

'You probably won't be able to answer this, but do you know where we are likely to be posted?'

'The stock answer to that, Millward, is "Even if I knew, I couldn't tell you". To be honest, it could be anywhere in the Empire. It all depends on how the campaign goes. I'm assuming, of course, that we will send a force to the Continent. It might well be that the Surreys will be posted for garrison duties abroad to release a regular battalion. It is equally possible that the battalion will be thrown willy-nilly into combat. The Army has a reputation for changing its mind at short notice, so expect the unexpected, to coin a phrase.'

'I have to go where King George pleases.'

'A very proper answer.'

'We may be serving together, we may not. Good to meet you, anyway.'

Captain Maitland stood up. They shook hands.

* * *

When James reported to Aldershot, he found several of his acquaintance on the same course; one of them, Cartwright, had been a year ahead of him at school. They exchanged greetings.

'What have you been up to, old son?' Cartwright asked.

James mentioned Classics and cricket.

'You were one of those people, Millward, who were good at everything. Very dispiriting for the rest of us.'

'You didn't do so badly yourself. Captain of Football.'

'Yes, but that can't compete with a Cambridge Blue.'

'What about afterwards?'

'Father's office, ship broking. At least I got a year away in Singapore. Then back to London. I signed up as much to get away from the office, never mind King and Country.' Cartwright sighed. 'I am afraid it might be all over soon and I will have to go back to civvy street again. What do you think, Millward? All over by Christmas?'

'I sincerely hope so, but I think it very unlikely.'

'Why so?'

'Because Germany has a big army and they believe France and Russia are ganging up on them and they will have to fight a war on two fronts. Therefore they are attacking France first, before it has time to mobilise fully. And then deal with Russia.'

'Dear boy, do you have access to the German High Command?'

'It makes sense and is obvious now that they are advancing through Belgium. And we are pledged to support Belgium.'

'So what sort of war will it be?'

Just then a senior officer entered the room and they stood up. He outlined their training programme – musketry, map making, manoeuvres, munitions, communications and much else besides, including how to write a military letter.

'You will have to work fast,' he went on. 'We want you in your regiments as soon as possible. Any questions?'

Cartwright put up his hand.

'People say that it will be all over by Christmas, sir. Is that likely?'

'One must be optimistic but I fear not. I myself witnessed German Army manoeuvres before the war. They have a formidable force and their plans are well-laid. We have to stop them reaching Paris at all costs. Therefore we will be putting as many men as we can across the Channel. You may find yourselves in action sooner than you think.'

James was working as hard as he had ever done. Reveille at six, breakfast, parade – his boots shone until he could see his reflection in them – classroom instruction, lunch, weapon training in the afternoon, debriefing, dinner in the mess, study and preparation for the morrow before collapsing into bed. At drinks before dinner, Cartwright tended to monopolise him and after a few days James tired of his breezy manner and his trite conversation. Instead he started a conversation with another cadet officer, who, as James observed, worked efficiently but did not volunteer much comment. He carried his drink over to the table where the man was sitting.

'Can I introduce myself? Millward.'

'Please sit down. I'm Horton.'

They chatted desultorily about the training. Then Horton said, 'Your reputation goes ahead of you. I have never met a county cricketer before...'

'Only Minor Counties.'

'And one who scored a century off Sidney Barnes.'

'Nearly a century.'

'Good enough.' Horton laughed.

'Who told you about me?'

'Oh. Cartwright.'

'Same school, but we were not chums there.'

'I can understand why.'

'Am I allowed to ask about you?'

'Well, nothing much to tell. Minor public school, King's College, London. Banking. Felt I needed a little adventure after a so far uneventful life.'

'I expect many of us are of the same mind. I also regard it as my patriotic duty to join up. I can't think of any reason why I shouldn't.'

Horton was about to reply when the gong sounded for dinner. James was accosted by another cadet officer and so they could not continue their conversation.

Over the next few weeks, James got to know Horton a little better. There were no sudden revelations, just a gradual dispensing of information as Horton came to trust James. Though he appeared as English as the others, his name was originally Hartmann and he was born in Vienna. His father was a doctor who emigrated to England because of the anti-Semitism of Viennese society. The family were not observant Jews. Moritz Hartmann was baptised as Maurice Horton at an early age. His father set up a practice in London dealing with nervous disorders.

James asked if he had experienced any anti-Semitism in England.

'Well, I don't look very Jewish, at least the stereotype of a Jew. I have heard plenty of anti-Semitic remarks but not directed against myself.'

'Do you have any memories of Vienna? I have never been there.'

'Very few. But my father insisted on our speaking German at

home, and I am still pretty fluent. It has been useful in some banking matters I have had to deal with.'

'I was brought up in India, and I did know a little Urdu because my sister and I spent so much time with the servants. I have forgotten it all now. Does the Army know that you can speak German?'

'I have kept it dark. There is a certain amount of anti-German sentiment around. I don't want to have my loyalty questioned and possibly to be liable under the new Defence of the Realm Act as an alien. But I suppose a knowledge of German could be useful on the battlefield. I am young and fit enough to fight and I don't want a cushy staff job.'

At the end of six weeks a forty-eight hour leave was granted, and they went to see their respective fathers. James found Mr Millward in his study.

'I have killed the fatted calf for my warrior son. Mrs Wilson is preparing roast beef, I have opened a decent claret, and we will have a pint of champagne to start with.'

'*Dulce est desipere in loco.*'

'Sounds like Horace. What does it mean?'

'It's good to get tipsy on occasion.'

'Well, this is an occasion.'

He opened the bottle and poured.

'Cheers.'

'Cheers, Pater.'

They drank.

'Well, how are you getting on? Do you have a field marshal's baton in your knapsack?'

'I don't think I would like to be a field marshal in this present war. Now we know a little more about the German forces that we have to face, we will be hard pressed by sheer weight of numbers. As for the present, I am being worked very hard, which is good, but there is only so much that the classroom can teach you about soldiering. I can't wait to have command of my own platoon and, with a bit of luck, I will have a reliable Sergeant who will keep me out of scrapes.'

'I see that you are growing a moustache.'

'No young officer is complete without one.'

'Have you met any congenial colleagues?'

James told him about Cartwright: 'Not my cup of tea. He called me "old son" at our first meeting. I avoid him as much as possible without being openly rude. The others are as you would expect. But I have chatted a lot to a man called Horton. He is an interesting character.'

James told him what he had learnt about Horton.

'I suppose there must be quite a few like him,' said Mr Millward, 'not Jews necessarily but immigrants, keen to serve their new country. We must be grateful for them.'

'It looks like Cartwright, Horton and I will be in the 2/7th East Surreys, though that could change at any moment.'

'What are your instructors like?'

'All regulars, and most of them committed to the task of turning out new officers as fast as possible. Though there is an undercurrent of resentment that they are not at the front. Battle brings medals and promotion into dead man's shoes. Our weapons officer makes no bones about it.'

Over dinner, Mr Millward told James about a new project.

'You remember I was on a committee looking into the problems that might surround a withdrawal from India. Interesting, but all speculative; there was no knowing what situation might arise to cause us to consider withdrawal. Well, that has been put aside. I have been approached to sit on a committee to examine aspects of civil defence.'

'Civil defence? Is there a possibility of a German invasion?'

'We have to consider what can be done to protect people from the consequences of aerial attack, or shelling from the sea. Modern naval guns have a long range.'

'The best thing is to stop aircraft or ships getting anywhere close.'

'True. But we are looking at ways to ensure civil order and maintenance of essential supplies for civilian life.'

'I see. I must ask, why you?'

'I am at a loose end. I'm supposed to be a good committee man, and I have experience of civil disorder in India. It's another way to serve the country. In the meantime, I am writing memoirs of my time in India. They probably won't ever see the light of day, but it is a useful exercise for me, and will give you and Beth something to think about.'

'I look forward to reading it. Have you heard from Beth at all?'

'I didn't hear for three weeks, apart from a quick note to say that she had just landed in France. However, this came about a fortnight ago. It is addressed to both of us.'

Dear Father and James,

I hope this finds you both well. I have been thinking of you, but day-to-day concerns dominate. Sometimes I wonder how I am going to get through the next five minutes, when we are working fourteen hour days. But be reassured, I am well, though very tired.

I have been been driving a lorry most days fetching wounded from the front. This can be difficult since there is so much traffic on the roads, which are not of the best. The Army has been retreating since the battles of Mons and Le Cateau and there has been a big battle on the Marne. I am no judge of these matters but the retreat has been anything but orderly. What has made it worse is the stream of refugees from the war zone, pulling carts with all their belongings and even driving their cattle. Not only do I have to drive the truck, but I have to help out with the wounded. Three days ago I had to stop because a man lying in the back was writhing about. The other soldiers called me to do something. All I could do was give him water from my bottle and soothe him. He had a bad wound in the stomach. I held him in my arms but he died shortly afterwards. His mates covered him up with a tarpaulin and on we went. I told myself that I had to be strong, if only for the sake of the others. That night I did not sleep. My supervisor said I could have a rest day, but I said I must carry on; can't have too much brooding.

More VADs have arrived and it has been decided that we are to work in pairs, because there have been cases of women being attacked by drunk soldiers. It seems that on the retreat soldiers had to forage for themselves in abandoned farms, and drank what they could find. Of course, we are greeted by wolf whistles and saucy remarks, but I don't mind. If the sight of a woman cheers the boys up, so be it.

(A few days later. I can only write now and again.)

Things have been stabilised now, but there are still wounded to deal with. Now the Army has started digging in, support behind the lines is better organised. We have been told that we won't have to go forward so much as the Army now has its own medical teams. But there is still plenty to do. I have a chum, Cynthia, and we work well together. I don't know much about her, but she has a lively sense of humour (very necessary, I can assure you) and she stands no nonsense from anyone. She doesn't drive, but she is a good navigator. All the road signs were removed during the retreat. She also speaks French. I haven't had to use my German yet.

Just heard that Cynthia and I are to go north. The Army is shifting operations to the area round Ypres, just inside Belgium, and the French are taking over our old sector. Our lorry, which we have called Clarence (why, I don't know, but Cynth says that it reminds her of someone she knew), has been loaded with all sorts of gear.

(Near St Omer)

At last we are in a hutted camp. It is being fitted out as a hospital. It even has baths! Though you have to queue, as there are only two for all the girls. I have met my first German. He is a POW and comes from Hamburg. I was very tempted to ask him about the Oldenburg regiment but the Sergeant in charge of his work detail moved him on quickly when we started speaking. Stefan is always there at the back of my mind. I would love to see him again, but it is more important to me that he survives this dreadful war.

Now that we are more settled you can find me at this address: BFO235 (VAD). It will take some time to find us, since we are not a regular unit, but it will get here in due course. Please write when you can. The soldiers look forward to letters from home; sometimes I have to read them out because they are semi-literate, if that.

The weather has turned autumnal. There are some nice days but it can be cold and windy. Can you please send some woollens from my wardrobe.

I have to catch the post. This will go by civilian mail, otherwise it would have to be censored.

With my love,

Beth

James read the letter twice.

'She's a tough girl, your sister,' said Mr Millward.

'I'll say so. To be frank, despite the dangers and discomfort, it's a new challenge for her, just the thing to get Stefan in perspective.'

'We must write at once. I didn't want to reply without having seen you. I've got Mrs Wilson to look out things to send to her.'

'You write, Pater. I will write too.'

On Sunday morning James did not accompany his father to church (Mr Millward had been a more regular attender since his wife died) but sat down to write to Beth. He described his training and the characters he had met. Then he went on:

...Father and I have been very impressed with your fortitude in the face of horrible experiences. I hope you have not been having bad dreams. We always knew you were a practical person; your motto has been 'Just get on with it'.

Back home it is beginning to become apparent what a bloodbath it has been. The war will NOT be over by Christmas. Although nothing has been said officially, the view here is that the BEF, despite their superior musketry, have suffered heavy losses through the sheer weight of the German offensive. The French have lost huge numbers. It is therefore quite likely that Territorial Reserves will be sent to France as soon as they can be trained. Our officer training course is being accelerated and we could be across the Channel in the Spring.

I haven't seen Marjory since I joined up and we have not corresponded. I must say I have not missed her and she has not tried to contact me. I suspect your opinion of her was the right one. But there will be other girls in due course. My colleague Horton and I had a conversation on the subject the other day. We decided that it was unfair to form too close an attachment with a girl when we were going to war, in case we got killed. We must be realistic…

* * *

After Christmas the 2/7th East Surreys were finally integrated as a unit, based at Talavera Barracks in Aldershot. James had charge of 4 platoon in B Company. Horton had 3 platoon. Cartwright had been assigned to D Company, the HQ Company. All the men were now equipped with uniforms and rifles, and much of the early training was in Musketry on Ash Ranges, which necessitated a march of nearly an hour from the barracks. This had the benefit of warming the men up before the long wait to take their turn on the firing point. James's Platoon Sergeant was 'Lofty' Milner, so-called because of his diminutive size. Nevertheless, when required he could be very fierce and the platoon soon learned to keep on his right side. He was a veteran of the Boer War. James was one of a succession of subalterns he had had to lick into shape, and at first he was inclined to play the old soldier with James. But when he discovered that James was a cricketer and it turned out that he was the best marksman in the platoon, and he had also noted James's firm but fair treatment of the men, he afforded him due respect. In the weeks and months to come, they worked well together. James had Private Wallis as his batman, an amiable rogue, about James's age. He had joined the Army as a boy soldier, but he had opted for a cushy billet and was content to avoid promotion. He was efficient in his ministrations, but James could not trust him entirely; what kept Wallis out of trouble was his fear of losing his position.

At the beginning of February the battalion entrained for Winchester and then marched for five miles to a village where there were billets for B Company. The officers were billeted at the Rectory. Most of the soldiers were provided with tents on farmland, but 4 and 3 platoons squeezed into two old barns. These buildings leaked and were infested with rats, which gave the men a foretaste of what they would experience in the trenches. But most of the training was in open warfare, platoons in the attack, and then company manoeuvres. The Village Hall was used as a mess and the School was turned over to the Company for the men in the evening, where they could smoke and read. There was an old piano for sing-songs. On Sundays there was a Church Parade for all except the Roman Catholics; the local Rector led the service. While cleaning James's boots, Private Wallis remarked that he had never given much thought to church, but the prospect of going into battle had changed his mind.

Some days were taken up in Divisional Training. These entailed long marches, whatever the weather. As often as not, the battalion was simply assigned a route and a destination, where there would be a soup kitchen and sandwiches, and then told to march back the way they had come. Although the men became fitter in the process, there was little enthusiasm for these exercises, even among the officers. To relieve the boredom the men were encouraged to sing. There were occasions when the route chosen proved impossible, such as boggy ground along a river, and Major Burton, James's Company commander, ordered a diversion onto firmer ground.

'I bet the silly sods at HQ never recce'd this area,' he said.

'Let's hope they do a little better in France,' said James.

'"Time spent in recconnaissance is never wasted", said Burton. 'That was drilled into us at Sandhurst. Mind you, it is a bit difficult to carry out a recce when the enemy line is twenty yards from yours.'

'But the principle still applies. And we will have balloons and aircraft to help.'

'When it is raining, or a storm is blowing? I prefer to rely on my own observations if at all possible.'

The battalion was ordered to reassemble at Bramshott Camp, near Liphook. A large inter-Divisional exercise had been arranged, to be inspected by Kitchener and a host of generals. It was to be a 'battle' between divisions, the 9th and 14th fighting the 10th and 12th. Each division started from a different area and were expected to converge at a point near the village of Witley. The 2/7th East Surreys for the purposes of the exercise had been assigned to the 9th Division, composed of Scottish regiments.

James briefed his men the night before.

'We are a small cog in a large machine. Our battalion will form the right flank of our brigade, that's Brigadier-General Moncrieffe. We are in the van and the other two brigades will follow in reserve. There will be umpires to monitor our progress and our contact with the "enemy". When we do, we will either be ordered to attack or form a defensive perimeter. There will be no live firing, but I gather that thunderflashes will be used to encourage us to keep our heads down. This may be a pretend battle but it is a real rehearsal for what is to come. Therefore I want all of you to be on the alert. Mistakes will be made but learn from them for the future. And whatever you do, don't ask a Scotsman if he wears anything under his kilt.'

Private Sellar put up his hand. 'Is it true, sir, that at inspection the sergeant carries a stick with a mirror on the end?'

'You'll have to find that out for yourself, Sellar, but… be careful.'

That provoked laughter.

'Very well, men. Reveille at 05.00. And make sure you have a good breakfast. It will be a long day.'

Not only was it long, but very windy and wet. The 2/7ths trudged through mud and puddles feeling the water dripping down inside their uniforms. Farm tracks indicated on the plans either did not exist or led the wrong way. A mobile canteen with hot drinks for lunchtime had been given the wrong grid reference and never appeared. The men, who had started the morning with singing, relapsed into sullen silence. Burton called a halt at midday, at a derelict farm. The barn still had a roof of sorts and he told the men to get under cover and eat their rations. Not everyone could squeeze in and some had to stand against walls in the lee of the wind. Cigarettes were lit. James, Horton and the other officers huddled under their ponchos. James's pipe refused to light.

'These things are sent to try us,' said Horton.

'Less of your philosophy, Horton,' said Burton. 'Let's be practical. We are three hours march from our start point. I have been following my compass – here's another aphorism for you, Millward: "Always trust your compass" – and we must be within a mile of our objective. Mind you, with visibility down to a hundred yards or so, it is impossible to be sure. I sent a runner to the Colonel, who should be half a mile that way. I await his return with interest. I'll give him half an hour. We are due to start our battle at 13.00.'

Twenty-five minutes later the runner appeared and produced a note from his breast pocket.

"Am waiting for confirmation from staff that things will go ahead. Maintain position until further orders."

The wind and rain eased a little. Burton told the men inside the barn to change places with those who had remained outside. James sought out Sergeant Milner.

'Get the platoon to fall in by that tree.'

When they were assembled, James addressed them.

'Not only will we have the enemy to contend with, but also the weather. Our enemy today have not condescended to put in a appearance. We are stuck here waiting for further orders. We are cold, wet and tired of hanging about. Therefore, we will do some exercises.'

He took off his webbing and the men did the same. They did some running on the spot, first jogging then sprinting.

'Imagine you are boxing. Your opponent is in front of you. Now work your fists and arms... Good. Now imagine you are swimming backstroke.' James demonstrated.

When all were warmed up, James called a halt, and said:

'That's all, for now. There's an old Army saying: "Any fool can be uncomfortable."' Sergeant Milner nodded. 'So make sure you have an extra pullover in your pack, and some gloves, if possible. If you are shivering with cold, your reactions will be slow and you will not fight well.'

An hour later a runner arrived from the Colonel with a note. Burton read it, called the officers and announced that they were to return to camp, two hours march away.

'At least the men will be fit, if not battleworthy,' he remarked sardonically.

In spite of the directions issued by the staff officers, the 9th and 14th divisions had failed to make contact with each other, let alone the enemy.

'You would have thought,' observed Burton, 'that two groups of ten thousand men each would have found each other and made common cause. If they can foul things up in England with not a Boche in sight, how do you think they will manage in France?'

'No plan survives contact with the enemy,' said James.

'I would not dignify today's fiasco with the term "plan". It should give Kitchener something to worry about.'

Chapter Fifteen

✻

The German advance into France and towards Paris had been checked at the Marne. Their next objective was to reach the Channel coast and secure their right flank. They were then held up by the British Expeditionary Force at Ypres in Belgium, twenty miles from the coast. Losses on both sides were enormous. More than half the original BEF had been killed or wounded, or had gone missing, since it had crossed the Channel. Such a rate of attrition could no longer be sustained in open warfare. Therefore, and with winter approaching, both sides settled down in trenches which ultimately stretched from the coast to the Swiss border. It was during this winter that the Christmas Truce was observed, though not approved by senior officers. At the second Battle of Ypres, in April and May 1915, the Germans attacked and using gas for the first time made small gains, but the salient around Ypres, though reduced, was not broken.

Beth, Cynth and their VAD colleagues were transfered to nursing duties. They received some rudimentary training at a base hospital in St Omer, and then were moved up to a casualty clearing station just behind the lines. When the wounded started to come in, she learned very rapidly how to deal with shell-splinter or shrapnel wounds, gangrene, dysentry and the effects of gas. The VADs were supervised by professional nurses, but when casualties began to come in thick and fast from regimental first aid posts, in the first instance they had to use their own initiative and there were never enough doctors. After a few days she had grown less squeamish as there was simply no time for tender feelings. Dirt and stench were everywhere. She had dreaded witnessing her first amputation, a lower leg, but the surgeon talked his way through the operation and she became absorbed in the technical details. At the beginning of June 1915, when Second Ypres ended and she had been on duty for two months without a break, she was given a fortnight's home leave. The first thing she did, after kissing her father, was to take a long hot bath. She did not do very much with her leave, apart from sleeping and eating ('You are too thin,' said Mrs Wilson, the housekeeper), going for walks and writing letters. One day, her father took her up to town to see *Tonight's the Night*, a popular musical comedy at the Gaiety Theatre. This frothy piece was just the antidote to the Western Front she needed. She felt rejuvenated by the end of her leave, but she was sad to have missed her brother. He had left with his battalion for France the week before she came home.

* * *

The 2/7th East Surreys marched from Bramshott Camp and entrained at Liphook Station. A crowd of well-wishers had come to see them off. They reached Folkestone Harbour Station at midnight and embarked at once.

'Makes you think,' said Horton, as he and James stood on the after deck. 'The lights of Folkestone will be the last some of us will see of England.'

'For King and Country,' said James. 'I hope I have left my affairs, such as they are, in good order.'

'I made my will during my last leave.'

'So did I.'

'We have had months of training and now comes the test. A sobering thought.'

'Well, I just hope I won't let the side down.'

'That's the cricketer speaking. I am of the same mind.'

'Do you pray, Maurice? I have started to, just these last few months.'

'Not really. A prayer won't deflect a bullet, though maybe a Bible in your breastpocket might. If I am to die, I hope it will be quick. Better that way than a lingering death in agony from terrible wounds.'

'Indeed.'

The ship reached Boulogne at 2.30 in the morning. The battalion marched to a rest camp, where it stayed for seven hours. The older men got their heads down straightaway, but the young men were too excited to sleep much. James awoke to the sound of distant gunfire. Horton was already up.

'That's where we are going,' he said.

A short march took them to a station, where they picked up the train which had come with all the battalion kit from Le Havre. It made slow progress past St Omer and stopped at Wizernes. From there they marched three miles to their billets. The officers of B Company were in a farm house and the men in the barns. The other companies were billeted in nearby villages. Army rations could be supplemented by purchases of milk, eggs and wine from the locals, though the wine was pretty rough.

The battalion spent two or three days in the billets. Then orders came through to pack up and move; two hours' notice was given. After a day's march it was united with the rest of the Brigade and the following day with the Division. The 2/7ths were at the rear of the column and the going was slow and the heat oppressive. The march resumed the following day in pouring rain and the cobbled surface of the roads was hard on the feet. That night, barns afforded some shelter. The next morning a Zeppelin was seen over the front line to the east, but it was chased away by British aircraft. While the battalion continued in their billets, the officers went to Armentières and spent some days with the 1st Leicestershires, receiving instruction in trench warfare; the line was two and half miles from the town. The town had sustained some damage and James and Horton were having a drink in a café when a German bombardment started; they ran for shelter.

'Rather undignified,' said Horton.

The battalion spent the next two months in training or acting as a reserve, relieving other battalions for a few days; there was a lot of marching in hot weather. For the most part their time in the trenches was quiet, though they could take no chances. Around Festubert they suffered from flies and the stench of decomposing German bodies from an earlier battle. James's dugout was too small for him to lie at full stretch and intermittent enemy shelling during the day prevented him from sleeping after the night's exertions: repairing trenches and barbed wire, and patrolling. He received a parcel of food and a bottle of whisky sent by his father; it had been posted a month ago and had been following him round from billet to billet.

He wrote back:

...Thank you very much for the parcel, which is much appreciated. I am getting heartily sick of bully beef. To celebrate, my chum Horton and I broached the bottle. We were just beginning to feel a little euphoric from the alcohol when a shell burst near us; the shock showered us with soil and knocked the bottle over. Fortunately I had put the top back on. Obviously the shelling is frightening, but I have so much to do that I simply get on with it. Dawn Stand-to, breakfast, constant checking of sentries, latrines and equipment, and ordering up supplies of ammunition, food, whatever is needed. Then there are daily reports to write for Company HQ, and correspondence. And maybe there is time for a nap. When the CO calls for a meeting, that means threading one's way along the trenches. It's easy to get lost! So we have given trenches names, such as Park Lane and Bond Street. Stand-to at dusk and if there are no alarms or other duties one can go to the Company Mess for a drink and a meal.

Despite the rain it has been warm. There is mud everywhere. My boots are still wet and I am getting through socks fast. But it is better to be uncomfortable than the other thing! My man Wallis does his best and does not grumble. So far the platoon has lost two men, one killed and another badly wounded, both from shell splinters. They were a bit slow to take cover when a whizz-bang came over.

Any news of Beth? I wrote to her at the address she gave

but I have no way of knowing whether she received it. I did hear from a college chum. Apparently our old scout has been killed at Ypres. He must have volunteered to join up, despite his age; he was a good soul and leaves a young family behind.

We are due to be relieved two days from now, but you can never be certain of anything. We may stay here after all, or be moved back for some R and R. I could do with it, if only to have some clean clothes and a good night's sleep...

* * *

During the spring and early summer attempts by the British and French armies to break the stalemate of trench warfare came to nothing except for a significant loss of life on both sides. Two factors created difficulties for the Allies: shortage of shells and the advantage to the Germans of defending well-prepared positions. It was easier for the defender to plug gaps by bringing up reserves which did not have to move across a war-torn battlefield, whereas the lines of communication and supply for the attackers were more fragile the further they advanced. It became more and more difficult to hold onto ground that had been won.

The French were pressing for a co-ordinated attack by all the Allies on the Central Powers. They were particularly anxious to recover possession of north eastern France, where the bulk of France's heavy industry and coalfields were. The British wanted to delay until the spring of 1916 when more guns and shells would be available; they were also concerned that the new armies raised by Kitchener, the War Minister, would not be fully trained or equipped until then. Nevertheless General Joffre, the French C-in-C, insisted. The French were to attack in Champagne with a diversionary thrust at Vimy Ridge. To the north, the British First Army, under General Haig, would attack across the coalfields round Loos, south of Lille. Haig was unhappy with the plan because the land round Loos was mostly flat and open, and there was good cover for the defenders – miners' cottages, slag heaps and winding gear. However, it was decided that chlorine gas would be used, which, Haig hoped, would incapacitate the defenders sufficiently for a breakthrough to be made; from that gap, infantry and cavalry would spread round the countryside and send the Germans into retreat.

The prospect of a 'Big Push' was no secret, though the details were yet to be confirmed. James shared the optimism of his fellow officers.

'This could be it,' he remarked in the Mess. 'Break the line, advance to Brussels and the Germans will be suing for peace.'

Burton, his Company Commander, was less sanguine: 'Huh. Many a slip. I'll believe when it happens.'

His pessimism was justified. Aerial reconnaissance revealed that the Germans had a second defensive line up to two miles behind the first, on a reverse slope so that it was out of sight for the most part, and beyond the range of field artillery behind the British line. There were concrete machine-gun posts in between and a number of heavily fortified redoubts (the biggest was the Hohenzollern Redoubt) on the front line and one on an elevated position to the southeast of the village of Loos, designated Hill 70. This could bring down enfilading fire on troops attacking the second line. All along both lines was thick barbed wire. One of the objectives of British artillery was to blow a way through it.

The attack was set for the end of August but was delayed twice until the last week in September. The 2/7th and other battalions in the division were encamped at Annezin, a mile from Béthune and about five miles from the line. The town was crowded with officers and men of many regiments and the locals happily catered for their needs. There were bars, restaurants, cafés, barbers' shops and some branches of British stores. London newspapers were on sale. There were also discreet establishments down side streets with curtained windows. Officers and other ranks enjoyed the amenities, but frequently Military Police came round announcing that men of particular regiments should report to their units at once, perhaps with action ahead of them. Therefore there was an air of desperation about the holiday spirit of those on short leave.

There was a hospital in the town, and on the canal there were barges ready to take the wounded to the rear. The nurses came into town to enjoy their brief moments off-duty. James was seated at a café on the main street with Horton, watching the traffic of people. A group of soldiers from a Highland regiment had been imbibing freely and were making a lot of noise. They were rounded up by MPs and put on a lorry back to camp.

'Poor chaps,' said Horton, 'denied their fun, maybe the last they will have. No wonder they wanted to drink.'

'I can sympathise. Béthune's bars are not quite the Duchess of Richmond's Ball on the eve of Waterloo, but the feeling is the same.'

'The worst thing is the waiting. We all know that there is something big in the offing, but we don't know what part we ourselves will play. Once we get started... Have you heard anything more on the grapevine?'

'Just that we will have difficult ground to cover if we are to reach the German line. And shells have been rationed.'

'Let's hope they don't waste them, then. I have heard that in some sectors they have blazed away without coordination with the infantry, and even shelled our men by mistake, and not just the odd rounds, either.'

'Well, we musn't tell the men that. Only good news to give them hope and a sense of purpose. Keep our doubts to ourselves.'

Horton nodded and sipped his coffee. Then he noticed three nurses coming down the street.

'Turn round, James. That could be a sight for sore eyes. Shall we invite them over for a drink?'

'Of course. We may need their ministrations in due... Good God... that's my sister.'

He got up and went over.

'Beth...'

'Oh. James. I didn't see you at first. We were so busy chatting.'

'Come over for a drink, all of you, and meet my colleague Maurice.'

They shook hands.

The girls sat down at the table. The waiter produced another chair and took orders.

'Delighted to meet you. We have fifteen minutes left before our time runs out. The proprietor only allows one hour; he has so many customers.'

James asked the girls where they were based.

Cynth seemed to be the spokesman.

'Beth and I and Carol now work on the hospital barges, which take the wounded down the canal to Aire and then on to the coast at Calais. We are not really nurses, only VADs, but we have nursed just the same.'

'Since we have been in France,' said Carol, 'we seem to have done everything except fire a gun. We have been drivers, mechanics... we even know how to put up a tent. It's been very unpleasant at times... I have been hungry, tired, cold, wet and covered in mud from shell bursts. Sometimes I think the Boche are aiming their artillery just at me.'

'But you wouldn't be anywhere else just now,' said Cyth.

'Not in boring old suburbia anyway. And I will have some stories to tell my grandchildren.'

James noticed Beth had not said anything.

'Maurice, can I leave these two in your tender care?'

'Of course. You have a lot to talk about with your sister.'

Beth and James walked away towards the canal. They sat on a bench.

'I'm sorry to have missed your leave, Beth. Did you get my last letter?'

'Yes, I did. And I wrote to you.'

'It hasn't arrived yet. We have been moving around. But much better to see you in person.'

'Well, you look just the part, the dashing young officer. I like your moustache.'

'This dashing young officer is getting a second pip and a little more pay.'

'Have you been in the line?'

'Several times, for short periods while other units go for R & R. It has been relatively quiet. We haven't had many casualties. We are here now because of the Big Push that's coming up. No more cushy billets after this. But I think that the battalion, at least our company, has been well trained and is ready for it. We shall see when the time comes. What about you?'

'I am in with a good pair of mates. We work well and laugh together. I have probably seen more deaths than you have so far, and unless you can laugh on occasion, you would go potty. You can bathe wounds, change dressings, administer painkillers and clean up the unmentionable, but we also have to comfort the dying. Nothing much you can do. Just hold their hand and soothe the brow.

'They are so young, some of them. One will cry out for his mother, another will talk wildly about some event in his childhood, which was not so very long ago. I was once asked by a boy if he would be going to heaven.'

'What could you say?'

'You know I am not that way inclined, but I gritted my teeth and told him that God loves everyone, including sinners, and he need have no fear. That appeared to calm him. He died five minutes later.'

She pulled out a cigarette and lit it.

'I'm smoking too much, but it calms me. The other girls smoke as well. It has become a symbol of equality with men. At this rate we will have the vote soon.'

James looked at her quizzically and held out his pipe.

'Equality,' she said, 'doesn't extend to smoking that disgusting thing. I am serious, though. If I survive this war, then I may well rejoin the cause. We talk about it amongst ourselves a lot.'

'I'm sure there will be many changes.'

'There had better be.'

'Fighting talk, Beth. That's what I admire about you, actually one of the many things. You don't give up easily.'

Beth sighed.

'Sometimes it's perhaps better to concede defeat.'

'How do you mean?'

'It's Stefan. One of the reasons for coming to France was to embark on a completely new episode in my life.'

'It certainly is that.'

'Yes. But I wonder if he is still alive, I wonder where he is, whether he is safe, whether he is still thinking of me; and if we do meet again, what will it be like. If only we could communicate. I try, but I can't bring myself to rid my thoughts of him.'

'I understand, Beth. We have talked about girls, Maurice and I and one or two of the other chaps. A lot of the men have sweethearts at home. And they talk a lot about sex. They also say that they are afraid that they might die as virgins. Out here, the restraints of life at home no longer apply. That is why a lot of young single men resort to back street establishments.'

'Not all the men I have nursed have had war wounds.'

'Notices go round warning of sexual dangers.'

They fell silent. Then Beth laughed.

'Here we are, miles from home, discussing venereal disease. Our parents would be shocked.'

'Well, my eyes have been opened to all sorts of things since I joined up. I must have been very innocent.'

'Me too.'

She looked at her watch. 'Damn. I must report back soon. You know, I never used to swear - well, hardly ever - but now we girls eff and blind with the best of them.'

'Very unladylike.'

'Ah, but we are part of the war machine. If men swear, we can swear too. It's liberating. It helps to let off steam. I must go.'

'How long are you going to be here?'

'No idea. I presume that we will be supporting the Big Push, so we won't be too far from the action.'

'Can we meet again?'

'I hope so. But how?'

'I know. I will ask the proprietor of the café to take messages from you and keep them for me, and I will leave messages with him as well. It may not work, but worth trying.'

They got up. They had never been demonstrative together and their embrace was awkward.

'Come back in one piece, James.'

James smiled. 'And you, Beth, take care of yourself.'

She walked away without looking back.

For a few francs James persuaded the owner of the café to take messages. He left one to say that he would be there the following week at the same time, but when he called at the appointed time, there was a message saying that she could not make it and suggested two days hence. James replied that he was likely to be away that day, but when he came into town he would seek her out at the hospital barges.

When the Big Push came a few days later, they had not managed to meet.

* * *

The First Army would be attacking on a front of six and a half miles, too wide for 533 guns. If the second German line two miles behind was to be shelled as well, that meant bringing up howitzers into vulnerable positions. Sir John French, the C-in-C of the BEF, had been lukewarm about the plan. He said: 'We shall not be helping the French by throwing away thousands of lives knocking our heads against a brick wall.' When he proposed to Joffre that the British attack should mainly be with artillery, Joffre demanded an effort in full force. French told Haig that to achieve any result would cost many lives. However, Kitchener insisted that the utmost should be done to assist the French even though the losses were very heavy. The order having been given, Sir John still harboured doubts and this became evident when he was slow to send up the Reserve, IX Corps, after the initial attack; a gap had not yet been opened up in the German line. For this, he was heavily criticised and later sacked from overall command of the BEF. Nevertheless, he had good reason for his doubts. The battalions of IX Corps were inexperienced and had only recently arrived in France, and he was afraid that Haig would have to commit the Reserves too early, thereby reinforcing failure.

There was no attempt to conceal the coming attack. In four days beforehand a quarter of a million shells were fired in the direction of the enemy but the front was too wide for a blanket bombardment to be achieved. Moreover, the Germans were in well-prepared defensive positions, not just in the trenches but among the slag heaps and quarries, providing enfilading fire. But the British commanders hoped that the release of gas would nullify these advantages and allow their troops to reach the enemy lines and capture them. By the 24th September, over five thousand cylinders of chlorine gas had been manhandled up to the front line trenches ready for release. High command, mindful of public opinion which had condemned the Germans' use of gas earlier in the year, referred to it as 'the accessory'. The problem with gas was that a wind was needed, strong enough to carry it to the German lines, but not so strong that it dissipated the gas cloud. At his forward HQ Haig ordered his aide-de-camp to light a cigarette. The smoke drifted eastwards, and the leaves in the poplar trees rustled. That was deemed sufficient for the release of the gas. At the front, gas officers had warned of the wind's unpredictability, but without gas to disable the enemy, the British attack would be even more fraught with danger.

As it happened, the gas was carried gently in a diagonal between the opposing lines and some blew back into the British trenches, causing over two thousand casualties, though only a very few died of its effects. The gas was inclined to linger in hollows and in the German trenches. The German gas masks were more efficient and the troops lit braziers in the trenches to cause the gas to rise. The British gas mask, called 'the goggle-eyed booger with the tit', was uncomfortable to wear; many soldiers took the risk and tore them off because they made fighting at close quarters much more difficult.

The 47th London Division, of which the 2/7th East Surreys formed a part, was poised to attack on the right of the British line. Its primary objective was to occupy Loos. If successful it was to carry on and capture Hill 70, about a mile beyond the village. The route lay across fields between pitheads and slag heaps. Hill 70 was the highest point of the area and there was a German redoubt at the top. The British had no detailed information about the strength of the enemy facing them in this sector. It was hoped that a determined charge would carry the men through.

Chapter Sixteen

❋

During the late afternoon of the 24th September the 2/7th East Surreys marched the six miles from their camp at Annezin to the reserve trenches just to the east of the village of Grenay. There had been heavy rain on the 23rd, the first for three weeks, and the 24th was drizzly. Because divisions were on the march, progress was slow, and to meet the timetable the 2/7ths, at the rear of the column, had to divert into muddy fields. Each man was heavily laden, with rifle, bayonet, 200 rounds of ammunition, extra rations, gas mask, a pick or shovel and some grenades, called cricket balls; there was a short fuse sticking out of the top which had to be lit with matches. There was intermittent shelling by the Germans, but directed towards the trenches and the head of the columns, so that the 2/7th were not troubled.

They arrived at the reserve trenches after dark.

'I hope we are in the right place,' observed Maurice. 'Our guide seemed a little uncertain. I didn't see any street names.'

'Burton's navigation is usually pretty good,' said James. 'We will find out at dawn. The most important thing is for the field canteen to reach us so that we have a hot meal before the action starts.'

The field canteen was slow to reach them, which caused some grumbles. The trenches were deep and cramped, and anyone moving had to step over dozing men and kit, which occasioned more grumbles. There was rain again during the night and by dawn the men were stiff and cold. The rum ration came as a relief. James and Maurice sipped from a hip flask.

'We need a clear head, so not too much.'

James tried to light his pipe but his matches were damp.

'Damn. Should have kept them in my pouch.'

Maurice obliged with a petrol lighter.

'My new acquisition. It'll make the tobacco taste a bit funny at first.'

'Thanks.'

James got his pipe going and Maurice lit another cigarette.

'Have you said your prayers, James?'

'I have.'

'I have petitioned my Jewish God as well. Just to make sure.'

'We're going to need all the divine help we can get.'

'Do you remember Sir Jacob Astley's prayer before the Battle of Edgehill? "O Lord, thou knowest how busy I shall be this day. If I forget thee, do not thou forget me." Sums it up well.'

* * *

By dawn the sky had cleared a little and peeping through a periscope they could see the pithead structure called Tower Bridge, and to the right a huge slag heap. British shells were falling on it in an attempt to destroy any machine gun nests. Two miles away was the dim outline of their objective, Hill 70.

At 5.30 a.m. the order came to don gas masks. They could see the green cloud heading towards the enemy, but then some gas headed in their direction. Fortunately the wind changed slightly and picked up a bit so that it blew the gas between the lines until it dissipated.

'Thank God for that,' James said to Sergeant Milner. 'I hate these things.'

He took off his mask. Milner did the same.

'All the men checked?'

'All correct and ready to go, sir.'

'Now we wait.'

Two hours later orders came that they should move up to the front trenches. There was another wait.

'Let the men have their rations. There's no knowing when they will next eat.'

Fifteen minutes later came the order to advance. They climbed up the ladders left behind by previous occupants of the trench and started to run.

The battalion was in open order. Officers kept an eye on the colonel, who had slowed to a walk. They passed through the former front line of the German trenches and threaded their way along the communications trenches, stepping over the bodies, mostly German but some British. There was no shelling, so they climbed out of the trenches and made faster progress. Within half an hour they reached the cemetery on the outskirts of Loos and took cover, while messengers were sent to Brigade. James and Maurice were eventually called to confer. Captain Burton had a field notebook in his hand, from which he read a message.

'All good so far. German resistance is less than we expected and Loos has been occupied, well, what's left of it. Tower Bridge is in our hands. So we are to proceed as before, well spaced out. We are the right flank. The other news is that eighteen pounders have been ordered to target the wire around the hill, so with a bit of luck – actually, a great deal of luck – there will be passages through it to the enemy trenches. Once again, advance at a walk to save our breath until we come under fire. Then go full tilt. All clear, gentlemen?'

'All clear, sir.'

'Our objective is to hold the hill which other battalions ahead of us will have captured.' Suddenly there was the noise of firing by machine guns and the crump of mortars.

'Sounds as though things are getting hot. We leave in fifteen minutes.'

The 2/7th formed up and began to walk forward. Immediately they were met by retreating troops, some of them without their rifles. Wounded men bleeding profusely were carried by comrades; there had not been time to apply field dressings. B Company picked its way through the corpses and the wounded. One private in James's platoon stopped to give a man, who was plucking at his legs, some water, but Sergeant Milner took one look and dragged him on.

'He's a goner, lad. We must keep moving.'

There was a shrapnel burst overhead. Several East Surreys fell. Burton yelled 'Leapfrog, leapfrog!'

Immediately, following their training, James's platoon flattened themselves on the ground or dived into shell holes and gave covering fire to Maurice's platoon as they rushed ahead. After twenty yards, Maurice's platoon took cover and James and his men rushed ahead. The manoeuvre was repeated, though there were casualties. James looked around him as best he could and reckoned that he had lost about ten men. The slope of the hill was getting steeper and they were more exposed to enemy fire and grenades. As Maurice's platoon passed him, there was another burst of machine gun fire sweeping along the line and taking in the whole company, and more men went down. One of them was Burton.

A hundred yards ahead of them was the wire. The shelling by heavy guns had not made gaps but created a tangled mass on which bodies lay like washing hung out to dry.

Maurice was not far from James. He wriggled across and shouted in James's ear.

'So much for holding a captured position. We can't leapfrog any more. We must join forces, what's left of us, and make a concerted rush. There looks like a gap of sorts in the wire over there, to the right. We might be able to use it to enfilade them.'

James nodded, and signalled to Sergeant Milner. He nodded and gathered the men together. Maurice's sergeant did the same. The two half platoons covered most of the ground before the machine gunners, who had been concentrating on the attack immediately in front of them, noticed the flanking manoeuvre and swung their guns round. James carried on, closely followed by those of his men who were left, and jumped down into the enemy trench. Maurice was not so lucky. A burst of fire caught him in the open and he died instantly.

James reloaded his service revolver. Ten yards ahead was a bend in the trench.

'Give me a cricket ball,' he said to Wallis, who had been following him closely all the way.

'Matches.'

Wallis fumbled in his pocket and brought out a box. He lit the fuse and James threw the grenade round the corner and ran along the trench. There were two dead Germans lying on the floor. To the right was a communication trench going uphill.

'This way,' said James.

A soldier came out of a dugout and James shot him. Another appeared round a corner and Sergeant Milner fired, toppling him. As they continued past him, Milner bayonetted him in the throat and seized his weapon, throwing it out of the trench.

James's party reached the top of the hill. They were well to the rear of the German front line and were occupying twenty yards of trench. James took a quick count of his men: twenty-two. Immediately he ordered them to construct a barricade at each end from what they could find. In that stretch of trench was a dugout with some furniture, a chair, a table and a couple of mattresses. The barricades might hold up the enemy for a few moments. While the men were building them, James looked around the dugout and found some food and a bottle of schnapps. These he gave to Milner to distribute. He located some papers and studied them. He couldn't make much of the German but he reckoned that this sector was manned by the Oldenburg regiment. The papers he folded up and put in his pocket.

Below them and around a curve in the hillside, more waves of attacking British soldiers were falling like ninepins. So intent were the German gunners that they did not notice the small British party in their rear.

James called the men together.

'Well done, men. We are at the top of the hill. Our orders were to hold the hill when it had been captured by other units. The other units never made it past the wire and I suspect that many of our mates are dead. There are three options open to us. First, we make our way down the hill, but that will mean presenting our backs to the enemy. Second, we stand here and fight to the last man. Third, we surrender. But first we have to show the world that we gained our objective.'

He produced a Union Jack from his pack.

'We are going to raise the flag.'

A short pole was found and the flag tied to it. James stuck the pole into a crevice in the parapet and wedged it with stones. He was about to speak again when there was the crump of a heavy shell nearby. The shock knocked over the flagpole. James put it back up.

'That must be British, firing ahead of the poor bloody infantry. If anyone sees the flag, it might warn them off. Having got this far, I would hate to be killed by one of our own shells.'

There was another crump. James had to put the flag up again.

'Right. Decision time. Sergeant Milner, take half the men and make your way down the hill, keeping well to your left. I will stay here with the rest. We will defend ourselves but if the odds seem hopeless, we will surrender. It is remotely possible that other units will make it to the top but I doubt it. We were the last to go into action and I don't know of any reserves in our sector. While you slip away, Milner, we will create a diversion.'

Milner's men moved the barricade to get past and replaced it.

'We're ready, sir,' he called out.

James ordered his men to prepare grenades.

'Who are the best throwers?' Two men came forward.

'We have ten grenades. Just light them and throw them as far as you can. The rest of us will put down suppressing fire.'

James picked up a spare rifle and took the lead in firing at the backs of the Germans in the trench in front. This distracted them from chasing Milner and his men, who were visible running as fast as they could down the hill. However a burst of machine gun fire brought Milner down. He was at the rear of the party and had stopped to aim at the gunner. The other men continued to run until they were out of James's sight.

A few minutes later, from his vantage point James saw that the German trenches had ceased firing. British stretcher bearers had appeared at the bottom of the slope.

James realised that their time was short. He looked round and saw that German soldiers were cautiously coming from behind. He called the men together.

'We are trapped. I think we have done enough today for King and Country. Give me a handkerchief, white for preference.'

He took the Union Jack down from the pole and fixed a white handkerchief.

'I will carry this towards the Boche. Meanwhile keep your heads down and your hands up.'

Holding the pole in front of him, he climbed slowly out of the trench and stood up. He ostentatiously threw away his revolver. As the German officer approached him, a burst from a British shell fell to his left, the splinters shredding his left arm. He continued to hold up the pole until delayed shock overcame him and he lost consciousness.

* * *

The Battle of Loos was mishandled from the start. The attack on the Hohenzollern Redoubt on the 25th September cost the lives of 800 men and 40 officers within five minutes of the advance, though some units were able to outflank it. Their position became increasingly difficult to hold because there were no reserves available at hand to relieve them. The Reserves (IX Corps), after a seven mile march in pouring rain and along crowded roads, only reached the front line in the early afternoon of the 26th. The Germans were fully prepared for their attack. There was a bombardment of only twenty minutes before the British climbed out of the trenches and made their way forward in parade ground order. German machine guns opened up from the second line at a range of 1,500 yards and fired at will; barrels overheated. Infantry stood up on the parapet to have a clear field of fire, not bothering to take cover. In four hours over 8,000 British soldiers were killed or wounded. By early evening, the Germans stopped firing; it was reported that they were sickened by the slaughter. Stretcher bearers came forward from the British lines, and the Germans sent their own men out to rescue the wounded in front of their trenches. The corpses lay out in the open for several days, and the stench of putrefaction became overwhelming.

The fighting continued on and off for another fortnight before petering out on 13th October. Around the village of Loos the British gained of a mile and a half of ground, but were unable to break the second German line; Hill 70 continued in German hands. Elsewhere along the front gains were minimal. The British lost about 45,000 men, killed or wounded. Many officers of all ranks were killed, three of them major-generals. The Germans had barely 25,000 casualties. The French had insisted on the joint effort, but their 10th Army further south in Artois failed in its objectives and suffered very heavy casualties.

Sir John French was blamed for the disaster, because of the delay in bringing up the Reserves. There had been initial successes on the 25th but Haig complained that he had not been able to exploit them, and instead of the much-vaunted breakthrough the battle became a slogging match of attack and counter-attack over the same stretch of ground. The battle revealed many deficiencies of staffwork in supply, co-ordination of artillery and infantry and in troop movements. Questions were asked in Parliament. In December, French was replaced by Haig as Commander of the BEF.

* * *

James opened his eyes. Above him was a canvas awning which flapped in the breeze; he could see grey sky beyond. He was lying on a palette and was shivering. He felt a sneeze coming on and tried to reach into a pocket for a handkerchief, but his left arm would not move. He tried to sit up but was so dizzy that he fell back with a groan.

'You've come round, sir,' said a familiar voice.

'Wallis? What are we doing here? Where are we?'

'We are prisoners, sir. We surrendered, as you ordered.'

'What exactly happened?'

'You got out of the trench with a white flag to surrender but a British shell burst very near you. You fell over. I came out after you. I called out to the German officer, saying that I was your servant. He put down his pistol and came over to look at you. He spoke good English: "Tie a tourniquet round his upper arm. Use the lanyard from his revolver." I did as instructed. The other men came out and were marched down the hill, but Hoskins was told to stay and help me lift you. We carried you down the hill and through the second line. We are now in a field dressing station. Are you in any pain, sir?'

'I wasn't but it is really coming on now.'

James looked at his arm. It was hanging loosly and his sleeve was soaked in blood.

'Well, thanks to you, Wallis, and Hoskins, too, I am not lying in some ghastly shell hole being eaten by rats. Are you two OK?'

'Not a scratch, sir, either of us, but we are bloody hungry.'

'Let's hope our hosts can rustle something up for you. Oh…'

He groaned as a wave of pain racked him.

'Wallis, my left hand pocket. There should be a flask there.'

Wallis felt around and found it. It was dented but intact.

'Open it, Wallis. Have a swig yourself first.'

Wallis obliged and moistened his lips before putting the flask in James's right hand. He took a long draught.

'Put it back, Wallis, please. I will need more later on.'

The whisky did not do much to relieve the pain but warmed him a little.

'Good for morale, if nothing else,' he observed.

Just then the German officer entered.

'I am Hauptmann Köller, Oldenburg Regiment.'

'Lieutenant Millward, East Surreys. Thank you for not shooting me or my men.'

'You made a formal surrender after a gallant action. It was unfortunate for you that other units did not support you.'

'What will happen to my men?'

'They will become prisoners. They are not wounded.'

'Can I ask that my man, Wallis, stays with me?'

'Hm. I don't see why not. He can help with your treatment.'

Another officer came in. Köller introduced him.

'Oberst von Lichenau.'

'I am sorry I can't get up, Herr Oberst,' said James.

'No, no, my dear chap,' said von Lichenau. 'You must rest. I will have our orderly look at you.'

James felt in his right hand pocket. 'I found these papers in a dugout. I can't read German and I don't suppose they are of tactical significance.'

Köller glanced briefly at them and tore them up.

'A list of men to go on latrine duty. Not much use to Allied Intelligence.'

James laughed. 'Do you mean to say that I fought my way up the hill, just for that?'

'I'm afraid so.'

'Can my man have a bite to eat? He has had nothing to eat all day.'

'We'll see.'

The officers left. A few minutes later Köller returned with an orderly clutching a knapsack with a red cross on the outside. The orderly unbuttoned James's tunic and felt his chest. James did not wince. He then pulled down his trousers, grunted and indicated to Wallis to pull them up again. He produced a pair of scissors and cut away the sleeve of his jacket.

'Have you passion?' he asked James.

'Er…'

'He means are you in pain,' said Köller.

'Yes. Quite a lot. Ah…'

The orderly brought out a long bandage and poured some liquid onto it.

'This will hurt,' said Köller. 'Wallis, hold him down.'

The orderly wrapped the bandage round the shattered arm. James cried out. The pain was overwhelming.

The orderly wrapped another bandage round the first and tied it tight. With another long bandage he tied the arm to James's side so that it could not move.

He got up and spoke to Köller, who led him outside.

'More whisky, sir?' asked Wallis.

James couldn't speak, just nodded.

Wallis held the flask to his lips and poured a generous amount into his mouth. James gulped it down.

After a few minutes he ceased groaning and relapsed into sleep. Later a soldier came in and handed Wallis a bit of *wurst* and a hunk of bread.

'*Danke, Kamerad,*' said Wallis. The soldier smiled and said in English: 'You are welcome.' Wallis ate greedily.

By now the evening was drawing on. Köller returned and James stirred.

'Lieutenant Millward. Can you hear me?'

'Loud and clear.'

'Good. Do you want a smoke?'

'I have my pipe somewhere.'

'It was in your pocket, sir,' said Wallis. 'I'm afraid it is broken.'

James sighed. 'So it's not just my arm.'

'No,' said Köller, 'but would you like a cigarette?'

'Please.'

'I'll light it for you.' James drew on it deeply and coughed, which hurt his arm.

'Huh. All my pleasures are being taken away from me, one by one.'

He inhaled with more care.

'Now I have spoken to the Colonel,' said Köller, 'and this is what is going to happen. It seems that the rest of you has some bruising but there are no internal injuries that we can detect. However, your arm needs extensive treatment and there is little we can do out here. There is also the fact that there are our own casualties who need treatment and obviously have priority. Therefore we are going to hand you back under a flag of truce. Can you walk?'

'I haven't tried yet, but I see no reason why not, with Wallis with me.'

'Good. I will have some food brought to you. You will leave some time tomorrow.'

'Thank you. Let's hope my side respect the flag of truce.'

James had a sudden thought.

'Why aren't you interrogating me to find out what is the British Order of Battle and what General Haig's plans are?'

'We know them already,' said Köller. 'And we know that all you will give is name, rank and number, and I am not going to beat any more information out of you. What is your number, by the way?'

James told him.

'We can pass that information on to the Red Cross.'

Köller went out.

'Wallis, I need to try and walk. Will you help me up?'

James managed to swing his feet onto the floor. Wallis put his arm under James's right shoulder. James straightened his legs and stood upright.

'There. Stage one. Now for stage two, the walk. I feel very wobbly, so please stick by me.'

'Where are we going, sir?'

'The latrine.'

Slowly, but with increasing confidence, James walked over to a small tent marked *Nur Offizieren*.

'This looks like it. You wait outside, Wallis, and keep guard.'

Wallis held the tent flap back for him. James had difficulty with undressing and dressing one-handed.

'I had better get used to it,' he said to himself.

When he had finished, Wallis led him back. He sat down on a stool beside the palette.

'I'm exhausted. Why don't you get your head down somewhere? You deserve a nap.'

Wallis went off. James suddenly realised that he was desperately hungry. As if in answer to his unspoken prayer, a German orderly soon came in with a bowl of soup, vegetables mixed in with chunks of meat. It didn't smell very appetising, and he found difficulty balancing the bowl on his knees while using the spoon. In the end he lifted the bowl to his lips and gulped it down.

It was now dark. James was about to lie down when a figure with a candle lifted the flap of the awning.

'I wanted to make sure it was you,' said Stefan.

Chapter Seventeen

❋

'Stefan?' James peered at him. 'My God! What are you doing here?'

Stefan held up his cross. 'I comfort the wounded, of whatever nationality. That is what I will say if we are found talking together. How are you? Is your arm very painful?'

'Painful is an understatement. But I have no other injuries, apart from some bruising. I presume it was a shell splinter that got my arm. I'm lucky it wasn't worse. Bit of a fluke, really, considering.'

'James, you did something gallant, which we respect.'

'Gallant, but hopeless. We surrendered because we were unsupported and I did not want my chaps to be killed in a hopeless cause. Somewhat ironic that a British shell did for me.'

'You are being handed over tomorrow. I will come too. I hope that your side will respect the Cross.'

'Stefan, it's not worth the risk to you. You have other men to look after.'

'I want to give you the best chance of reaching the British lines. And besides, I have a personal reason.'

'What's that?'

'I couldn't look Beth in the face when and if we meet again if I didn't do my best to save you.'

'Do you still carry a torch for her?'

'Oh yes. The war has come between us and she may well meet someone else. But until then I... well, I can but hope. Do you have a lady in mind?'

'No. A friend of mine and I agreed that it was unfair on a girl to have an arrangement when we might well be killed. And my friend was killed today. I think he expected to die. It was mercifully quick.'

Stefan sighed. 'That is war. There is no apparent reason why one man should die and another not. I have no answer when men ask me that. All I can say is they should pray for strength to endure and they will be comforted.'

'Do they believe you?'

'Those who have not seen battle are scornful. But once the shells start falling… Some of them are very young. They joined up in a burst of patriotism hoping for military glory. The reality is rather different. Their concern is to survive the next day and not let their mates down.'

'Same as our chaps.'

Stefan felt in his pocket for a cigarette. He gave one to James and lit it for him.

'James, your family were very welcoming to me when I was in Oxford. I will never forget it. How is Beth?'

'She is nursing in Béthune when I saw her last, a week or so ago. But she might have been moved on.'

'Will you take a message to her? One I have been composing in my mind since the war began in case the opportunity arose. Do you want to know what I will say?'

'Of course not. So long as it doesn't upset her.'

'Will you take it?'

'Yes, I will.'

'Thank you. I must go. There are others to attend to. Try and get some sleep.'

'Stefan, I hope we can meet again in happier times.'

Stefan went out and James tried to compose himself to sleep. But his arm started to throb abominably and defied his best efforts to distract his mind. Eventually he fell into a fitful slumber. He awoke to find Wallis standing by him with a cup of coffee.

'How are you, sir?'

'If you really want to know, bloody awful. Thanks for the coffee.'

The coffee was lukewarm but he drank it eagerly.

'Sir, Mr Köller said that we were to move in fifteen minutes, before the shooting starts.'

'Right, help me up.'

When he was standing he attempted a step.

'My legs feel like jelly, and my head is swimming. There were times last night when I wished I had been taken out instantly like Mr Horton.'

'Don't think like that, sir. You are alive and you will feel better.'

'You're quite right. I mustn't moan. Come on, let's get it over with, whatever the next hour will bring.'

It was getting light when Wallis put James on a wagon and climbed up beside him. Köller was there and shook hands with James. Stefan slipped an envelope inside James's jacket, then sat beside the driver; his orderly walked beside the horse.

They went parallel to the trenches and reached a point a mile and a half south of Hill 70.

'From now on, we must walk,' said Stefan.

They turned towards the front line and made their way with difficulty up a communication trench past soldiers busy with early morning duties. There were some curious looks at the British officer with a bloodstained arm and some curses when they got in the way, but Stefan was wearing his pastoral robes and with a smile wished everyone good morning. They were met by the officer in charge of this section of the trench. He looked at his watch.

'Better be quick. The Tommies will be opening up soon.'

The two front lines were here about a hundred and fifty yards apart. The orderly had brought a large white sheet of plywood with a large red cross painted on it. As instructed he stood on the firestep and held it up over the lip of the trench. The office took a megaphone and shouted down it.

'Hey, Tommy, do you hear me? Don't shoot for the next ten minutes and we won't shoot either. Do you hear me, Tommy?'

He waited. After a couple of minutes a voice came back.

'We hear you, Fritz. What's on?'

'Two of your men and one of ours will come forward to the middle. Your officer is badly wounded and we can't look after him. Our man is a padre. He will be carrying a cross. Understood?'

There was another couple of minutes before a reply came.

'Yes. Understood. Get on with it.'

Stefan climbed up a ladder and stood in the open holding his cross above his head. Wallis helped James up the ladder. Supported by Wallis on his right, and with Stefan on his left he walked slowly and unsteadily towards the British trench. The air was very still and there was no sound apart from the twittering of birds. It seems that both sides were watching intently to see what might happen.

At the mid point, Stefan turned to James and spoke softly.

'To quote your Shakespeare: "If we do meet again, why, we shall smile. If not, why then, this parting was well made."'

James grinned in spite of the pain.

'Amen to that. Thank you, Stefan. I will give your love to Beth.'

He held out his hand and Stefan took it. Then Stefan turned and walked slowly back to the German lines.

Wallis urged James forward.

'Come on, sir, before they start to get twitchy. Only fifty yards to go.'

By this time James was almost faint and Wallis had to drag him. When they reached the British trench helping hands lowered James down onto a stretcher; Wallis went with him. He was carried down a communication trench to a First Aid post. Though he was drifting in and out of consciousness, he was able to explain the nature of his injury. A medical orderly started to unwrap the bandages, but having taken one look at what lay beneath, he tied them up again. He wrote a note on a pad, put it in an envelope and tucked it in the breast pocket of James's jacket.

'You his man?' he asked Wallis.

'Yes.'

'Well, stay with him. He will need all the help you can give him. I don't like the look of his arm; it might be gangrene.'

Though the battle was still raging four miles to the north around the Hohenzollern Redoubt this was a quiet part of the line and there were no other casualties that morning. James was put on a horse-drawn cart and was carried the six miles to Béthune. The road was potholed and as they neared the town the road became very congested. Casualties were coming in from the battle and supplies were being carried to the front line. Occasionally German shells came over. By the time the cart reached the Casualty Clearing Station James was feverish. He was laid on a bed in a hut and a VAD nurse looked him over. She took out the note the orderly had written and gave it to the doctor who was on his rounds. He unwrapped the bandages and examined the arm.

'Phew. This one for the theatre in thirty minutes. Get him ready.'

He gave James a large shot of morphine and passed on to the next casualty. The nurse brought a small bag and filled it with the contents of James's pockets - tobacco, identity card, wallet, hip flask, and Stefan's note. She had to cut the leather strap to remove the watch. Then she sealed the bag, labelled it and put it in the locker beside the bed. Then she stripped him of his clothes and put them in another bag. Wallis was hovering by the door of the hut.

'I am his batman,' he told the nurse. 'What do I do now?'

'You can help me put this gown on him. Leave the arm open.'

Wallis had not seen the full extent of the wound and he blanched at the sight and the smell of the wound.

'Go outside if you want to be sick.'

Wallis dealt with the rest but averted his gaze from the arm. When James was dressed in the gown, Wallis asked what he should do now.

'Report to your unit, I should think.'

'I will need a chitty, otherwise I will be arrested.'

'Go and see the doctor. Actually, I will come with you.'

The doctor scribbled on a note pad.

'What unit?'

'2/7th East Surreys, B Company, 4 platoon, Lieutenant Millward's batman.'

'Very well. Don't lose this.'

Wallis left the hut and wandered into Béthune, where he was promptly arrested by two Military Policemen. After being questioned by their sergeant, he was put in a cell to await confirmation by his unit. He was given a bowl of stew, which he devoured in short order. He stayed in the cell for two days until an officer from the 2/7ths came by to verify him and he was released, with a pass.

'How has the battalion done, sir?' he asked.

'Huh. What's left of it. We have been pulled back.' He looked at his watch.

'Meet me by the church in two hours. I'll take you with me.'

* * *

Meanwhile, James was given a sedative and another shot of morphine. He was carried to the theatre and within a very few minutes the arm was amputated below the shoulder and the blood vessels tied. The surgeon filled out a form:

Reg. no. *1572* Date: *27-9-15*
Name: *James Ronald Millward*
Rank: *Lt.*
Regt or Corps: *2/7 East Surreys*
Diagnosis: *severe injury to left arm and gangrene*
Treatment: *amputation of arm*
Prognosis: *will be able to walk soon after operation but further military service unlikely*
Further treatment: *the wound must be regularly washed with Eusol to avoid further infection*
Notes: *a fit young man. Heart and other organs in good order*
Signed: *GR Slater, FRCS. Capt. RAMC*

When James woke up he was lying on a bed with two bags beside him. It took a bit of time for him to work out where he was. He was on a barge which was still moored to the canal bank at Béthune. He could see the town through the window. He looked around. There was a line of beds with men with various injuries. Some were moaning, others lay silently. A nurse came in, looked at one in the bed at the end of the row, felt his pulse and pulled the sheet up over his head. Two orderlies came in a few minutes later, put him in a large bag and carried him away. At the other end of the row a man was smoking a cigarette, which made him cough violently. Nevertheless he carried on.

James had a headache and felt queasy. He was very thirsty. His left arm ached. Another nurse came in and went to him.

'You are awake, Mr Millward. Is there anything you want?'

'Something to drink and eat. And my left arm hurts all the way down.'

'I will bring something. And your arm... you have had an operation. It had to be removed.'

'But my hand...'

'Mr Millward, it is not unusual to feel pains in limbs when they have been amputated. The nerves and sinews in your shoulder are beginning to adjust to the new situation.'

'God... and the rest of me. Anything more?'

'All in good shape, considering. We will let you stand up and walk about in due course. But you must be very careful of the stump. Don't fall over.'

'Er...'

'Your wound should heal well. But you will have to learn how to live with one arm. It will take a bit of time.'

James was left to his thoughts. All sorts of images rose in his mind: batting one handed, he would take a left hander's stance, leading with the right elbow, as he had been taught with the left; driving, he would have to have some one to change gear, unless the gear lever could be put on the right, as in some cars, and he would have to steer with his knee; eating, would he have to have someone cut up his food for him? That would be the most humiliating. Or would he have to survive on porridge and soup? Before he could imagine more disabilities, he fell asleep.

He was woken by the doctor's round. His temperature was taken, his chest listened to and he was prodded and poked. The results were entered on a board at the end of the bed.

'Hm. All seems to be in order. He can get up and be dressed. I'll look at his arm tomorrow.'

With that, the doctor turned to go to the next patient.

'Just a minute, Doctor,' said James. 'Do you have a VAD nurse on the staff here, Beth Millward?'

'I've no idea,' replied the doctor brusquely and turned away.

When the round was over, the nurse came back to James.

'There is a Beth Millward here. I think she is on another barge.'

'Ah. She is my older sister. Would it be possible for her to come and see me if her duties permit?'

'I'll see what I can do. Now we must get you up and dressed. The more you move about the better.'

'I haven't washed for several days.'

'We gave you a complete wipe-down before the operation.'

'But my clothes. They must be torn and filthy.'

'We had to burn them. But we have a supply of underwear and overalls. They may not fit very well, but they'll do. I expect someone from your unit will bring your things from camp.'

James was dressed, taken to a table and given a bowl of stew, a hunk of bread and a mug of tea. Then he was walked up and down the line of the beds. Within a short time he learnt to counteract the loss of his arm and keep his balance. The nurse watched approvingly.

During the next two days, James grew more confident. He chatted to other men in the ward, and realised that compared with their wounds, he had been lucky. Their stoicism made him ashamed of his bouts of self-pity. He was even allowed down the gangplank to take the air on the bank.

One day, as he was sitting on a bench, an officer came up. It was Captain, now Major, Maitland, whom he had met when he had enlisted.

'Millward?'

James stood up.

'Sit down, old chap. How are you?'

'Still sore, but I am alive. For which I have to be very grateful. Are you still with the East Surreys?'

'I am now an Intelligence Officer with the 47th Division. I want to hear how you got on.'

James told him about the attack on Hill 70, and his decision to surrender, when completely cut off.

Major Maitland listened carefully.

'We put up a Union Jack but the shelling continued and that is how I got my wound. I gather my men went into captivity, but they were very young and that seemed better for them than fighting to the death, ten men against the Boche and under fire from our own side.'

James paused, then added lamely. 'I didn't have much time to make a decision. Did the other men who had been with me get back safely? We covered their retreat as best we could.'

'Yes, they did. Now tell me about your treatment by the Boche.'

'They allowed my man Wallis to stay with me. He brought me back to the British line. I hope he is OK. The Boche didn't want to keep me, since I was badly wounded. They said that they respected my gallantry, whatever that means exactly.'

'Did you give them any information?'

'I gave them name, rank and number. They said they wouldn't interrogate me as they knew all that I was likely to give them. They just wanted me out as soon as possible.'

'Did you learn anything that might be useful to us?'

'I was unconscious most of the time. There was a Lieutenant Köller and a Colonel von Lichenau and it was the Oldenburg Regiment. They spoke good English. I don't speak German.'

'I see. And the priest, the one who came with you into No Man's Land?'

'He was the regimental padre.' James paused and took a deep breath. 'The thing is, I knew him at Oxford before the war.'

'What is his name?'

'Stefan Haase. He was doing a D.Phil in Biblical Studies, at St John's College.'

Major Maitland absorbed this information.

'I suppose this war is bound to throw up instances of meeting former friends and acquaintances on the other side,' he said.

'Tell me about the 2/7ths. I saw Captain Burton and Lieutenant Horton killed.'

'The casualty list is long,' said Maitland. 'The colonel ordered a retreat when he saw that there was little hope of breaking the German line with the men who were left. Only about a half of the battalion made it back to the British lines.'

'The artillery reduced the wire to a complete jumble, and made it even more difficult to get through. We spotted a place well to the right, which was intact and were able to slip through it. The Germans weren't concentrating their defence there. So we were able to go up their trenches to the top of the hill. Well, I have told you the rest. From what I saw of their defences, they were well fortified and dug in. Our men did not have a chance.'

'It was the same all along the front, especially around the Hohenzollern Redoubt.'

'I have been thinking, sir,' said James.

'Yes?'

'My surrender. I am sure I did the right thing. But with so many other men being killed, perhaps we should have been a forlorn hope, as in Wellington's day.'

'That will be for an enquiry to decide.'

'Enquiry? Oh, I see. Court Martial for cowardice in the face of the enemy.'

'Not necessarily. I will be presenting evidence to an ad hoc board, which will examine the whole conduct of the battle. As far as you are concerned, I have interviewed your man Wallis and he substantiates your story, as do the other survivors. I doubt if you will be called. I think that the enquiry will concentrate on the higher command.'

'Well, how high is high? The gas was a failure. I would say, from my worm's eye view, that intelligence gathering was poor; we had no clear idea of what we were attacking. There were few instructions, our cricket balls are no match for the German potato mashers, which accounted for those of our men who approached the wire. I could see the damn things being thrown down the hill at them. Food was late or inadequate; my men had not eaten since the previous evening. The artillery failed to breach the wire, and there was no communication with them once we were engaged, as I know to my cost. I imagine our dead are still lying out on the hill. What a lousy show!'

'I agree things did not go as we wanted.'

'It was my first experience of battle and now I know the meaning of the term "poor bloody infantry".'

'Well, there is still more fighting to come. Maybe we will make the desired breakthrough.'

'More wasted lives, I suspect. I have also been wondering what will happen to me now. I can't fight.'

'You will go back to England and have further treatment. Thereafter, you may get an honourable discharge.'

'So that I can get back to teaching? I still want to serve. There must be something I could do, using my brains this time. What about Intelligence? Or staff work? I'm sure I could do better than what they're doing now.'

'Well, maybe and maybe. The main thing, James, is to get your arm…'

'Or what's left of it.'

'Sorry, get yourself back to full health despite your wound. You will have some leave. Then we shall see.'

James sighed. 'Of course you are right. But I would be grateful if you could put in a word for me.'

'I'll see what I can do. By the way,' said Maitland, holding up a kitbag, 'I have brought your spare uniform and clothes. One or two other things as well. Let me know if there is anything else you want from your kit.'

He got up. They shook hands.

'Tell Wallis,' said James, 'I am grateful for the care he took of me, beyond the call of duty, and I would like to keep in touch with him, if I could have his details.'

'Very well.'

Maitland went off. James extracted a cigarette from the pack in his pocket. He lit it by holding the matchbox between his knees.

More practice needed, he said to himself.

He puffed at the cigarette and decided that he would go back to a pipe as soon as he could; he threw the cigarette away half-smoked. He carried the bag onto the barge and dressed himself in his uniform. It took him some time, especially with the braces, and he fumbled with buttons. He could not tie the tie, nor his shoelaces. He wondered what to do with the empty sleeve. In the end he tucked it into the side pocket of his jacket. Then he brushed his hair, put his wallet and other things, including Stefan's letter, in his pockets, and felt better.

A nurse came in. 'Someone is waiting to see you, Mr Millward. On the bank.'

James got up and walked carefully in case he tripped over his shoelaces.

He saw Beth sitting on the bench. She came towards him and was about to throw her arms around his neck.

'Steady, old thing. My shoulder is still sore.'

Beth did not say anything but looked at him with tears in her eyes. Then she took his hand and led him to the bench.

'Before we sit down, could you please tie my shoelaces. I can't manage by myself.'

Beth obliged.

'Are you in any pain, James?'

'Sore, but it's getting better. I am told that the stump is healing well. How are you?'

'There have been a lot of casualties coming in and we have been rushed off our feet, barely time for a smoke. Some terrible injuries.'

'There are quite a few like that on the barge. I think I have been lucky. Have you heard from Father recently?'

'Last week, a brief note to say that he was well and busy, but terribly worried about you going into battle.'

'I will write to him as soon as I can. I will have some leave when I get home.'

James told Beth about the attack on Hill 70 and his surrender and wound.

Beth said nothing, so he went on.

'When I was lying there, Stefan came to see me.'

'Stefan?'

'Yes. He is the Padre of the Oldenburg Regiment. I promised I would give you his love.' He felt in his pocket.

'Here is a letter for you.'

Just then a nurse came out and shouted to James that the barge was about to move off. James kissed Beth. She started to weep again.

'Chin up,' said James. 'See you back in Blighty soon.'

Chapter Eightteen

❋

My dearest Beth,

You have never been far from my thoughts and many times have I composed a letter to you in my mind. Now an opportunity has been vouchsafed to me, through my meeting with James. James was severely wounded but he showed great fortitude. Clearly he needed urgent treatment which we could not provide. Therefore our colonel decided that he should be returned. I was able to assist without revealing my connections to him. If and when you receive this I hope he will be well on the road to recovery. I pray for him.

I did receive your last letter, the day England declared war. I have been with the regiment since the start. I witnessed some terrible things during our march through Belgium though I am glad to say our regiment was not responsible for the worst excesses. Since then there have been three major battles in which the Oldenburgs have been engaged, though not always in the front line. I have been fully occupied in my pastoral duties.

I was able to return home for a few days earlier this year and I am happy to report that the family are well. The children are growing up fast; it is always a delight to see them after the squalor of war. My brother's firm is now totally devoted to military production, and I expect the same is true of firms in England.

So much for me, Beth. I would love to write more but time is against me and I mustn't reveal anything that could give aid and comfort to the enemy! Though I know very little directly of our military affairs. What about you? James told me that you were nursing behind the British lines. I knew you would not stand aside. You must have had some terrible experiences, but I am sure you are strong enough to deal with them. War has certainly deepened my faith, since I know God is with us even in the direst of circumstances.

As I said before, do not wait for me. There will be other men and all I wish for is your lasting happiness. Should we ever meet again, as James said to me, may it be in happier times.

With much love,
Stefan

Beth read the letter three times, then folded it back in the envelope. The shock of seeing James and then the letter left her numb. She returned to her barge and went about her duties in a trance. That night she sobbed herself to sleep, weeping for James, for Stefan and herself. In the morning, she rebuked herself for her tears, realising that her emotions ran in three separate channels; worry for James, frustration at not being able to reply to Stefan and express her own feelings for him, and consciousness that their time for a relationship was running out.

* * *

James spent three days in hospital in St Omer and then crossed the Channel on a regular ferry. The other passengers were men, and some nurses, on home leave and some senior officers. His stump, though still very tender, was healing well. Fortunately, the crossing was calm and he had no trouble in keeping his balance. He was embarassed when he had to ask a fellow passenger to cut up the food provided.

'Don't worry, mate. My pleasure. That's some Blighty wound. How did you get it?'

'At Loos. Shell burst.'

'One of those *minenwerfers*, eh?'

James nodded. The lie was easier than telling the truth.

'I was just lucky that it did not do more damage to me.'

A brigadier walked past as he was standing by the rail. He glanced at James, then looked again.

'East Surreys?'

'Sir.'

'That was a bad show, Loos. Sending Territorials against the Hohenzollern Redoubt.'

'I was on Hill 70, sir.'

'The whole plan was misconceived from the start. It was a battle in the wrong place at the wrong time. You lot bore the brunt.'

'I gather there will be an enquiry, sir.'

'It will make uncomfortable reading, I can tell you.'

'Were you in the battle, sir?'

'No. I was on the Intelligence staff at HQ. We advised very strongly against the attack, and our worst fears were realised. But Grand Strategy demanded that we make a bold gesture in support of the French. They suffered heavily as well, with just as little to show for it. Same as Gallipoli. Huge loss of life for nil returns. It makes me very angry. We are fighting this war like a bunch of amateurs. Shouldn't be criticising the brass hats in front of you, but you have suffered from their ineptitude.'

The brigadier paused.

'What are you going to do with yourself when you are discharged?'

'I haven't thought that far.'

'Well, we could use your brains. Here's my card. What's your name?'

'James Millward.'

'Millward? Where have I heard that name recently? Oh, never mind.'

He made a note, then said: 'Good luck with your recovery, Millward. Get in touch when you are ready.'

* * *

Over the next few weeks James's stump continued to heal well, and he spent some time at home with his father. He developed techniques for doing things one-handed. He purchased shoes and boots with straps rather than laces and ties he could slip over his head. The major difficulty of cutting up food remained. He persuaded the cook to prepare his food so that he could use just a fork or spoon. When he was dining out, he soon lost his embarrassment about the matter. If he was sitting next to a woman the request became an opening conversational gambit.

In due course he was summoned to the War Office, where he was interrogated by two colonels, neither of whom he knew or were from the 47th Division. James did not know what to expect. After some thought he decided to give a straightforward narrative of the events on Hill 70, and justify his actions only if asked directly. The colonels listened in silence to his statement, and one made notes. When James had finished, the colonels told him to leave the room. Ten minutes later he was summoned back.

'Why did you surrender?'

James gave his reasons.

'Hm. Are you blaming senior officers for lack of support?'

'No, sir. I think the fog of war accounts sufficiently for our predicament on that hill.'

'I see.'

The other colonel asked about his brief period of captivity.

'Did you learn anything about German defences?'

'I saw that the second line was well-defended; it would be very difficult and expensive in lives to break through it. But bear in mind that I was slipping in and out of consciousness at the time. Perhaps Wallis, my batman, can give you a better idea.'

'Why did the Germans let you go?'

'Lieutenant Köller told me that they could not deal with my wound, as they had their own men to look after. It seemed easier and more humane to return me to the British lines.'

'What regiment were they?'

'The Oldenburg Regiment. I only talked to Köller and the colonel, whose name I forget, and a medical orderly.'

'Did you give them any information?'

'Only my rank and number, which they would give to the Red Cross.'

'They did.'

Papers were shuffled.

'I have a note from a Major Maitland to the effect that you knew the padre who accompanied you into No Man's Land.'

'I knew him at Oxford before the war.'

'Tell me about him.'

James did so, but omitted the relationship with Beth.

The colonels looked at each other and picked up their papers.

'Well, that will do for now, Millward. Dismiss.'

James stood up, put on his cap and saluted.

Out in the street he pulled his pipe from a pocket; he had filled it in advance. Using his new petrol lighter he lit up. It took him several attempts because of the breeze. When he had it going he walked to Trafalgar Square, reflecting on the interview. The colonels had not been hostile and seemed to have accepted his account. He wondered if his personal conduct was at issue, or whether it was part of a general enquiry into the battle, as Maitland had suggested. He felt some apprehension, but there was no point in worrying about the outcome of the interview; time would tell. He looked at his watch. Twenty minutes till he was due to meet his father for lunch at the club. He went up into the National Gallery and bought a brochure from the desk. His purse was in his left-hand pocket. He reached across for it, put it on the desk and asked the girl to take the money. She looked at him more closely than at first.

'I'm sorry for your wound,' she said.

'All in the line of duty,' he replied. 'I survived, which is more than my colleagues did.'

The girl smiled nervously, not knowing how to react. James smiled back.

'Battle of Loos. A bit of a shambles if you ask me. But I lived to fight another day.'

'Er... with one arm?'

'I still have a brain, which could be of use to His Majesty.'

James wondered why he was talking like this to a total stranger, but the girl was pretty.

'Thank you for the brochure. Look, I have to go for lunch. But I will come back afterwards. If you are not too busy, we could chat for a bit.'

'Yes, of course.'

'I'd better go.'

Lunch with his father was a perfunctory occasion and the food was basic fare. Mr Millward was busy with one of his committees and was obviously preoccupied with a day-long meeting, from which he had escaped for an hour. James did not volunteer much about his interview; there was nothing to be said until he had heard the outcome.

When they parted on the steps, Mr Millward asked him where he has going.

'As I am up in town, I thought I would go to the National Gallery. You tend to forget about Art in the trenches.'

'Will I see you tonight?'

'I'll be home before you. I want to change out this uniform into something more comfortable.'

'Are you still in pain?'

'From time to time. And I need to bathe the stump.'

With that, they went their separate ways. James nearly changed his mind, with the thought that he was making a fool of himself with the girl. But then, he had nothing to lose and life didn't stop just because he was, as the French called it, *un mutilé de la guerre*; if he were in Paris, he would have a seat reserved for him on the buses.

When he got to the desk in the National Gallery the girl was not there. He sat on a bench pretending to read the brochure. One or two people came in and gave him curious looks. He was just about to get up and look at the pictures when the girl came back to the desk.

'Hello,' he said. 'I'm James.'

'And I am Beatrice.'

'A pretty name. Dante had an ideal girl called Beatrice.'

'We have a painting of her by Rossetti. Apparently he saw her only twice but that was enough for him to fall deeply in love with her.'

'I didn't know that. Are you a student of Art?'

'In a way, yes. I have had no formal training and I have no talent with a paint brush, but I was encouraged by my mother to study the history of painting. That is how I came to work here.'

'Is your mother an authority?'

'She has published some books; she is a fan of Ruskin, and knew him in her younger days.'

'I will look out for her books. What is her name?'

'They will be hard to find. She published them privately. Eustacia Valentine.'

James was silent for a moment.

'Um… forgive my asking, but did your mother have a lady's companion on her travels? It would be five years ago.'

'I was still at school, so I didn't go on her trips then, but I met the woman a few times.'

'Do you remember her name?'

Beatrice shook her head.

'Was it Beth Millward?'

'Why, yes. Mother always spoke highly of her.'

'Beth is my sister.'

'Really? What a coincidence! Where is your sister now?'

'Nursing in France.'

'Oh, I hope she is safe.'

'I saw her briefly when I was on a hospital barge. But we didn't have much time together.'

Just then an official of the Gallery came past and stopped when he saw them deep in conversation. He looked disapproving.

'You should not be talking to the staff like that.'

'I am just buying a brochure,' said James.

The official saw James's left sleeve and his manner changed.

'I see. But Miss Valentine has her duties to perform.'

'She had been very helpful. I will not detain her too long,' said James. 'Miss Valentine, do you have any books on Rossetti?'

The official went away. Beatrice laughed. 'He promised my mother to protect me from the attentions of young men.'

'I can assure you that my attentions are extremely honourable. I have been dedicated to Art since… since just before lunch. Can I see you again?'

Beatrice found another brochure, this one on Rossetti. James handed over his purse.

'In answer to your question,' said Beatrice, 'yes, you can.'

* * *

Over the next few weeks, James took Beatrice out for tea a couple of times and one day they spent the afternoon together. They walked in St James' Park. The weather, though sunny, was cold and James had an overcoat. Beatrice took his arm, but she had to disengage while he doffed his hat or blew his nose.

'Take my hand instead,' said James. 'It will be easier.'

'It's the thought that counts,' she giggled.

It was too cold to sit down, and they strolled around the park, deep in conversation. Beatrice told him about her family and her schooling.

'No scandals, no wicked uncles. A cousin was killed in South Africa, but I barely knew him.'

'What about your father?'

'He was an MP till my grandfather died, and then he had to go to the Lords. He is not very active there, more a business man than a politician. Prefers to sit on boards. We have an estate in Shropshire and he goes up for the shooting in the autumn. We spend Christmas there. I used to enjoy it when I was younger. You know, parties for the tenants, carol singing round the village, Christmas Day Service when Father would read the lesson.'

'Sounds fun.'

'Up to a point. But all my friends are here in London. And Shropshire is awfully cold in winter. Deep snow has its charms…'

'For about five minutes.'

'You're right.'

Just then a woman came up to James and thrust a white feather at him, trying to pin it on his coat.

'You should be fighting out there in France,' she shouted. 'Instead, you are cowering at home enjoying the girls while all true men are dying for their country.'

James was about to expostulate, but Beatrice, without a word, leant across and unbuttoned the coat, showing the empty sleeve of his jacket.

The woman tried to resume her tirade, but Beatrice's glare silenced her. She mumbled something and turned away.

'Come on, James, we need some tea.'

James did not say anything until they were seated at a café and Beatrice had ordered for them.

'Such a silly woman,' she went on. 'Did she upset you?'

'Not her. But now I have been home for a while, the novelty of my situation, which carried me through the early days, has worn off. Seems an odd thing to say, but it is true.'

'I understand.'

'I am having dreams about my days at the front and I am not sleeping well. The tears well up. So many of my colleagues and friends wiped out in barely an hour. I shouldn't say this, but the battle was an useless gesture to appease the French, with negligible gains. For me, the crowning futility was the fact that I lost my arm to a British shell when we had reached the top of the hill we were attacking. And then I was interrogated by a pair of colonels about my conduct, because I had surrendered and, incidently, saved the lives of my men. They are prisoners, but they have a life ahead of them.'

'Can you tell me about that day? It might help you.'

'I kept quiet about it when I got home. Never told my father and he never asked. I think he realised that I would when I was ready. So it has all been bottled up inside me.'

James felt in his pocket for a handerchief to wipe away a tear.

'Sorry, so unmanly. I haven't cried since I was a boy at prep school.'

Beatrice touched his hand. 'Let the tears come. Never mind what other people might think.'

The two women at the next table were staring at him.

'How did you get back to the British lines?'

James composed himself and told her, mentioning his previous acquaintance with Stefan.

'I console myself by thinking that I have got off pretty lightly compared with the wounds other men have suffered. I have a lot to be thankful for, not least in getting to know you.'

Beatrice did not reply but leant across the table and kissed him. The women on the next table were visibly disapproving.

'You can take me home,' Beatrice said. 'It's not far. Bruton Street.'

At the door, Beatrice took his hand.

'You now know the address. Please write to me, and then I can write back.'

'When can I see you again?'

'I have to go with my mother up to Shropshire for a week. But when I get back...'

'You can begin my education in Art. Show me your favourite paintings.'

He kissed her lightly and turned to go.

'Never mind those nightmares, James. They are all in the past.'

He smiled. 'If only it were that easy. But I will try.'

* * *

Despite Beatrice's urging, the nightmares did not go away. One evening, over dinner, he suddenly decided to tell his father the whole story. Mr Millward listened in silence.

When James had finished, he said: 'When you came home, I thought you were bearing up well, perhaps too well. And now there is a reaction, as was to be expected. I do not know how to advise you, since I have never experienced anything of the kind.

All I would say is that you should, if you can, look forward rather than back. What was it Vergil said?'

'I think you mean *dabit deus his quoque finem.*'*

'I'm glad you haven't forgotten your Latin. And the business of life with one arm. I know it is frustrating but you seem to be managing.'

'I still swear when I am thwarted.'

'Have you thought about cricket?'

James laughed. 'Oddly enough, that was one of the first things that came to my mind. But there are more serious repercussions. The interview with the colonels. They questioned me about the decision to surrender. I wonder if I am to be accused of LMF.'

'LMF?'

'Lack of Moral Fibre. Perhaps I am making this up but I felt there was an implication that I and my men should have fought to the last. More heroic, but quite useless in view of our position. We were totally unsupported and coming under fire from our own side.'

'If you ask me, you showed more courage in saving the lives of your men, whatever the consequences for you.'

'But the Brass Hats prefer a last ditch stand. Looks better in the newspapers.'

'I think that your predicament in microcosm has called into question many aspects of the conduct of the war. There is a lot of talk in Whitehall, *sotto voce* of course. There are complaints about grand strategy, lack of shells, insufficient training, poor staff work, the lot. And on top of all this we have a Prime Minister who allegedly writes love letters to his mistress during cabinet meetings. What we need is someone to take a grip.'

'Maybe Lloyd George is the man.'

'A slippery piece of work. But he does have determination and can be quite ruthless.'

'They call him the Welsh windbag.'

---

* God will make an end to these things also.

'Well, there are times when words are important. James, I have to ask. Are you staying in the Army?'

'No one has told me to leave, yet. I'm not sure what I could do. I would be a liability in combat, a liability to others. Possibly a staff job. But I am not a professional and the long service types look down on Territorials. I'll have to wait and see. If nothing happens for a couple of weeks I'll go and bang on a few doors. A Brigadier did give me his card. And I am being paid for sitting at home.'

* * *

Three days later a brown envelope arrived from the War Office, addressed to Lieutenant JR Millward, MC. The citation for the award of the Military Cross read:

> Amidst heavy enemy fire and significant losses, Lt Millward pressed forward the attack through the German lines to the crest of the hill. Finding that he could not hold the ground, despite being severely wounded he ensured that his men were able to retreat in good order.

The notice would appear in the next issue of the *London Gazette*. There were also instructions for him to claim the medal at the War Office.

Mr Millward commented: 'I would have thought that some general, or even royalty, might have pinned the medal on your chest.'

'MCs are two a penny, Pater. I suspect it was awarded to give the 2/7th East Surreys something to be proud of from an otherwise disastrous day. Funny, though. I haven't had a word from the battalion since I got back. Perhaps they have disowned me for surrendering.'

'I expect they are too busy writing to the relatives of those killed. There were a lot of them.'

'And the citation leaves out quite a lot. It wouldn't do for a hero to be wounded by his own side. And I am sure many others are much more deserving.'

'James, just accept the medal as a military necessity. Be proud of what you did. The fact that you reached the top of the hill meant that your colleagues did not die altogether in vain.'

'I suppose you're right.'

'Pardon my mentioning it but I see that you are going up to town more recently.'

'Er... yes. I'm seeing a girl.'

Mr Millward poured him a glass of port. 'Good. Now think about her and not the hilltop in France.'

Chapter Nineteen

❀

Now that he was feeling better and the stump was behaving itself, James was becoming bored. There being no further communication from the War Office, he wrote directly to the Brigadier whose card he had been given and received a prompt reply. He was invited to the Military Secretary's Office for an interview. This was in a building just off Whitehall (and not too far from the National Gallery, he noted). At the Front Desk he was directed down a corridor on the ground floor. He knocked on the door and went in. A secretary invited him to sit down and rang through to an inner office. He was invited in.

'Do sit down, Millward,' said the Colonel behind the desk. He was wearing the ribbon of the DSO.

'I have read your file and your exploits. I hear that you are anxious to continue in the King's Service for the duration.'

'Sir.'

'In this office we have files on officers of the rank of Major and below; we read their annual assessments and make recommendations to Selection Boards. As you can imagine, our work has increased enormously in the last year with Kitchener's armies. So much so that we need all the men we can get, and our secretarial staff has grown considerably. The work may seem dull initially, but you get to learn a lot about the Army and your fellow men. And don't forget, every subaltern worth his salt should aspire to red tabs. So you could be selecting the brass hats of the next generation. Care for a drink? Whisky and soda?'

'Er… thank you, sir.'

The colonel got up from his chair and clutching a stick hobbled over to a sideboard. James saw that he had a prosthetic leg. He poured a generous shot for James and a smaller one for himself.

'Bottoms up.'

James took a tentative sip.

'I don't dispense drinks every day, but it tells me something about the man I am employing. You did not refuse, but you didn't down it in one. So, welcome to the Old Crocks Battalion. I have six officers under me and between us we could make up two complete human beings. The only one who looks normal is Watkins, but he has only one eye which works and he is very deaf. All of us have MCs or are Mentioned in Dispatches. Two things we never talk about, even in jest, are how we won our medals, and, of course, our wounds. Clear?'

'Yes, sir.'

'Very good. I will introduce you to the chaps. As from tomorrow you can add a pip to your uniform, as acting Captain. Let's go through.'

* * *

Beth was given home leave in the spring of 1916. Although she spent some of it at home with her father and brother, she tried to see as many friends in England as she could in the time allotted. To James she seemed to have lost some of her sparkle. She never referred to Stefan and James took care not to mention him. When asked if she was unwell, she gave a brusque reply.

'Of course not. I haven't had time to be ill.'

One day she came home from staying with some friends and sat in the lounge brooding. James gave her a drink.

'Sorry I have been behaving like a cow,' she said. 'I am angry. Angry with the people at home, who have such a unjustifiably rosy view of the war. I try to tell them the reality of the Front but they will not listen. Then I describe to them some of the casualties I have to deal with and I don't spare them the gory details. They think I'm exaggerating, and say that they read in the newspapers that Loos was a significant step on the road to Berlin. Then I tell them about the lives lost in front of the Hohenzollern Redoubt and on Hill 70, and that you were lucky to come out of the action only losing an arm.'

'I am angry, too. I have discussed it with Father and it seems that there is disquiet in Whitehall.'

Bath took a large gulp of her drink and lit a cigarette.

'I promised myself that at home I would not swear, but I bloody well hope so.'

'That sounds like the old Beth.'

'But not with the language. I haven't told you how glad I am that you are making very good progress with your stump, and you seem in good heart.'

'I am getting used to it and all that it entails. Besides, I have got to know a girl, which is good for morale. I have no prospect of going back into battle, and therefore I can take a girl out with a good conscience.'

'Who is she?'

James was about to tell her when she stopped him. 'Not now. Tell me when you have a definite arrangement.'

'Funny. She is rather like you in some ways.'

'What do you mean?'

'She is no shrinking violet.'

Beth thought for a moment.

'This violet badly needs watering,' she said. 'I am exhausted, not so much physically, though I have been sleeping pretty well since I got back, but mentally. I am weary of the pain, the squalor, the terrible things war does to young men. In my mind's eye I see them running round when they were small boys, with everything in front of them, and all the hopes and aspirations that their families had for them. Now, if they are lucky, they are killed outright. The unlucky ones suffer appalling injuries and despite our best endeavours die just the same, having experienced agony of mind as well as body. It's not something you can ever get used to, James. People talk about having a clinical approach, being objective, leaving your emotions outside. That worked for me at the start, but no longer.'

'Do the other nurses find the same thing?'

'Cynth and I have talked about it. I think she is tougher than me, but she admits to weeping in private, out of sheer frustration at the futility of it all.'

'Will you go back?'

'Of course. But I need a complete break first.'

'Where will you go? Have you friends who will go with you? What about Cynth?'

'I want nothing and nobody to remind me of the war, at least for a little while.'

'Could be difficult to achieve. Scotland?'

'Possibly. Somewhere I can be by myself, go for walks, read books. It is impossible to be alone at the Front.'

* * *

She booked herself into a small guest house in Northumberland, run by nuns as part of their establishment. The only restriction placed on her was silence at the communal meals, if she wanted to attend them. She went for long walks along the coast and read books, both those she had brought and those she found in the library. She worked in the garden and fed the chickens. One morning the Mother Superior came to see how she was getting on. It was a sunny morning and she was on her knees, weeding round vegetables.

'Are you enjoying getting your hands dirty, Beth?'

'It is very cathartic, Mother. Soil is clean. Blood and gore are not.'

'I see. Would it help if we talked? Sometimes it is easier to talk to a stranger. But only if it will ease the tension inside you. Think about it.'

That afternoon she asked to see the Mother Superior. Beth talked for nearly an hour while she listened. Everything that had been whirling around in her mind came pouring out, including her love for Stefan. While speaking she had been pacing up and down. At the end she sat down and burst into tears.

The Mother Superior waited until Beth's sobs had subsided.

'I don't give advice, Beth. A way out of your difficulties must come from inside yourself. But there are things I can say. The work you do in France is horrible. No wonder you need a break from it, but it has to be done. I believe you have the fortitude to carry on with it as a public service, whatever your views on the conduct of the war. As for your love for the German priest, loving also involves pain, but it has its reward in deeper happiness than you can find anywhere else. That is a conventional sentiment for a religious to utter, but it is no less true for all that. Can you share his faith?'

'We have talked about it but he has not tried to convert me. I am still agnostic but I am getting closer. I couldn't be his wife otherwise.'

'I agree. Try praying. It is a way of opening a conversation with Him. Sorry, that's advice.'

'I have tried praying. But I have no peace of mind and my work troubles me more than ever.'

The Mother Superior stood up and came across to where Beth was seated. She placed her hands on Beth's head.

'*Pax tecum. In nomine Patris, Filii et Spiritus Sancti. Amen*'.

Then she went out and Beth was left alone. The touch of the hands had been like an electric shock. She didn't want to move as the tears began to flow again. At last, with a great effort she got up and went to her room and lay on the bed. Within a moment she was fast asleep.

* * *

After his mission of mercy Stefan went to the Oldenburgs' HQ and reported that the British officer and his servant had been successfully restored to their lines. Later that morning Oberst von Lichenau took him aside.

'Haase, why did you go into No Man's Land with our wounded prisoner? I can understand your Christian duty, but wasn't it more than what was strictly required in the circumstances?'

'I felt that the circumstances were unusual, and that it could inspire a reciprocal gesture from the Tommies if the occasion arose.'

'I can see that. But to put yourself in the firing line like that... Oh, never mind.'

'There was more than just a sense of duty, sir, I must confess. I knew the officer concerned from before the war, when I was at Oxford. I stayed with his family during the long vacation. I had to make sure he got back. And he needed treatment badly, treatment which we could not give him.'

'Very well. I think the less said about this the better. There are people in our regiment who would say that we should have shot him and his men out of hand, since prisoners are a nuisance and have to be guarded and fed. I am not of that opinion, since we would like our prisoners in Allied hands to be well treated. But I fear that this war will turn much nastier. The Allies are frustrated that they are not achieving a breakthrough, and we are on the defensive most of the time.'

'What can we possibly get out of this war, having started it? I am finding it more and more difficult to justify our actions.'

'I would like to turn the clock back, too. But now I have to get on with the job I have been ordered to do. How long have you been with us, Haase?'

'Since June 1914.'

'You have done more than your statutory period of service. You have served us well. But we need someone who is more committed to the war effort. With all due respect to your cloth, we can't have a pastor who voices doubts. I will speak to the Chaplain-General and ask for a replacement.'

Within a few days, Stefan was on the way back to Germany. Only when he got back to his brother's house did he realise how tired he was.

An interview with his Bishop followed in a few days. He was not unsympathetic at first.

'I can see that you need a rest. There is mental as well as physical fatigue, and priests are no less liable to suffer than others. Give it a month and you will be able to rejoin the fray.'

'I won't be going back.'

'What? That will never do. All of us must support our men at the Front.'

'The colonel wants someone more committed to the war. I told him of my doubts, but I have never voiced them to anyone else.'

'But…' the bishop spluttered.

'I will serve in other ways. More pastors are needed here, back home.'

'You have never had a parish.'

'No.'

The bishop glared at Stefan for a few moments.

'You with your tender conscience. Go home and think about your position. And pray. I will see you again in a week.'

Stefan shared his problems with his brother and sister-in-law. Dietrich said that most people would think he was a coward in refusing to go back to the Front.

'Do you think I am a coward, Dietrich?'

'It took considerable courage to expose yourself to enemy fire, when you needn't have done so. As for your feelings about the war in general, I should keep them to yourself, even if you may well be proved right.'

'What do you think, then?'

'I give employment and a livelihood to men who produce war matériel. If I stopped, the men would be out of work and liable for conscription. I cannot concern myself with what the generals do with my product. My humble, and private, opinion is that, having started this wretched war, we must win it, or at least have a negotiated peace before more damage is done.'

'Times are already getting harder for the poor,' said Hannah. 'The blockade is causing a shortage of food in the cities. Things are not so bad in the country, and we can afford good food, but many can't. I am trying to organise a food bank in Bremen. Fewer and fewer people are willing to make contributions. What we collect disappears in minutes.'

'I'd no idea things were that bad at home,' said Stefan. 'The army is not badly fed on the whole. So far.'

'What will you do now?' asked Hannah.

'I have to do something to avoid conscription. In the short

term, I will ask the Bishop for a parish, even as a locum. If I look further ahead, I would like a teaching job in a theology faculty, maybe at my alma mater; I could combine this with a parish. And in the long term...'

'Yes?'

'In the long term, apart from everything else, I would like to marry Beth, if she will still have me.'

* * *

When Beth's leave ended, she was sent on a nursing course. This was intended for those going out for the first time, but it was thought that some, including Beth and Cynth, needed a refresher. Like old lags anywhere they sat at the back of the class. Both were wearing their 1914-1915 medals, which rather disconcerted the lecturer. There were supposedly new nursing methods being taught, which drew from Cynth the comment not so *sotto voce*: 'a statement of the bleedin' obvious'. The lecturer pretended not to hear and went on to talk about personal conduct and hygiene. Finally she asked them for any comments. Cynth was about to answer, but Beth cut in.

'There are three things that come to mind. Firstly, for all the regulations and procedures we have, improvisation by both doctors and nurses is the order of the day; there are many situations that are not covered by the book. Secondly, by the end of your first week you will feel utterly exhausted, and after that you will be fighting weariness all the time; it will be difficult to keep your perspective and temper and you will see things that horrify you. And last, though I am sure that you are all proper young ladies, do not be tempted to seek relief in intimacy. Venereal disease is rife.'

'And you don't know where they've been,' added Cynth.

There was a shocked silence.

'Well, you did ask us,' said Beth.

Beth and Cynth returned to France at the end of May 1916. For the most part the Front was quiet, but there were extensive preparations for the new Push. A new field hospital was being constructed at Amiens, shells were stockpiled and fresh regiments were training in camps along the north bank of the River Somme. Beth and Cynth were moved up to a casualty clearing station just outside the town of Albert, two miles from the Front. All around were gun emplacements, firing, it was said, a million and a half shells in the last week of June. The attack went in on July 1st, at a cost of of 20,000 killed or missing and nearly 40,000 wounded on the first day. By the time the offensive had petered out in the middle of November, the British had suffered ten times that number of casualties. Only later was it revealed that the Germans had suffered the same, and even more. The ground over which the battle was fought was a sea of mud, caused by the exceptional rainfall that summer and early autumn.

In those months, Beth worked unceasingly, with only a few days' local leave when there was a lull in the fighting. There were German prisoners to nurse as well. Beth took especial care of them, imagining that one might be Stefan and comforting them as best she could; she interpreted for the doctors. Her knowledge of German became known and she was even asked to attend interrogation of prisoners. She soon realised that the aggressive style of some officers was not eliciting useful replies. The prisoners were frightened and disorientated, often simply repeating the questions back, or saying what they assumed the interrogator wanted to hear. So she rephrased the questions in gentle terms, with the result that more information was gained. She did not receive much thanks for her efforts, since the fact that a woman had such a good command of the language was resented by the male officers.

By October, she was at the end of her tether, and was granted extended leave. She went home and slept for the first few days. When she resurfaced she wrote to Frances Stevenson, asking if they could meet 'for a chin wag after such a long time'. She had a reply by return, inviting Beth to lunch and the afternoon at her flat.

'I have asked David for a free day; he said I must work until noon, so our lunch will be rough and ready. But I have a nice bottle of wine we can share.'

Beth arrived at the flat just as Frances came bustling along with a basket of food. They went up in the lift.

'I'm getting lazy about the stairs.'

The flat was small but had a good view over Westminster. While Beth picked out the various buildings Frances prepared cold meat, cheese and a salad and chatted away.

'Now David is Secretary of State for War after the lamented Kitchener, he is busier than ever. The generals are not used to having a civilian in charge. David and Willie Robertson are at odds over the Somme. David thinks it has been a ghastly failure and says so openly. Willie, as CIGS, thinks that David should back him up in everything.'

'I don't know about grand strategy,' said Beth, 'but I have seen and tended to the victims of it.'

'Where were you?'

'In a forward clearing station near Albert. We were working sixteen hour days. Men were lying everywhere as there were not enough cots to go round. All one could do was to comfort them and offer them a drink while they waited for treatment. And they often died before they could be dealt with.'

'I thought that preparations had been made to accommodate a large number of wounded.'

'But not that number on one day.'

'Hm. Have a drink.'

Frances poured glasses of wine.

'Cheers.'

'Cheers.'

They sat down to eat.

'No wonder you said that you were exhausted and depressed. I have seen a film of the battle made on the spot. It didn't make for pleasant viewing: men entangled in barbed wire, men shot down, wounded men carried back and their faces contorted with agony. And the dead bodies lying out in the mud. All those who talk about military glory should see it. It would soon disabuse them of their ideas. And you can be sure that it won't be shown publicly.'

'So what is, er… David's plan?'

'The generals want to keep a hold on what little ground we have gained, and continue to wear the Germans out. Have a push in another sector next year. David is finding his feet in his new role at the moment, but he thinks that unless there is a change right at the top things will continue to drift.'

'Do you mean Asquith?'

'Yes. He must go.'

'Will there be an election?'

'Not in the middle of a war. It is not a party issue, just a change of personnel. And anyway, we could not vote.'

'True. If I were to vote I'd choose a party that promoted peace and banned war. Idealistic. But I have seen too much of war at first hand.'

'Have some more wine.'

'Just a little, otherwise I will fall sleep.'

When they had finished eating, Beth asked if she could smoke a cigarette.

'Yes, do, and you can give me one.'

They puffed away. Then Frances asked about Beth's German friend.

'It's sad that you haven't been in contact since 1914. Have you met someone else?'

'No, and I am glad of it. He would only go out and get himself killed. There will be plenty of widows when it is over.'

Beth told her about Battle of Loos and her brother's wound.

'And he was helped back to the British lines by Stefan, who is a chaplain with the Oldenburg regiment.'

'Your friend?'

'Yes. And he sent me a loving letter which he tucked into James's jacket. What distresses me is that I cannot reply. I have so much to say to him. Absence does make the heart grow fonder.'

Frances was silent. She got up and cleared away the plates.

'Give me another cigarette. Thanks.'

'Maybe,' she said, 'just maybe, I can help. There are ways and means. Although we are at war with Germany, there is a very discreet channel of communication open to the Chancellor's office. David has met Bethmann Hollweg and they exchanged messages before the war. I can't say more than that. If you were to write a letter to your friend I could have it sent. Can you write in German?'

'Yes.'

'That will make it less suspicious. You will not get a reply by the same channel, and you will never know until this is all over if it was ever received, and perhaps not even then. And the letter will be opened and read, so confine yourself to personal matters.'

'Well, thank you, thank you very much. But I don't want to get you into trouble.'

'I will have to get David's blessing and he will tell me directly if it is impossible. In which case I will send it back to you.'

For the rest of the afternoon they chatted, Frances telling some amusing stories of Westminster politicians.

'Do keep all this to yourself but, surrounded as I am by men all the time, it is fun to share their follies and foibles with another woman. I also keep a diary. David knows I write one. It is an account of our personal as well as working relationship; it also serves as an aide-mémoire. Maybe one day I will write a personal history of our times.'

'Is it frank?'

'No point if it wasn't.'

It was time for Beth to go, as Frances had to check a speech to be made by David. Beth thanked her for her hospitality.

'It has been a pleasure to see you again,' said Frances. 'As for your letter, don't tell anyone about it. Send it to me here and I hope I can do something with it.'

Back at home, Beth devoted much thought to the letter and then translated the final draft into German. She wanted it to be idiomatically correct. She put Stefan's name and home address on the envelope and put it inside a bigger envelope, which she posted to Frances.

She didn't hear anything for three weeks. But then a card came from Frances, just a postcard with a picture of a pigeon, on which she had put an exclamation mark.

Chapter Twenty

❄

Stefan stayed with his brother for three months after his return from the Front. He occupied himself by starting a project that he had had in mind for some time, a study of the book of Isaiah. Access to libraries was limited because of the war, but he was able to correspond with former colleagues at Heidelburg. He felt guilty that he was not contributing to the household, but Hannah told him not to be silly.

'The best thing that you can do,' she said, 'is to help with the children. Our younger maid has left us to work in a factory, where she will be paid better. I don't blame her. And have a drink with Dietrich of an evening. The factory is having problems with supply of raw materials and the goverment is pressing for greater production. He needs someone to let off steam to. He doesn't want to burden me with his worries, so he becomes moody and reserved.'

'I'll do what I can both ways.'

He helped the children with their homework. When Hannah was busy he walked them to school and back. At night he heard their prayers. When Heinz and Annelore were confined to bed with chickenpox he sat with them, reading stories and playing card games.

One day Dietrich returned from the factory is a particularly bad mood. Supper was a silent meal. Hannah cleared away and left the men to it. Dietrich produced cigars and a bottle of brandy.

'I have been keeping these for happier times, but I need a restorative. And a sleeping draught. Otherwise I will lie awake worrying.'

He poured glasses and lit their cigars.

'Right. This is my latest problem. Since the summer, quite a few of my men have been conscripted for the Army, though I have been able to hold onto my managers and foremen. My men are well paid by comparison with other workers, because of war production, and they are given an extra food allowance for heavy work. To fill the vacancies I now employ women – our former maid works as a machinist – but they are not given the ration supplement given to the men for the same work. I have had to deal with numerous complaints. I am accused of discriminating against female workers, and I have to explain that I am at the mercy of government regulations. When the women threatened to walk out, I was faced with a dilemma. I now need female labour to fulfil my contracts with the government. So I suggested to the union that I would set up a women only canteen, providing cheap meals. The food comes from local suppliers to whom I pay cash. Which is illegal. Now the men are demanding access to the canteen. In the past I could invoke a spirit of patriotism, but now it's every person for themselves. Ordinary workers are suffering, I know. Just ask Hannah. It is becoming more and more difficult to feed families adequately.'

'And is the problem the Allied blockade?'

'In part, but not totally. I have been looking at some figures. If they are right, we had to import a lot of stuff anyway before the war, but since then we are reliant on our own resources. We can still import foodstuffs from Romania, when the Habsburgs let us.'

'But I have not noticed you personally going short, if I may say so.'

'True, but we have not had a holiday since the start of the war, not even to the coast. We do not entertain as we used to do. Hannah is very long-suffering; she has not bought a new outfit since 1913. Same with my suits. These are small sacrifices in the grand scheme of things. But we don't know what is round the corner and we are trying not to be extravagant. You have been away quite a lot recently, but have you noticed how much prices have risen all round? We have had inflation before but this time I see no end to it. I wonder what sort of world Heinz and Annelore will grow up in.'

With that, Dietrich announced that he had to go to his study. Stefan was left to his thoughts. He was beginning to feel trapped in his brother's house, grateful though he was for their hospitality. Therefore it was with a certain relief that he received a letter from the Bishop, inviting him to St Martin's Church in Bremen, whose incumbent had died suddenly. This was a brick building beside the Weser, dating from the thirteenth century. Not only was it in need of constant maintenance, which was not forthcoming in wartime, but also the congregation was elderly and dwindling. Whenever rain threatened, buckets were put out in the nave. Stefan lived in the pastor's apartment, which was cold and draughty; the windows did not shut properly.

He spent a lot of time preparing services and sermons. In one of his early sermons he spoke about his researches into Isaiah, which led to a consideration of the nature of scriptural authority. After fifteen minutes he saw that his congregation was either asleep or their eyes were glazed over. The following Sunday he spoke about good works, and care for one's neighbour. These were 'the fruits of faith'; Christ, he declared, had come to serve, not to be served. In difficult times, there was a tendency to put oneself first and disregard the needs of others; think of the Good Samaritan. He sought the advice of a senior layman, a parish warden. He explained that he had been away at the Front for most of the war, and only now was coming to understand the predicament of ordinary people. By training he was a Biblical scholar, and had done little parish work. How best should he minister to his flock?

'Because our church has long been associated with the civil authority, it is blamed for all the faults of the administration. We had a full congregation at the start of the war; everyone was very patriotic and prayed for our boys at the Front. But when the breakthrough did not come and it became a war of attrition and food became scarce and therefore expensive, we lost many members, not only us, but most other churches as well. Families no longer come and people have stopped giving money for alms.

We are not well endowed despite being the oldest church in Bremen, and so we rely on the diminishing goodwill of a declining congregation.'

'What do you suggest I do? I have had little support or advice from the Bishop.'

'Well, get out and about. Make pastoral visits. Our previous incumbent didn't bother since he had a full church. I may be doing him a disservice but I had the feeling that latterly he had given up. It might have been his illness. Anyway, there were few to mourn him at his burial service.'

Stefan embarked on a round of parish visiting, including those who had given up attending church. At first there was hostility, but when people learned that he had been a military chaplain and had lived alongside soldiers in the trenches he was received more warmly. Admitting to his own inexperience, he did not offer advice, but just listened. At the end of a visit, he gave a blessing, which seemed to give comfort to most. Where there was a particular hardship, he made a note and raised the matter with the city council, so that he was often seen around the Rathaus. Most of his appeals fell on deaf ears, but once or twice he convinced the authorities to grant an exemption or increase an allowance.

In the summer of 1916, bread riots in Hamburg provoked similar disturbances in Bremen. The autumn was cold and wet and the potato crop was severely reduced by a fungus. The government forced farmers to provide turnips instead; turnips were winter feed for cattle and pigs. As a result, animals as well as humans lost weight. Meat was in short supply. Milk was diluted. Agricultural labourers were conscripted into the Army and some farms were abandoned, or worked by women and men over sixty years of age. Prisoners of war were drafted onto farms, but they were suspected of sabotage and often absconded. The winter of 1916-17 was bitterly cold and coal supplies fell short. People succumbed to tuberculosis, pneumonia and lung diseases. The 'Turnip Winter' was long remembered.

From a military point of view, the revolutions in Russia during the autumn of 1917, culminating in the collapse of Russian armies, enabled the transfer of divisions to the Western Front. Preparations were made for a new offensive in the late spring of 1918. However, the Revolution inspired more civil unrest in Germany. In Bremen and other cities, there were widespread strikes, led by those who wanted to bring down the government of the Reich. The workers in Dietrich's factory were reluctant to strike; in view of increasing military expenditure and increased profits that would result, he had given them a pay rise. Neverthless they came out in sympathy, but only for two days. Pay rises were always welcome, but they were soon swallowed up by the rising cost of food. Even with money in their purses, women had to queue long hours for limited supplies. The habit grew of buying whatever became available, even it was not needed immediately. There were many complaints, justified or not, of profiteering by farmers and shopkeepers; they were accused of creating an artificial shortage by hoarding supplies to obtain a better price. There was a universal suspicion that you could obtain plentiful food if you had money and knew the right people. It was natural that people should put the needs of their own families first; Stefan's exhortations to love one's neighbour had little effect. He tried to live within the official calorie limit, but by the end of a day he was sapped of energy and found it hard to concentrate. When Hannah visited him she was shocked by his appearance and insisted on his coming to spend a few days with them. After much deliberation and with guilty feelings he accepted.

While he was there a letter arrived with an official postmark. He opened it with trepidation, thinking it might be a notice of conscription. It was a letter from Beth, headed by official stamps, certifying that it was a legitimate communication and not subject to censorship. Her letter was dated nine months previously.

My dearest Stefan,
If this ever reaches you, it will be a little miracle, for which I give thanks. I am at home again, after months in

France. I have been given a long leave, though whether I return to nursing duties this coming winter is another matter. I am very weary. My father is not in the best of health, though he won't admit it. My brother despite the loss of an arm, is back in uniform, working in London. He is in good heart, since he is now courting a girl. By a coincidence, she is the daughter of the lady I attended as a companion before the war. I didn't really know her then, but now I approve of his choice, and I hope he pops the question in due course.

You will be surprised to hear that I went on a short retreat last summer. It was balm to my soul. I am saying my prayers, though I wouldn't yet describe myself as a full-fledged believer. See, I am following your advice.

Wherever you are and whatever you are doing, you are never far from my thoughts. I hope you and your family are safe and well. I can't say more, but only pray that at some time we can be together again.

Ever yours,

Love,

Beth

Stefan read this letter three times, conjuring up in his mind recollections of their last time together. July 1914 seemed a lifetime away. But memories, he reflected, could only sustain one so far. He had a mission to fulfil, a mission that was proving more and more difficult through shortages and civil unrest. He preached to his congregation, married them, baptised them and buried them, but he could not feed them nor protect them from violence on the streets; such spiritual comfort he tried to give them fell on deaf ears. As time went on he felt more and more helpless. He began to have serious doubts about his pastoral skills. And if he lacked confidence, how could his flock have confidence in him? And although he had always regarded himself as reasonably self-sufficient, he felt increasingly lonely. He could not find solace in his study of Isaiah; academic work now seemed dry and irrelevant. The proper Christian response to his troubles was to look upon them as a test of his faith and to pray for inner strength. Hadn't St Paul taught that one should rejoice in suffering, to share the suffering of Christ upon the Cross? But he was not St Paul but a very much weaker vessel. He spent more time in prayer, adding to his list those of his congregation who were in especial need, and the number grew.

One evening, when he had had a particularly busy but fruitless day, he was kneeling at his prie-dieu trying to find the words for his intercessions. His mind went blank and the words would not come. He reproved himself for weakness, but to no avail. Shaking his head he got up, lay on his bed and fell fast asleep.

He awoke twelve hours later. He got up and made a cup of coffee. He was physically refreshed and he noticed another change in himself. Instead of repeating his morning prayers, he just said to himself 'Here am I, Lord. Do with me what you will.' He had another cup of coffee and lit a cigarette. He looked out of the window. The sun was shining, though frost glinted on the pavements. He put on his boots and a coat, and was about to go for a walk along the river, when the telephone rang. It was the Bishop; he didn't go in for civilities.

'Haase, leave what you are doing and come and see me at once.'

Stefan for once did not feel intimidated by the peremptory demand. He simply replied 'Will do,' and put the phone down.

He deliberately took a long way round to the Bishop's office, enjoying the sunshine and the fresh air. When he arrived he was shown immediately into the presence.

'Ah, there you are. Sit down and listen.'

Stefan couldn't help smiling to himself; the bishop was just like his old schoolmaster.

'Right. Something has come up. There has been a communication from the Swiss Government. Their embassy in London handles matters relating to our prisoners and internees over there. They are requesting a pastor for the Lutheran congregation, in-

terned at a camp which is called...' he looked at the paper, '...
the Alexandra Palace. It is in London. Our government has
agreed that we should send somebody, and the English, it is felt,
are likely to give their approval.'

Stefan's mind whirled. The Bishop went on.

'I know that you have been finding things difficult at St Martin's, difficulties, I may say, which are shared by all pastors.
However, I think that for many reasons, not least your familiarity
with the English, you are the person I shall recommend. Of
course it has to have approval at the highest level, but first I must
ask you if you would consider yourself for the post. In case you
are wondering, your salary would continue to be paid over here.
I don't know what conditions are like at the Alexandra Palace.
You would be an internee until the war ends, one way or another.
What do you say?'

Without hesitation, Stefan said that he would like his name to
go forward.

* * *

Two months later, with a laissez-passer from the Swiss government, he crossed the North Sea on a neutral Danish vessel and
arrived in London. He was met by a representative of the Diocese of London and three policemen. After the formalities of im-
migration, with his two suitcases he was hustled into a black van
and driven to the Alexandra Palace. At the gate, one of the policemen said:

'Here you are, Reverend. The Ally Pally is your home now for
the duration.'

Stefan looked up the slope at the massive building of ornate
design on top of the hill. It was surrounded by a park, with a
lake. The perimeter of the grounds was marked by a barbed wire
fence with wooden watchtowers. On a flat area a game of football was in progress. He could see people, either alone or in company, walking round inside the fence. Others were engaged in
physical exercises led by an instructor.

He was taken into an office by the gate. His particulars were recorded and his luggage was searched. Nothing amiss was discovered. And so, accompanied by an armed soldier, he went up the hill to the main entrance of the building. At one side was a small suite of offices marked 'Camp Commandant'.

He was ushered inside and told to wait, so he sat down on a bench and was eyed with curiosity by the ladies at their typewriters. One of them asked if he would like a cup of tea.

'Yes, please, if you would be so kind.'

Tea was brought, with a biscuit on the saucer.

'Thank you. I am hungry.'

An hour later, he was summoned to the Camp Commandant himself, Major Baring. He told Stefan to sit down. Then he looked at some papers.

'Tell me about yourself.'

Stefan did so, and Baring listened without interrupting. Then he said that they must have been in the same sector at the same time.

'I was at Loos when I was shot in the chest. They patched me up after a fashion but that was the end of active fighting for me.'

'I understand, sir, that all the people here are civilians.'

'Yes, but they are subject to military regulations. But obviously they have rather more freedoms that soldiers would have. For example they can receive parcels and letters, which are censored. We allow them the freedom of the grounds.'

'Do any try to escape?'

'Some have tried, but they were soon recaptured. They were treated to a spell in a proper prison, where conditions are much tougher. Likewise if they have misbehaved seriously or have committed some crime. As you probably know, there were thousands of Germans over here working before the war, and many of them stayed. But anti-German feeling grew, and they were abused in the street and their businesses vandalised. So it was partly for their own protection that they were interned.'

'Are there families?'

'Yes. There is a nursery and a school set up for the internees' children, and most of their activities are organised by themselves. There are two doctors. We supply the food and they cook it.'

'Has there been a pastor before?'

'Not as such. There are quite a few Romans, and a priest comes once a week. The Diocese of London sends us a priest from time to time, but not on a regular basis. Therefore they have petitioned us for a Lutheran pastor... and here you are.'

'Is there a leader, or committee which acts on their behalf?'

'Indeed.' He looked at his watch.

'They should be waiting for you outside. I have a word of advice for you. This is like a little town and it has its own politics and disputes. Be a shepherd of souls and steer clear of politics.'

Stefan nodded.

'We will not talk again,' he went on, 'unless it is really necessary, because you must not be seen to be too close to the camp authorities. Work through the committee.'

Stefan was so busy in the next few days finding his feet that he had no time for reflection. The committee was helpful, up to a point, but his most useful contact was Father Peters, the Catholic priest. With him he worked out a schedule for conducting services in the hall set aside as a chapel. Peters told him how to obtain candles and the elements for Communion, and on his visits brought in a newspaper.

'This will help you to be up to date with things, even if from your point of view the news will be onesided.'

'What is morale like, Father? I have been made welcome but without much enthusiasm.'

'My German is limited, Stefan, but fortunately most of them speak English. Looking out from the top of the hill they can often see places where they lived and worked, and it is very frustrating. Some of them have been in England for twenty years. Consequently they are depressed and apathetic. Over the last year I have noticed that the community spirit, which used to be strong, has faded. There used to be societies, lectures, concerts and shows, which we encouraged, but these have fallen by the wayside. People still take exercise, it's true. You've seen games of football and the walkers and runners. But when you have been round the same circuit every day for three years, it's hardly surprising that motivation is poor.'

'I can see that,' said Stefan. 'But they will not know that the rations they are getting here are considerably more substantial than people are getting at home, and I suppose they don't have to pay. Back home, food is more and more expensive, and the effect on people's health is marked. Tuberculosis is increasing and pneumonia is not just an old man's disease. Parents starve themselves to feed their children. And there is a lot of civil unrest.'

'All the people here want is the war to end as soon as possible. News is filtering through to them that Ludendorff's Big Push, after initial success, has run out of steam. There seems little point in carrying on fighting.'

'I agree totally, Father. I thought the war was folly to start with, and I have the melancholy satisfaction of having been proved right.'

'But you were a military chaplain.'

'A pastor has to go where the sheep are. I have done my share of route marches and digging, but I have never carried a rifle.'

Father Peters always made time during his visits to have a few words with Stefan. They both agreed that tensions within the camp were growing. There were fights among the men over trivial things. Escape attempts were becoming more frequent, which always ended up in the cells. An attempted rape had been reported. And there had been several serious cases of influenza, three of which had ended in death. As the summer approached, when sunshine and warmth might have improved health and morale, more and more people were getting ill, not just a day in bed but prostration. Peters told Stefan that the same was occuring outside the camp. The medical authorities were alarmed by the outbreak.

Stefan was grateful for their conversations and, feeling that he could trust Peters, asked him to take a letter out for him, past the authorities, and post it.

'Of course. Let me have it on my next visit; it will be dispatched instanter. And I will treat you to a stamp.'

Three weeks later, Stefan received a reply. Beth's letter had been sent inside another envelope addressed to Father Peters. Stefan opened it with trepidation.

My dearest Stefan,

To think we are within only a few miles of each other! So near and yet so far. And you got my letter! It helps to have friends in high places. One day I will explain it to you.

After my spells in France, I have been nursing at a rehabilitation centre for wounded officers. It is in a country mansion not far from home and is set in beautiful grounds. I walk or wheel the patients along the paths and chat to them. There are some pretty gruesome injuries which have to be dressed but the whole atmosphere is much more relaxed than in France. Those who make it to us are not likely to die in agony within hours!

The other blessing of the place is that I can get over to see Father fairly frequently. He is soldiering on but feeling his age more and more. But so long as he is busy, I am happy with that. The other news is that James is engaged to be married, to a girl he met at the National Gallery. She is younger than him by a year or two. No date has been set. James works at the War Office and seems content there. He is getting quite adept at living with one arm. His current ambition, apart from marrying Beatrice (she is lovely, by the way), is to play cricket again. He is practicing his batting, only with a left-hander's stance. Father has been throwing balls at him.

So far, we have not had a case here of the terrible 'flu that seems to be going round. In a closed community like the camp, it could run riot. Please take care. I want you in good health when we meet.

There are reports here of starvation in Germany and civil unrest. I hope your family is safe. And they say that the Army is disintegrating. I just wish that the whole thing can be over before more lives are lost.

Write when you can,

Ever yours,

Love,

Beth

Not long after Beth's letter, Stefan received another, from Hannah. It had been stamped by the censor and the Swiss Post Office.

...Things are very bad here. It looks as though the factory will have to close as government contracts are drying up. Dietrich has been trying desperately to find other markets so that he can keep his people in work, but everything is falling apart. He is getting very depressed and drinking too much.

My chief worry, though, is for the children. They have both had the 'flu but have been very slow to recover. I try to feed them up, but good food is hard to get. They have both lost weight and their spark has gone. One of the boys in Heinz's class died, but he did have asthma as well.

You probably won't be able to write, but pray for us...

Chapter Twenty-One

✳

The war came to an end at eleven o'clock on November 11th, 1918. The Kaiser had abdicated two days earlier and a republic was proclaimed. Soldiers were demobilised or just dispersed anyway, eager to return to their homes. In the ensuing weeks, there were attempts to establish a constitution after the manner of the Russian Revolution the previous year. Street battles were fought in Berlin, Munich and other cities between those who wanted soviet-style workers' councils and those, especially the Social Democratic Party, who wanted to resume parliamentary government. A new National Assembly was elected on January 19th, 1919; women voted for the first time. Because of the unrest in the capital, the Assembly met in Weimar.

Dietrich Haase struggled to keep his factory going. The workforce was keen but there was little for them to do. During the war, and for some years before that, production had been devoted to the military and it was a battle to find new markets. As military contracts came to an end, Dietrich had to lay off workers, especially women, since former male employees, back from the war and encouraged by their unions, were demanding their old jobs. Eventually, in spite of intense competition he negotiated a contract with the railways, but only by cutting his margins to the minimum. Thus the factory stayed open and its workers were paid.

There were troubles at home, as well. The children had recovered from influenza but they went through the gamut of childhood illnesses. Hannah fed them as well as she could in the current shortages and she did not refuse food to beggars who came to the house, though the amount she could give them was small. It was hoped that with the Armistice the British would stop the blockade of German ports, but it did not end till the summer of 1919. It was estimated that a quarter of a million died of disease or starvation in the interim.

* * *

The internees were buoyed up by the hope that with the announcement of the Armistice they could return to their homes or Germany. But that did not come for nearly another year. Whereas during hostilities being interned was seen as an inevitable misfortune, now that the war was over there was bitter resentment at their continued confinement. Some people went on a hunger strike in protest; others marched round the perimeter holding up placards and shouting to passers-by outside. There was also the complaint that insufficient medical treatment was being provided in the face of the epidemic of influenza. Stefan felt he could no longer stand aside from the protests, as he had been urged to do by the Camp Commandant, and joined a deputation to the camp authorities. Their response, repeated several times, was that there was still only an armistice, not a peace treaty, despite the obvious fact that Germany was in no fit state to resume hostilities. Then it was asserted that there was still much antipathy among the British public towards them. Finally, the Camp Commandant declared that he had no authority to release the internees, though he would be glad to do so; it was a matter for Parliament. At which point Stefan asked if he could write to the local MP. This was refused pointblank, but Stefan sent a letter via Father Peters. There was no direct reply to his letter, but Peters later told him that their case had been raised in Parliament. The Home Office minister had promised to look into the matter, not just the internees in the Alexandra Palace, but in other camps round the country; there was a large contingent on the Isle of Man.

During a visit by Father Peters, Stefan discussed the idea of reviving a Lutheran congregation in London. Peters raised the matter with the Anglican Diocese of London, but initially there was a chilly response. However, Stefan received an unexpected visit a few weeks later from the Revd Michael Honeyman, one of the Bishop's chaplains, who had also served on the Western Front.

There was a church, St George's in Whitehapel, built in 1762, which had had a congregation of over a hundred. In 1915, the congregation was interned and it was shut up; the key was in the hands of the local council. Honeyman reported that although there was superficial vandalism on the exterior, the lower windows were securely boarded up and as far as he could see the roof was intact. He had no information about the church's endowment; presumably the funds had been sequestered on the outbreak of war. Stefan asked permission to write to the Lutheran Church authorities at home. Their reply took two months to reach him. However, it stated that negotiations had started with the Home Office in England. There had not been an outright refusal, but nothing could be done until internment came to an end.

* * *

Way back in February 1918, Beth had received a note from Frances. It read: 'We've won! Well, almost. Look at the papers tomorrow. David is very pleased and says that it should have happened long ago.'

Beth bought a selection of the morning press. The headlines announced that the Representation of the People Act had received the Royal Assent. It enacted that all men over the age of twenty-one were entitled to vote, and certain categories of women over the age of thirty. (Parity with men would not come for another ten years.) The leaders maintained that lowering the age for men was an acknowledgement of the service of millions in the war, many of whom were young men. The female vote rewarded the work of women who had taken the place of men in the factories. The lobbying and campaigning of Millicent Fawcett had succeeded where the antics of the Pankhursts had only aroused hostility.

Beth replied to Frances: 'Excellent news! All that effort has been worth it. I will have to wait two years till I am eligible. I promise I will use my vote wisely and in the best interests of the country, as I am sure our sisters will.'

Beth continued to enjoy her work among the wounded officers. She didn't mind teasing them with gentle flirtation, which raised their spirits. One day, a lieutenant in a wheelchair tried to stroke her bottom. She was shocked but responded at once with mock severity: 'Tut tut, Mr Gilmour. Behave yourself.' He apologised.

She knew that as a result of his injuries he would be impotent.

Wandering hands were one thing, but of much greater concern to her was her father's health. Over the winter of 1918 he had ceased to go up to town and he was losing weight. He had always been well turned out, even when sitting in the garden. Now he never wore a tie, his shirts were scruffy and he didn't take much care shaving; he spent much time staring vacantly. Beth's efforts to engage him in conversation were rebuffed with a show of temper. When James came to see him, he asked loudly 'Who are you? What are you doing in my house?'

James was very upset; he had intended to tell his father about his engagement, but wisely reckoned that would confuse him the more.

Mrs Wilson asked to have a word with Beth. 'I'm sorry, Miss Elizabeth,' she said, 'but I cannot look after the house and Mr Millward as well. What he needs is a nurse. I'm sorry to have to say it but he is ill in his mind. And he is not eating or drinking much; he has always had a healthy appetite. If you were to hire a nurse, I am happy to continue as housekeeper.'

Beth thanked her for her frankness. She said that she would resign at once from her own nursing nursing duties and live at home.

Within weeks, Mr Millward declined markedly. He refused to get out of bed, he was eating almost nothing and the carafe of water beside him was untouched. If he spoke it was in a whisper. At night Beth could hear him whimpering. Beth called a doctor, who listened carefully to Beth's description of the symptoms. He spent a long time examining Mr Millward. When he came downstairs Beth was waiting anxiously.

'Miss Millward, you have seen some terrible things in the war, but this is different. Clearly he is in the grip of senility. This can afflict anyone; it doesn't matter whether you are rich or poor, or a university professor or a labourer. You described to me the symptoms of a classic case. But that is not what is killing him – I'm sorry to be brutal – but I suspect that he has cancer, a particularly nasty type, cancer of the stomach. There is nothing we can do. An operation is out of the question. All I can do is to prescribe palliative drugs. I can recommend a specialist, but I think he would come up with the same diagnosis.'

'Is he in much pain?'

'Difficult to tell. In a way his dementia is a help. He cannot remember anything beyond a few minutes.'

'He doesn't recognise me any more.'

'I know, and it is very sad. As for the pain, I can prescribe him morphine – you know all about that – and you can treat him with it.'

'Is there any chance, however small, of him getting better?'

'Absolutely none, I'm afraid. But stick to the dose that I prescribe. There is a temptation to hasten the end, but resist it. Let Nature take its course.'

Two days later a messenger from the surgery arrived with the drugs. Beth had difficulty at first in persuading her father to submit to her ministrations, but in the end he accepted that they would ease his pain, which was now constant. Beth recorded the exact amount she administered. By now Mr Millward was slipping in and out of consciousness. She called James and told him that the end was near. James came over at once. He had not seen his father for a while and he was shocked by his gaunt appearance.

'It's eating him up inside,' said Beth.

'Can't we do something about it, you know, er... hurry things on a bit? You must have done it in France.'

'Never on my own initiative.'

'I see. Well, let's hope he doesn't last long.'

Together they sat with him. Beth nodded off but awoke with a start. 'I am so tired. It's like being back in the casualty clearing station.'

'Go and lie down properly. I will stay with him.'

Mr Millward suddenly stopped his rasping breathing. In alarm, James called Beth, but by the time she came he had started breathing again.

'I'm sorry. Thought he was dead.'

'No. It's not uncommon. Just count the intervals of silence and let me know if he doesn't start again. He is deeply unconscious. This could go on for some time.' She went back to her bedroom.

All through that evening James counted. While the breathing was regular, his thoughts wandered. Sometimes he prayed for his father's soul, not through any real conviction but because that was what one was supposed to do at such a time. At other times, he recalled the respect he had had for his father, and occasionally fear of him. It was hard to connect the past with this wasted figure in the bed. He wondered whether he ought to call the vicar. It was too late at night.

Sometime after midnight Mr Millward gave a loud rasping breath. James's attention had wandered, but he started to count. The breathing did not begin again. James decided to wait another ten minutes. Then he got up and called Beth.

'I think he has gone.'

Beth felt for the pulse and placed a mirror over his mouth. There was no response.

'What do we do now?' asked James.

* * *

The funeral and legal business over, for the first time in what seemed like ages Beth sat down to write to Stefan.

My dear Stefan,

I am afraid I have been very neglectful of you. These last few months have been difficult. My father fell ill over the winter and died two months ago. His funeral was well attended by friends and former colleagues. He is buried beside Mother; we assumed that would be his wish. The good news is that James and Beatrice have named a day for their wedding, at the end of October. James has bought a house in Ealing, which means she can continue her work at the National Gallery if she so wishes. James is still in uniform, though how long he will stay in the Army is uncertain. I gave up my VAD work when Father became ill and I have been at home ever since. And now we have the vote, though there is more to do, I have finished with the Suffragists.

I hope you will understand why I have not been in touch. What about you? I hear that you are still in durance vile. Why, oh, why? The war has been over for months and a peace treaty is in the offing. And your family in Germany? They must be having a terrible time. Ordinary people must suffer for the follies of politicians.

Is it at all possible that you can have visitors and even a leave out? I so want to see you again. It's been just over five years. There is so much to say which I can't put into a letter. If you don't feel the same about me now, please say so directly.

Hope to hear from you soon,

Love,

Beth

While waiting for a reply, Beth busied herelf with preparations for James's wedding. She had tea with Beatrice's mother, Lady Valentine, and they reminisced about their travels together.

'But, Beth,' said Lady Valentine, 'what has happened to you since those days? I know the world has changed for ever. So how have you fared in this great upheaval?'

'Where do I begin? Oh, well, Oxford, Suffragists, Nursing – so much to say, but those are the headlines.'

'I'm sure. Beth, you must be nearly thirty. Did you lose someone in the war, like so many others? You were, and are, a very personable girl. '

'Yes... and no.'

'What do you mean?'

'There is a man I love deeply - the only one – but he is unavailable at the moment.'

'Why is that?' Lady Valentine sensed her hesitation. 'I'm sorry, I shouldn't have asked.'

'Nothing immoral, I can assure you. It's... it's that he is German.'

'Oh'.

'Ask James about him. Just now he is interned in Alexandra Palace. If only I could see him again soon. We have not been together since 1914.'

Lady Valentine absorbed this information, while she lit a cigarette.

'Hm. Tricky for you.' She took a long drag. 'Don't think that you can take up exactly where you left off. You must rebuild the relationship. I expect you realise this already.'

'I long to see him, but I am dreading it. What will he think of me, with grey hairs beginning to appear?'

'Silver threads among the gold, eh? Happens to us all, my dear, unless you want to improve on Nature. But I shouldn't bother – too much trouble, and the roots will give you away. Just accept the fact that the war has aged us all prematurely. Your mother had a fine head of grey hair, I seem to remember.'

'She did.'

'Look, he will be as nervous as you are. Just be normal. Give him a kiss and take his arm. After that... you will soon find out if you are still suited to each other.'

* * *

Stefan was given permission to leave the camp for an afternoon. He was required to state the purpose of his exeat; he put down 'Church Business'. This was the truth, because he had an appointment with the Revd Honeyman, who explained to him how to obtain access to St George's, now that internment was due to end in a few weeks. But also, arranged through Father Peters, he had a tryst with Beth. They were to meet at a café at Highgate Wood, half an hour's walk and out of sight of the camp. Beth arrived early, but was so apprehensive that she could not sit down at a table but walked up and down keeping the café in sight. She kept looking at her watch; time seemed to slow down. Five minutes after the appointed time she turned round at the end of a leg to find him twenty yards away; he had not called out to her.

She took off her hat and he did the same. At a glance Beth noticed how shabby his clothes were; he had lost weight and they hung loose on him. He smiled and came towards her slowly, as if feasting his eyes on her. She waited, not daring to breathe. She could not think of anything to say.

He took her hands and kissed them.

'Here I am, Beth. The same old Stefan, but a bit frayed at the edges.'

She stroked his hair.

'Frayed or not…'

She did not complete the sentence but embraced and kissed him.

They did not go to the café.

'Let's walk,' she said and took his arm. 'In that way I can hold onto you in public without frightening the horses.'

Stefan did not want to describe internment, 'It is boring and soul-destroying', but he did tell her about the possibility of re-opening the Lutheran Church in Whitechapel.

'I haven't seen it yet, but I am told that the interior is very fine. Many of my congregation in the camp worshipped there. Not many of them want to go back to Germany. Things are pretty bad there. All their assets are here and they want to carry on their business, if the state will allow them.'

'Does that mean you will stay here?'

'Yes, if the Lutheran Church gives permission. There is no pastor just now and I could take it over for a while.'

Beth digested this information.

'Of course,' Stefan went on, 'all this is still up in the air. Who knows, I might be deported when internment is finished.'

'Please, God, no. I couldn't bear it.'

She had a sudden thought. 'You don't know, but I have friends in high places. How do you think my letter could reach you?'

She told him about her friendship with Frances Stevenson. Then she shook her head. 'A nice idea but in all honesty I couldn't ask. Besides, she is very busy at Versailles just now.'

They walked on in silence. Then he disengaged his arm and put it round her waist.

'Will this frighten the horses?'

In response she put her arm on his shoulder and rested her head against him, which brought a disapproving look from two elderly ladies coming the other way.

'What would those old bags say if they knew you were a priest?'

'Well,' said Stefan, 'a priest is a man and can sin as well as the next. But I do not think our love is sinful. I am not afraid to proclaim it before all the world. I'm sorry. I said "our love". Am I presuming too much?'

'No.'

'If you were to ask me where I would like to be in ten years' time, I would say that having had experience of pastoral work in war and peacetime, I think I could best serve God as an academic, a professor of Theology. That would not prevent me from having a pastoral mission as well, but not just that. I believe God has given me strengths and I will serve him best by using them. As St Paul says, there are many gifts that make up Christian ministry.'

'Where would this be?'

'I am very fond of Heidelberg, my alma mater, but there is Oxford, or even the United States.' He chuckled. 'You could travel the world with me.'

'I have nothing to keep me in England, except sentiment. My

brother is getting married soon and he will not need a big sister any more. It's in two months' time. Will you come?'

'If they let me out in time. I'll have to smarten myself up.'

'I'll see to that. Don't be embarrassed. Between my mother and father, James and I have been left comfortably off.'

Stefan demurred.

'Don't get all masculine on me. From what I read in the papers German finances are in a mess. Your salary in marks will be worthless over here. Swallow your pride. Pride is a sin.'

'Not that sort of pride. If you like I could tell you why.'

'Dear Stefan, this is not the time for a lecture.'

'I am teasing. I will look smart at James's wedding, with your help.'

They took another circuit of the park.

'Assuming that when you are released you are not deported, where will you live? There is always a place for you with us. It will be a lot easier for you than some squalid lodging in Whitechapel.'

'Er...'

'My housekeeper will be a chaperone if it worries you. It doesn't worry me. Besides you will be busy travelling up and down to Whitechapel and I will be busy getting James to the altar. It will be nice for you and James to get to know each again.'

'The last time I saw him was in no man's land. But never mind propriety. I am worried about money. Such savings I have in Germany will be worthless.'

'Surely the church will pay you in sterling.'

'I am paid what they call a retainer while in I am in the camp, but it is not much more than pocket money. I have been trying to save as much as I can. It may take time for the authorities to release the church's assets; we might have to prove that we will be a viable congregation. But we can't be a viable congregation until we have a church. It is a chicken and egg situation. There is a house for a pastor but I have no idea what sort of state it is in. Beth, do you have a magic wand? Just wave it for me and all will come right.'

Stefan looked at his watch.

'I had better be getting back. I have a sort of curfew. Will you walk with me?'

They stopped just round the corner from the gate.

'Can I see you again soon?' she asked.

'I am hoping to visit the church with Mr Honeyman next Thursday. Will you come too?'

'You won't be able to keep me away.'

They kissed. Beth headed off for a bus stop. Stefan walked slowly through the gate and asked to see the Camp Commandant.

The next afternoon, with the camp committee beside him, he spoke at a general meeting of the internees:

In the last days all sorts of rumours have been going around. I have just heard from Germany that your church, the *Georgkirche*, is to be reopened. I have been asked to be the pastor. I gladly accepted the post, and I hope that I will meet with your approval. I have been given permission from the Camp Commandant to be away from the camp during the day, to make the necessary arrangements. I hope that those of you who were regular members will help me.

The Camp Commandant tells me that the Camp will close in two weeks time. Those who have homes to go to can start leaving tomorrow. (Cheers) There is a certain amount of paperwork, as you might expect. I can also announce that each single man will receive £10, and married men £20, to tide you over. (More cheers) It is not over-generous but it is cheaper for the English to give it to you than keeping you confined. It is enough for a passage back to Germany. Don't spend it all at once!

A word of warning. There is no land of milk and honey beyond the barbed wire. It will be hard for you to find work if you want to stay in England, and Germany is no better. But you will be free men. Give thanks to God that you have survived the hardships that the war brought. There will be no closing ceremony. Just go and build a new life. *Gott sei mit euch.*

I promise that I will be the last to leave the camp.

* * *

Stefan, Beth and Mr Honeyman stood at the door of the church in Alie Street while a council official unlocked it.

'No one has been inside since 1915. I have to make a brief report so I will come in with you. You know, this area used to be called Little Germany.'

Stefan hesitated in crossing the threshold.

'Let us pray for a moment. Help us, O Lord, to restore this church, built by faithful hands to thy praise and glory.'

With that he took Beth's hand and led her into the building. Mr Honeymen followed.

At the east end was a huge pulpit with a sounding board above it and an altar below. On each side of the pulpit were the Ten Commandments in German on elaborately carved panels and above it the coat of arms of George III. There were galleries on three sides and on the floor family-sized box pews. The lower windows were still boarded up, and the upper ones covered with netting on the outside. At the west gallery was the organ. The plaster on the walls was undamaged and the polished woodwork gleamed in the sunlight. At the side, hymn and prayers books were neatly stacked. On a notice board by the door there were announcements of forthcoming services, which never took place.

The three of them stood in awe, while the council official poked around taking notes.

'It's a miracle that it has been preserved so well,' said Beth, at last.

'I think you have found a new mission,' said Mr Honeyman.

Stefan did not say anything but walked up to the altar and knelt. When he got up he turned to face Beth. His eyes were full of tears of relief.

Chapter Twenty-Two

✳

True to his word, Stefan was the last to leave the confines of the Alexandra Palace. At the gate he shook hands with the Camp Commandant and piled his luggage into Beth's car. They drove first to Alie Street to confer with the Church Warden, Gunter, who had volunteered to resume the post he had held in 1915. On the door was a notice of a service the following Sunday. Stefan left a bag with his clerical vestments. Round the corner was the Pastor's lodgings. The Warden had the key.

'I had a look the other day,' he said, speaking in German. 'It will need some repairs and redecoration before you can move in. We will do the work for you.'

'Was the previous pastor married?' Beth asked, also in German.

'He was, but his wife died well before the war, and he didn't look after it.'

Beth led the way in and made a rapid survey of the premises.

'Hm. We can make something of the house, though the garden will need a complete restoration. It looks as though the neighbours used it as a rubbish dump.'

The Warden looked at Stefan with a raised eyebrow.

'Will *Fraulein* Millward be helping you with the house?'

'Yes, I will be. Stefan will be much too busy with his pastoral duties.'

'That's right. Rebuilding the congregation will take a lot of time. And I will have to reassure the neighbours and local businesses that we are not the enemy. You and I, Gunter, will have to work together. And Miss Millward will be able to help us with that. We er... we hope to be married soon.'

'I am sure she will be a great asset,' said Gunter. 'And you speak good German, *Fraulein*.'

Stefan and Beth returned to the car.

'I hope I didn't jump the gun, Beth, about marriage. I had to explain your presence with me.'

'Well, if that was a proposal, it was an unusual one. But it will do.'

'Do you really mean that?'

'Of course. Otherwise the last few years will have been wasted.'

'I expected to have asked your father's permission first to plight my troth, and then to go down on one knee. And I haven't even got a ring for you.'

'Stefan, we have seen too much in life to worry about the lack of a romantic gesture. Yes, I will marry you, and the sooner the better. As for an engagement ring, I will wear one of my mother's, to prove my commitment.'

* * *

'James is coming tonight, and you can have a long chat. He's bringing Beatrice; I have to speak to her about various things. I have asked Mrs Wilson to lay on a spread.'

'After all those meals in captivity, a spread will be welcome.'

'You need building up. And I will raid Father's cellar for some decent wine to mark the occasion.'

'Amen to that as well. I haven't touched alcohol for a long time.'

'We must make plans. I love planning.'

'It will be good to look ahead. These last years have been so monotonous with dull routine, one day just the same as the previous one. And now... the future has come all at once.'

'Same for me.'

'What's the first plan? You are much more practical than I am.'

'First, to get you a decent set of clothes. I will commission James to organise that.'

'Very well. And second?'

'Teach you to drive and buy a car for you. It is a difficult journey from here to Whitechapel by public transport.'

Stefan started to object but she overruled him.

'If you are to do your pastoral work as you want to, you will need a car. I can't always be a taxi service.'

Stefan mulled this over. 'But…'

'Don't talk money just now. We can afford it.'

'All right. But now it is my turn to be practical. Before we go any further, will you be content to be a pastor's wife, wherever his faith takes him, starting with a pokey little house in Whitechapel, even if you do not share his faith?'

Beth was silent, and Stefan was afraid he had upset her.

After a short while she replied: 'You are right to ask me that. It takes me back to our conversation in Scotland long ago. You said that I should open myself to God by praying and being patient. I have followed your advice and it has helped me enormously. I see the years in between as a preparation for what I have to do now. So, my dear, the answer to your question is "Yes", with all my heart.'

She kissed him.

'Have I convinced you?'

'Beth, I have so many reasons to be grateful. I hope I can be worthy of your confidence in me.'

'Just be yourself.'

She was about to expand on this when the bell rang. She went to the door.

James ushered Beatrice in. Beth kissed them both and led them into the sitting room.

'Here's someone from your past, James.'

'Stefan! My dear chap. Last I heard you were under lock and key. Good, very good to see you. Beatrice, the last time I met Stefan I was lying wounded in a German trench. He saved my life.'

'I did my Christian duty. Beatrice, you are to marry a brave man who I am proud to say has long been my friend.'

'Why didn't you tell me about him before?' Beatrice asked.

'Because…' said James, 'because we don't want to relive those days. You know about my nightmares.'

There was silence.

Stefan broke it. 'When we were up in Scotland, James said we should be thankful - I remember your exact words - for a warm day, clear skies, love and friendship. Words of wisdom.'

James laughed. 'You spent the rest of the walk huddled with Beth, and you were conspicuously late.'

'No telling tales out of school,' said Beth. 'Beatrice, let's leave the two boys to it. It will all be boring reminiscence. So by it's time for dinner they will have got the war out of their system.'

Stefan watched in admiration while James filled and lit his pipe.

'I can manage most things, even driving. Have you tried steering with your knees? It can be done. Beatrice has to tie my ties and cut up my food if necessary.'

'She is a lovely girl.'

'And has been very patient with me. I do get frustrated at times, but she tells me not to be an ass.'

'Are you still in the Army?'

'I have one week till civvy street.'

'And then?'

'I will probably end up teaching, but with some reluctance. I don't want any more government service. Fortunately, I have what you might call a financial cushion before I have to make up my mind. We are going to Italy for our honeymoon. Bee thinks my appreciation of Art needs considerable improvement, and she is right.'

'I have never been to Italy. Sometime perhaps.'

'Talking of honeymoons,' James went on, 'there is a little matter of the wedding in three weeks time. Stefan, my friends from the regiment or from school or university are mostly dead. Now you are in England for a bit, as I understand. I regard that as providential. Please, will you be my Best Man?'

Stefan thought about it for a moment. 'Do you trust me not to drop the ring? I will be honoured.'

Stefan went to a box and took out a cigarette.

'I haven't had one for months. Tell me, James, what you were doing in the War Office, unless it is a secret.'

'No, nothing so glamorous. Army appointments. I was in an office full of crocks. Good fellows, all of them. We had all been through the mill. I enjoyed the work on the whole, but it is time to move on. You and I have been in the Front Line, and we can put that behind us. But your country was defeated and is being made to atone. All these war reparations that are being demanded. From what I read, things are tough enough in Gemany as it is.'

'I think the best reparation that can be made is to have an assured peace. President Wilson has a point. I suspect that the desire for vengeance comes from the French, which is understandable, but short-sighted. We have enough to cope with, without paying out vast sums that we struggle to find. I am fearful for the future, especially when I think of my nephew and niece.'

'Will you go back?'

'Not at the moment. I have a new mission here. And I want to go back to academic work in due course.'

Beth and Beatrice came in with a bottle of wine and glasses.

'If I hold the bottle, James, will you pull the cork?'

James obliged.

'Beth,' he said, 'isn't that one of Mother's rings?'

'Yes, it is.'

'And have you noticed, James,' said Beatrice, 'it is on the same finger as my ring?'

'Yes, well... Stefan, have you popped the question?'

'Actually, I did so before the war, by the river in Bremen, but it had to remain unanswered until now.'

James shook his hand.

'Congratulations. And Beth, have a one-armed hug.'

'So when is the great day?' Beatrice asked.

'When we have had you two married we can think about naming the day.'

'Will you be my Best Man, James?'

'An honour likewise. I will carry a spare ring in case I drop it. But… but I won't have to make a speech in German, will I?'

'Absolutely,' said Beth. 'We will teach you the words.'

'Oh dear. I had better start practising now. Look, here we are and there is the bottle. Let us have a toast. To Love and Friendship, Good Health, and especially to Us, who have survived. May we enjoy the blessings of Peace.'

* * *

James and Beatrice were married in Shropshire, from Lord Valentine's country seat. The little church was full, but, as James had indicated, there were not many on the groom's side of the aisle, just Stefan, Beth, two cousins, and a couple of colleagues from the War Office. Stefan did not drop the ring. Before the wedding he had been much exercised about his speech. A first draft Beth said was too solemn.

'I know it is customary for the Best Man to make jokes, even risqué ones. But, as a priest, I would find that difficult.'

'But you must have heard some doubtful jokes in the Army.'

'I know the jokes, but I don't know what would be suitable for this occasion.'

'I have a suggestion.'

'Very apt,' he said when she told him.

Stefan spoke about his meeting with James in Oxford and their growing friendship, cultivated in a certain public house. 'He also was kind enough to introduce me to his sister. We will marry soon, after nearly ten years of courtship. (Cheers) I will not say anything about the meeting James and I had in the trenches, but suffice it to say that he amply deserved his Military Cross.'

James shook his head. There were murmurs of 'What meeting was that?'

'What I can tell you is the courage and determination he has showed in overcoming his terrible injury. And now he can embark on a new challenge, maybe teaching Classics. I am sure he will become a headmaster in due course; he has those qualities of leadership and humanity needed for a demanding job. He is a very lucky man to have Beatrice at his side. As a priest, I give them my blessing, in my own language: *Möge Gott Sie segnen*, which, being loosely translated, means May you have the Wisdom of Solomon, the Patience of Job and the Children of Israel.'

This was greeted with much merriment.

* * *

The re-establishment of the Lutheran congregation was not without difficulties. Local tradesmen were initially unwilling to work for Germans, even for their church. However, some of the former internees who had managed to return to their homes in the neighbourhood lent a hand and the pastor's lodgings were made habitable up to Beth's standards. At the church there was vandalism, mainly daubing of anti-German slogans on the doors and walls, such as 'Hang the Kaiser', which had to be removed. The interior of the church was thoroughly cleaned and the organ retuned after four years of silence. Finding an organ builder took a long time. Eventually, with the help of Mr Honeyman, Stefan discovered someone who, as a young man, had worked on the installation of the organ in 1886. He said he was delighted to come out of retirement to service such a fine instrument.

Apart from conducting services and other pastoral duties, Stefan made a point of going round the area meeting other local clergy, who were generally supportive, and also shopkeepers and tradesmen. Beth came with him when she could. Dressed in his pastoral robes he talked to as many people as would listen and left his calling card. His message was simple. 'The war has changed all our lives. We are trying to make a new start with peace in our hearts.' In this way he got to know every building, even if he was not welcome inside. He learnt a lot about the social problems of the area, poor housing and drainage, ill-health, unemployment, crime and confrontations between communists and their opponents. He could not offer solutions but he could listen, and this earned some recognition and respect.

Until the pastor's lodgings were ready, every day Stefan drove to the church under Beth's supervision. From time to time he camped out there overnight; Gunter's wife made supper for him. When Beth judged that he was sufficiently proficient, she bought an AC 12 ('a bit advanced for you at the moment') and Stefan used the old Wolseley. He had no mechanical aptitude, but a member of the congregation looked after it for him.

The Easter celebration was the first service when the all the surviving congregation was assembled, about fifty people, and some others from the area, out of curiosity. The organ was still under repair, but was playable; the old organ builder obliged. Stefan invited Father Peters and Mr Honeyman. Peters with much regret declined as his Bishop had refused permission. Mr Honeyman administered the chalice. There was no choir, but the congregation sang lustily. The opening hymn was *Nun danket alle Gott*. Stefan used that theme in his sermon. This was the time to give thanks for peace after a terrible time and for the re-birth of the church, as it were a symbol of Christ's Resurrection. Stefan also praised and thanked all those who had devoted so much time and effort to re-establishing the church. Beth thought that he had spoken from the heart with none of the academic overtones of his usual sermons.

* * *

After Easter, Stefan told his congregation that he would be away visiting his family in Germany, but he would be back in good time for Ascension Day. Beth came with him. It was nearly seven years since Beth had met the family and she was unsure of her welcome, especially from the children. Heinz was now fourteen and Annelore twelve. Their response was as it had been before, Annelore all welcoming and confiding, Heinz shy and suspicious. Hannah was now grey, Dietrich's face was lined.

Stefan had told Beth of their difficulties and hardships during and after the war. She asked Hannah how things were now.

'We managed, but many didn't,' Hannah explained. 'The children were ill, food was scarce, and there was an air of total despondency. Thank goodness, there is more food available this year and the children have recovered, though adolescence has hit Heinz hard. He communicates in grunts.'

'I remember when my brother was at that stage. We scarcely spoke for months on end. But now we are the best of chums.'

'Is he the one whom Stefan met in the trenches? He was wounded, I gather.'

'James will not speak about it in detail, but he says that he has every reason to be deeply grateful to Stefan. He lost an arm, but seems to be getting on well. He is now married to a lovely girl.'

'I'm glad that something good has come out this wretched war.'

'Annelore, how is she?'

'She remembers your previous visit and wants to practise her English with you. Now, tell me when you and Stefan will tie the knot?'

'In the summer at the end of June. Will you be able to come? I do hope you will, all of you.'

'It depends on so many things, such as getting new passports. Can Dietrich leave the factory for a week or so? And, I have to say it, the cost.'

'You will be our guests throughout your stay.'

'But...'

'I have had this argument with Stefan. James and I have been left quite well off by our parents, so we can provide. You will be more than welcome. Stefan must have his family at his wedding.'

Stefan made the same offer to Dietrich when they went for a walk. At first, Dietrich raised the same objections as Hannah had done, but Stefan insisted.

'For Heaven's sake, what are brothers for? Please don't be stuffy.'

Dietrich spoke of his problems at the factory.

'Now the war is over, there is work, and the men want to work. But there is another element. The mark is falling. Raw materials are much more expensive. In terms of dollars, we have to pay six times as much as we did last year. The government printed money to meet borrowing. I understand that if we had won the war, we would repay it by exacting war reparations on the losers. But now we are the losers. And we have to start paying up next year – with what? I am very fearful. Sometimes, I think we should sell up, cut our losses and emigrate to America. But then we would have to start from the bottom again, and I am too old. If the children were younger, it might have been possible.'

'Do you have to go as far as America?'

'Wherever we go in Europe, we will be pariahs, not welcome. And our assets would be worthless. But we will come to your wedding. We have the warmest feelings for Beth. She stood by you and waited for you all those years.'

'I am very blessed.'

* * *

A few days before the wedding, Stefan, Beth and Dietrich and his family went to James's old school to watch a game between the school and the Old Boys. James had brought Beatrice and introductions were made. The children were fascinated by James; they had never seen a one-armed man before. Heinz asked in hesitant English how he played cricket.

'Well, Heinz, I can bowl, a slow ball, I can field...'

'Beth taught us cricket,' said Heinz.

'Did she, by Jove? Beth can do anything. Now when it comes to batting, I have to adopt a left-hander's stance' – he demonstrated with a bat – 'but it needs a very strong right forearm and wrist. I have been practicing.'

Heinz nodded knowledgeably.

Annelore could not manage the English, so she asked Beth in German why both sides wore white and how could you tell which was which.

Beth endeavoured to explain. Annelore looked mystified. 'Never mind, it will become clear once the game starts.'

The men, with Heinz in tow, went off for a walk round the boundary. Dietrich lit a cigar and James his pipe. James explained how he had lost his arm and Stefan translated when necessary. 'But now I have a lovely wife who is going to have a baby soon. It is very exciting, and a bit alarming.'

The ladies stayed by the Pavilion and Hannah ventured to ask Beatrice when the baby was due.

'Very soon. My back aches. I'm told that everything is in order. I just want it to be over.'

Hannah made sympathetic noises.

'In case you are wondering, Beth, having done the arithmetic, we did er… anticipate things. Don't be shocked.'

'My dear, you have made my brother very happy. So who cares?'

Beth repeated the point for Hannah, who nodded and smiled.

Annelore had worked out a sentence. 'Do you want a boy or a girl?' she asked.

'So long as it is healthy child, I will be content. What would you like it to be, Annelore?'

'I would like a girl,' she replied. 'Like a little sister.'

The Old Boys batted first. James went in number four.

'Rather flattering, actually. This is the first time I have held a bat in anger since… I hope I don't make a mess of it.'

The fielding side maintained a respectful distance as he got his eye in, playing straight balls with confidence and leaving those wide of the crease.

'Why doesn't he score runs?' Heinz asked.

Beth was about to explain when James cut a ball to the off and ran two runs. Applause.

The next ball, a faster one, pitched just outside the leg stump and James tucked it away past Third Man for three.

Heinz clapped enthusiastically.

At the end of the over a spinner was brought on. He bowled a good length and James's strokes were restricted. Nevertheless his defence was solid and more runs came. By lunch he had scored twenty.

'We need more runs quickly for a decent declaration,' he said. 'I am going to have a go.'

Two balls into the afternoon, he played across the line and was bowled.

'I have done my bit,' he told them as he sat down with Beth and the others.

'Will you bowl?'

'I doubt it. I will be quite content to field somewhere in the deep. I can still throw a ball.'

At tea, Beatrice said she was feeling very tired and could she be taken home. James went to the school captain and asked for a substitute fielder. Then he gathered up his kit and they left.

'I hope she is all right,' said Beth.

'It is hot,' said Hannah, 'and she must rest.'

* * *

During the night before the wedding, Beatrice went into labour and James took her to the hospital. James rang at eight o'clock in the morning. Beth answered the phone. 'Tell Stefan I am sorry but I can't be his Best Man.'

She called the hotel where Stefan was staying with Dietrich and his family. They was sitting round the breakfast table.

'Let us pray for Beatrice, a safe delivery and a sturdy child.'

Then he produced a ring from his pocket and gave it to Dietrich.

'Time for you to do your brotherly duty and be my Best Man. Will you?'

Dietrich was taken aback.

'You must,' said Hannah.

'It's not that I don't want to. I am just worried that I will have to make a speech in English.'

'That is a excellent excuse for making it short.'

A cousin of her father gave Beth away. She did not want any bridesmaids; she had hoped that Frances Stevenson might be a Maid of Honour, but she was too busy in Downing Street. Stefan had his brother's family and two of his congregation from Alie

Street. The vicar, coached by Beth, said a few words of welcome in German.

There were two hymns: 'O perfect Love' and 'Now thank we all our God'. When it came to the exchange of vows, Beth gave her bouquet to Annelore to hold.

The ceremony was brief and the photographs outside the church in the sunshine took longer. The Wedding Breakfast was at the hotel. Stefan said Grace in both languages. During the meal Dietrich was writing some notes on a napkin. When it was his turn to speak, he got up, braced himself and in a few words talked about Stefan the scholar, Stefan the padre and Stefan the pastor. He praised Beth for her steadfast loyalty to Stefan despite being separated by war. It was all a bit solemn but when he had proposed the toast, he sat down to great applause. Stefan refilled his glass for him.

There was a hum of conversation. Beth and Stefan circulated round the tables, thanking everyone for coming.

'Much as I love my friends and relations, I'm looking forward to being together on our own,' said Beth.

'Seconded,' said Stefan.

They resumed their seats. Then Stefan's attention was called by a waiter. He got up and left the room. Standing outside, looking dishevelled but with a broad grin on his face, was James.

'I've been up all night. Good news.'

He told Stefan. Stefan congratulated him and took him into the dining room. He wrapped on the table and called for silence.

'Fill your glasses, please. My brother-in-law is now a proud father, and his wife, Beatrice, and son are both doing well. To the new family.'

'To the new family' was the loud response.

'Another toast. To the proud Aunt.'

Beth stood up and embraced her brother. 'Hello, Auntie,' was all he could think of to say.

Stefan raised his hand. 'I have a question for the new father.'

'What will his name be?' shouted a guest.

'*Nein, nein,*' said Stefan. 'Much more important than that. When will you buy him his first cricket bat?'

First published in the U.K. by

Ashgrove Publishing

an imprint of:

Hollydata Publishers Ltd
27 John Street
London
WC1N 2BX

© 2023 David Willington

The right of David Willington to be identified as the author
of this work has been asserted by him in accordance
with the Copyright, Designs and Patents Act 1988.

No part of this publication may be reproduced, stored
in a retrieval system or transmitted, in any form
or by any means, electronic, mechanical,
photocopying, recording or otherwise,
without the prior permission
of the publisher.

978 185398 206 4

Book design by Brad Thompson

Printed and bound in the UK